Montségur

A Novel

Catherine de Courcy is an Irish author, historian and researcher. She was first drawn to the story of Montségur and the Cathars in 2008. Since 2011, she has immersed herself in the landscape around Montségur, visiting places associated with the Cathars, conducting research and following up on stories told to her along the way. As a professional writer, she has published fourteen books and many articles on a diverse range of topics including the history of zoos and Australian outback travel. She has lived and worked in Papua New Guinea and Australia as well as in Ireland. She now divides her time between Ireland and the Occitanie region of France.

Montségur

A Novel

Catherine de Courcy

MABEL WRAY PRESS

First published in 2017 by
Mabel Wray Press
Dublin, Ireland
mabelwraypress.com

Reprinted in 2018

ISBN 978-1-9997266-4-5

Design by Anú Design, Tara

Timeline of Historical Events

1209	Albigensian Crusade commences with massacre at Béziers
1211	Siege of Lavaur by Crusaders. After town falls, 300–400 people accused of heresy burnt alive on a pyre
1218	Death of Simon de Montfort, commander of the Crusade forces, killed at Toulouse
1229	The Crusade ends
1233	Inquisition into Heretical Depravity commences
1241	Count of Toulouse lays siege to Montségur
1242	Raid on Avignonet
1243, May	Siege of Montségur commences under command of General Hugues d'Arcis, Seneschal of Carcassonne
1244, March	End of siege at Montségur

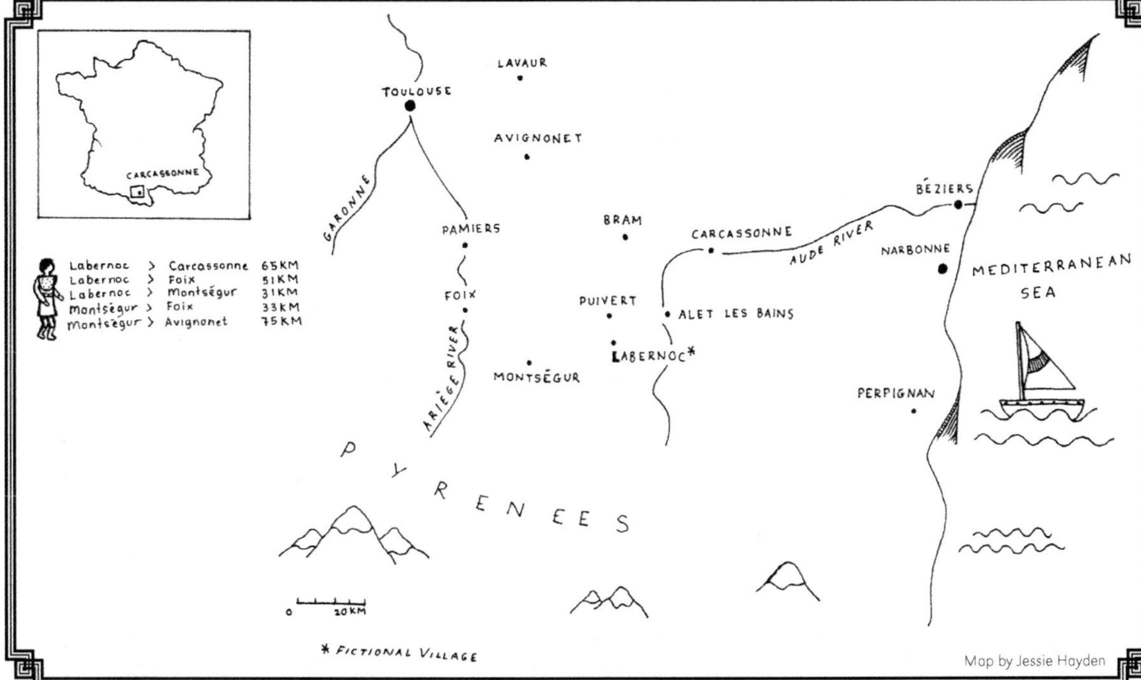
CARCASSONNE
Labernoc > Carcassonne 65KM
Labernoc > Foix 51KM
Labernoc > Montségur 31KM
Montségur > Foix 33KM
Montségur > Avignonet 75KM
TOULOUSE
GARONNE
LAVAUR
AVIGNONET
PAMIERS
FOIX
ARIÈGE RIVER
MONTSÉGUR
BRAM
PUIVERT
LABERNOC*
CARCASSONNE
ALET LES BAINS
AUDE RIVER
BÉZIERS
NARBONNE
PERPIGNAN
MEDITERRANEAN SEA
PYRENEES
0 20KM
* FICTIONAL VILLAGE
Map by Jessie Hayden

Historical Note

In the High Middle Ages, in what is now the Occitanie region in Southern France, the spiritual beliefs of a group of Christians, known today as the Cathars, were widely popular. Men and women travelled through the countryside bringing their Christian teachings and simple practices to townspeople and villagers. They had no churches, no statues, swore no oaths and had but one sacrament, the Consolamentum. This was administered to people who chose a life of prayer or to a believer who was close to death. The powerful lords of the region, including the Count of Toulouse and the Count of Trencavel in Carcassonne, tolerated the Cathars.

However the Roman church, concerned that it was losing control in the region, was determined to assert its authority as the one true Christian church. In the twelfth century, debates between representatives of the Roman church and the Cathar Christians were held. These were inconclusive and the Cathar influence continued to spread. In 1208, a senior papal legate, who had excommunicated the Count of Toulouse, was murdered. In response Pope Innocent III called for a crusade to purge the lands of Toulouse and Trencavel of these Christians, referred to by Rome as heretics. The King of France obliged and a vast army of crusaders moved south. The first act of the

Albigensian Crusade, as it became known, was the conquest of the coastal city of Béziers in 1209 and the death of thousands of men, women and children. The papal legate, Cistercian abbot Arnaud Amalric, reported to the Pope that 20,000 people had been slaughtered. The Crusade against Christians continued with great brutality under the leadership of Simon de Montfort, who was killed in 1218 at Toulouse. Peace was finally agreed in 1229. By then the Count of Trencavel had been killed, Carcassonne was under the control of the King of France and the autonomy of the Count of Toulouse was considerably weakened.

Yet, still determined to rid Occitanie of Christians who would not accept the authority of Rome, the papacy explored new ways of identifying and subjugating these so-called heretics. In 1233 Pope Gregory IX ordered an Inquisition into Heretical Depravity and charged the mendicant friars, St Dominic's Order of Preachers, with the task. The inquisitors had the power to order the arrest, prosecution and punishment of heretics; regional lords, now connected through feudal alliances to the King of France, were obliged to cooperate.

This story begins in the fictional village of Labernoc in 1237, five kilometres from Puivert Castle and 65 kilometres south of Carcassonne. All other locations in the book are genuine.

Montsegur: Main Characters

*Those marked with an asterisk are documented historical characters.

Esme, b. September 1221
Emersenda, d. September 1221, mother of Esme

ESME'S FOSTER FAMILY, LABERNOC VILLAGE

Jaufré, foster father, b. Béziers 1200
Ava, foster mother, b. Labernoc 1203
Matina, b. 1220
Raimond, b. September 1221
Alayda, b. 1223
Johann, b. 1241 January
Pedro, b. 1243 January
Bernard, Jaufré's brother, b. Béziers 1203
Julian, Bernard's son, b. 1223

THE HUNTER'S COTTAGE ABOVE LABERNOC

Guilhèm, hunter, b. 1211
Agnes, Guilhèm's mother
Serena, Guilhèm's wife
Bonassias, known as Bonnie, b. October 1237

LABERNOC CASTLE

Algaia, kitchen cook

Miguel Garcias, Bailiff, Labernoc Castle

Sibella, wife of Miguel

INQUISITORIAL PARTY

Friar Pierre Tiqué, b. 1201

Constable Jacques Barca

Constable Eric Del Gurbe

CARCASSONNE CASTLE

'Clement' – Guilhèm's alias in Carcassonne

'Pixie' – Esme's alias in Carcassonne

Nicholaus, hunter

Jacotina, head of the kitchen and second wife of Nicholaus

Pons, b. 1214 son of Nicholaus and his first wife

Rolfe de Turre, sergeant with the Castle guard

FOIX

William Bélibaste, consoled man. d.1321*

Philippe, b. 1199, Toulouse, father of Esme

Andreva, b. 1210, second wife of Philippe

José, a knight employed by Philippe to assist the Labernoc party

MONTSÉGUR

Bishop Guilhabert de Castres, 1165–1241. Bishop of the community*

Luisana, elder

Leyas, elder

Esclarmonde de Pereille, daughter of Raymond and Corba de Pereille, co-owners of Montségur*
Rixanda, healer, consoled woman
Brother Thomas, consoled man
Bishop Bernard Marty*
Bertrana, widow resident
Wilhelmina, widow resident
Pierre-Roger de Mirepoix, commander of the garrison, co-owner of Montségur and son-in-law of Raymond de Pereille*
Arpais de Pereille, unmarried daughter of Raymond and Corba de Pereille*
Philippa de Pereille, daughter of Raymond and Corba de Pereille and wife of Pierre-Roger de Mirepoix*
Luyon, Gerad, Dam, Yusu and Dimaz, male elders
Uswan, female elder
Othon, a knight and leader of the climbers

THE BESIEGERS

General Hugue d'Arcis, Seneschal of Carcassonne*

Prologue:
Foix January 1316

Esme heard a movement in the room and opened her eyes.

'Has he come?'

'Yes, Aunt. He's waiting in the forest across the river until it's dark.'

Esme reached for the hand of Stéphanie, her grand-niece, and squeezed it. She knew the risk Stéphanie was taking by bringing the holy man to her death bed.

'Have you got your stone ready, Aunt?'

Esme opened her other hand. A small stone lay in her palm. It was grey and almost perfectly round but with one jagged edge. There were several deep scratches on it.

Stéphanie rearranged the pillows and helped Esme with some water, then sat down beside her to wait for William Bélibaste. Her gaze fell to the stone.

'I wish I had been taught how to work with a stone, Aunt."

With a little effort, Esme waved her hand over the stone. It shimmered.

'Oh, there's that mist, the one with your stories, Aunt Esme. I haven't seen it for a long time. I thought I'd imagined it. Oh, it's gone again.' Stéphanie sighed as the mist vanished.

'Heart… watch...' Esme struggled to speak.

With a glance at the glazed window and thick oak door, which were both closed, Stéphanie raised her hands to her heart and stared at the stone again. The room became very still. Soon, Stéphanie saw mist. It came from the scratches on the stone.

Tears gathered in Esme's eyes as she smiled at the hazy images of men, women and children that formed. She was 94 years old and had known very many people in her lifetime.

There were footsteps. Esme closed her hand and the mist disappeared.

The door opened. A tall man dressed in a dirty hooded cloak stepped into the room and closed the door behind him. 'How's my favourite old heretic?' he asked quietly.

'Rogue,' Esme turned her head as the newcomer took her hands in his and dropped his head to kiss them.

'Please, sire, don't call my aunt a heretic,' Stéphanie said in a low voice.

William looked at the handsome forty-year old woman appreciatively. 'Beautiful lady, your dear old aunt is one of the original heretics. There are very few of us left.'

'Sire, I'd ask you to be careful, please. There are no heretics in this household.'

'Relax, young lady.' William threw off his cloak. 'It is nothing to be ashamed of. You're only a heretic if you disagree with the Roman church, and we have plenty to disagree with them about, haven't we, my friend Esme?' He settled himself comfortably into a fleece-lined chair beside Esme. 'Ahh, now that feels good. I haven't rested on as soft a chair in a long time.

Stéphanie, unsure of what to make of this scruffy man, left the room to fetch him some refreshments. The house was empty. Her husband had taken her daughters, all young women now, to visit relatives in Toulouse, and the servants were in their own quarters. When she returned with a tray of food, there was a distinct smell of roses in the room. William was talking animatedly. Stéphanie discerned a sparkle in Esme's eye.

'Do you know,' William said as he surveyed the tray placed on a small trestle table in front of him. 'your Aunt Esme is one of the few people alive who knowingly met direct descendants of our beloved teachers, Jesus and Mary Magdalene?' He tore off some bread.

'Did you, Aunt? Can that be true?'

'Oh yes, she met three of them, at least. All living on Montségur, and this sweet old lady,' William dipped the bread into the thick bean and vegetable stew, 'this mighty woman from a commercial family of Foix, she knew them well. And the things she witnessed, the goodness, the badness, and the written Word... ah yes, young lady, the written Word, she saw them all.' He pushed the bread into his mouth.

'Do you think you should be talking of such things, sire? Isn't that heresy?'

'Only the Romans say it is heresy,' William stirred the stew with another lump of bread. 'The Romans call any Christian who disagrees with them a heretic. Fear and nonsense. Now stop talking and let me eat.'

William ate quickly and noisily. Esme could feel her grand-niece's concern. Stéphanie had heard stories about the legendary men and women who travelled from village to village, praying, helping people to find their truth within themselves, and bringing solace to the dying. This was the first holy person Stéphanie had ever met and Esme could understand why she might be startled. But William, for all his careless ways, flirtatious behaviour and verbosity, was as true a holy man as Esme had ever known; there was a gentle presence around him and when he opened his eyes after praying, the other-worldly light she had once known so well was there.

Feel his presence, Esme urged Stéphanie through her mind. *Feel and sense his true presence.*

As William mopped up the sauce at the base of his bowl with bread, Stéphanie asked him quietly: 'sire, are you really saying that descendants of Jesus and Mary Magdalene lived on Montségur? We were told that Mary Magdalene was a...'

'Woman of high social status, married to Jesus and together they had at least one child, a daughter called Sarah who is much venerated around here,' said William, frustration in his voice. 'I am quite sure that you heard that at least once in your lifetime but you chose to accept the rubbish that the Roman friars told you.'

'Easy, William,' whispered Esme.

'Maybe, sire, you are right,' said Stéphanie with sadness. 'Maybe I was told and I chose to forget. But the Romans are in charge of our churches now and you know what they do with people who disagree with them. I won't put my children's lives in jeopardy.'

William pressed his hands to his heart and said softly: 'I beg your pardon, my lovely hostess. You are very generous and I have repaid your kindness with rudeness. I am sorry for sounding so rough. I am the only one of my kind left and I am terribly flawed.'

Esme sensed William's sorrow. She lifted her hand towards him: *Dear William, you have been so alone, I wish you had known the people of Montségur.*

William took her hand. 'I wish I could sit with you all day, Esme. I can sense the devoted people of Montségur through you. I wish I had known them, even for a moment.'

Esme's stone was hot in her hand.

Tell her, tell Stéphanie about Montségur, William. She can hear the story and hold it safely.

'Does your niece not know of your life in Montségur?' William asked.

Esme shook her head and gestured towards her stone: *it is all in here.*

'I know the story is in your stone, Esme. Maybe your good niece should know it too, if she is able to hear it?'

'You tell...' Esme whispered.

William sat motionless for a while. 'Esme, I have until dawn. I could try and read it from your stone. What do you think?'

Esme nodded reassuringly at her niece.

'I'd like to hear your story,' Stéphanie said. 'If Monsieur Bélibaste can tell me.'

'Before I start, Esme, dear friend, you may be asleep in the morning. I need to know if you still have Raimond's stone and do you want me to take that too?'

Esme pointed to the pouch around her neck. 'Yes, please.'

William took Esme' hands, kissed them, then sat upright in his chair, his fingers intertwined. He prayed silently as Esme placed the stone in her left hand and rested that hand on her right hand. William went into a trance.

A little while later, he spoke. 'We'll start on that day when your foster parents were condemned to death by the inquisitor, Friar Tiqué. You were fifteen.'

Part 1

1

Labernoc, October 1236

ESME LAY HIDDEN along the limb of a tall tree. From here she could see the village square at the top of the slope. The villagers huddled in family groups, silently watching the castle gate. Down by the river and clearly visible from Esme's tree stood the pyre, a crude platform with eight low stakes set on an enormous pile of wood. Above her, the craggy outcrops on the surrounding Pyrenees glistened in the sun and golden leaves floated in the autumnal breeze. Esme wanted to cry out to the heavens. Instead she kept her attention on the square. She saw Raimond in the crowd. He was standing between his two sisters. A space had been left around them.

Suddenly there was a thud and the heavy wooden gate of Labernoc Castle opened. A dozen soldiers marched down the short lane into the middle of the crowd. Using their lances, they forced the people back to clear the centre of the square. Raimond and his sisters stood at the front of the packed crowd.

Moments later, the imposing figure of Friar Pierre Tiqué on his magnificent brown horse came out through the castle gate. As he entered the square, he stopped and flicked his dark cloak out behind him. His cowl was perched on the top of his head so his eyes were visible as he slowly scanned the anxious faces. Nobody dared to catch his eye. Glancing over his shoulder, he advanced, revealing the terrible procession following him. Sixteen people, men and women, their arms pinned to their bodies by thick ropes, hobbled into view, barefoot and dirty. Eight burly constables in grey tunics, swords hanging off their belts, moved them along.

Esme's cry of horror at seeing her foster parents was drowned by the cries of the villagers. It was the first time she had seen them since their arrest four months earlier. Ava's long black hair was tangled, her face pallid and her woollen dress filthy. Esme could see her searching anxiously for her children. Beside her, Jaufré was walking bolt upright. His once powerful frame had shrunk and his hair had turned grey. He was glowering at the friar and muttering to himself.

Friar Tiqué waited impassively as the prisoners were assembled in front of him. Some were in a trance and were paying no attention to their surroundings. Others sought out their families, resignation and sorrow in their expressions. Only Ava and Jaufré were from Labernoc. The rest were from nearby villages or had been captured on their way to join the community on Montségur. People called out to their loved ones. Ava mouthed words of love to her own three children. Esme wished she was beside them so she too could receive those words of love from the woman who had mothered her from the day she was born.

Remaining on his horse, Friar Tiqué signalled that he was about to speak. The crowd quietened down, hoping against hope that he might show mercy. Reading from a prepared text in his native Occitan, Tiqué declared, 'You stand here accused of heresy; of denying the authority of the Pope in Rome; of teaching falsehoods in contradiction to the teachings of the one true Church. Here, before your...'

There would be no mercy. The villagers' voices rose again with protests and pleas.

The friar carried on. The crowd quietened down a little. 'Here, before your own families and neighbours, I give you one final chance to save your souls. Renounce your heresy, swear your acceptance of the authority of the Church, receive the sacraments and even now you can be saved.'

Jaufré stepped towards the friar shouting out: 'Priest of Rome, we are not heretics. We follow true Christian teachings'.

A stocky constable shoved Jaufré with his lance. Jaufré stumbled, pushing helplessly against his ropes, but remained standing. 'Friar Tiqué, you say you are Christian. We are ...'

The constable pushed him again, more forcibly this time. Jaufré landed on the ground. The crowd shouted out their support for their learned neighbour, encouraging him to challenge the friar.

'Jaufré of Labernoc,' said Friar Tiqué, watching Jaufré struggle to stand. 'You have defied Rome once too often.'

Jaufré regained his footing. 'You defy humanity.'

The constable lifted his lance but Tiqué raised his hand to stop him from striking. Jaufré seized his opportunity. 'I translate sacred scriptures so that we can learn from them. Our elders have followed the teachings of Jesus Christ for twelve hundred years.' The crowd hushed each other. Even in his emaciated state Jaufré's voice still held authority. 'You claim to follow the teachings of Jesus too. Why are you so afraid of people reading what He truly said?'

The constable made a move but the friar, his hand still raised, checked him. 'When common people interpret scriptures,' Tiqué said slowly. 'They worship false gods. Now, people of Labernoc,' he pointed the index finger of his raised hand at the crowd, moving from one person to the next slowly and deliberately. 'I warn you to forget this man and his falsehoods, or you too will be damned for all eternity.'

The cries of Jaufré's daughters, Matina and Alayda, were lost in the rising noise level as the crowd surged forward. The soldiers pushed back, bellowing orders and threatening violence.

'In the name of our beloved teacher, let my wife go! She is innocent.' Jaufré fought to be heard.

But the crowd was now yelling without restraint, their protests turning to pleas as they begged the friar to change his mind, begged their loved ones to do what the priest wanted, begged God to show mercy.

Jaufré stepped close to the friar and bellowed up to him. Tiqué's eyes darted around the square. He flicked his hand at the stocky constable, who struck Jaufré's head with his lance. Esme saw the pinioned body of her foster father fall to the ground. Bloody, he tried to stand up. Constable Barca, notorious for his brutal behaviour, kicked his head several times. By now, Jaufré was unconscious and possibly dead.

Constable Del Gurbe, Barca's violent comrade, drove a lance into Jaufré's left hip and dragged his leg backwards. There was a loud crack. Women screamed. The crowd was in uproar. Ava fell to her knees beside her husband.

Esme clamped her hands over her mouth to muffle her cries. The soldiers still had control but the threat of all-out violence was growing.

Signalling to his constables, the friar started down the track towards the pyre. A constable pulled Ava into a standing position and the procession was hurried along. Two more constables untied the ropes around the unconscious Jaufré, lifted him under his arms and dragged him to the pyre. His left leg trailed at an unnatural angle behind him. They passed the procession, walked around the back of the pyre and threw him onto the lowest side of the platform. A narrow ridge stopped Jaufré from rolling to the ground.

When the last prisoner had left the square, the soldiers manoeuvred themselves backwards to form a solid barrier on the road leading down to the river. The villagers kept the pressure on, shouting, crying out and protesting, but the tight group of soldiers controlled the road.

At the pyre, constables untied the prisoners and pushed them up the crude steps. On the platform, they were tied to a metal ring on one of the waist-high stakes. Ava stumbled up the steps and was caught by a castle soldier, who was assigned to help the constables. Esme could see her pleading with him. The soldier, glancing at the constables over his shoulder, moved her to a stake on the edge of the pyre near her prone husband.

With the condemned secured, the friar dismounted his

horse and approached. He raised a sheet of parchment in front of his face and rushed through the prescribed condemnation: 'I, Friar Pierre Tiqué, command you one last time to admit your guilt, recant your false beliefs, embrace the one true church and save your souls. You have been condemned to suffer the penance of death as unrepentant heretics, and therefore you are all forever excommunicated.'

None of those on the pyre appeared to be listening. Eight were standing upright and silent with their eyes closed. Esme guessed they were in a prayerful trance. Four people had collapsed and were lying motionless on the ground, their hands tied above them. One couple from a nearby village held each other's eyes and sobbed quietly. Ava, at the back of the pyre, was crouched down by Jaufré's prone body whispering to him.

Tiqué turned towards the bailiff, who stood nearby. The bailiff dropped his eyes and nodded in the direction of his soldiers, so giving the final order. The men lit torches from a small fire and moved along the dry hay at the base of the pyre. Heavy overnight rain had dampened it and it crackled loudly as it let off thick clouds of smoke. The wind picked up and blew the smoke towards the friar.

At that moment, Esme saw Ava push frantically at Jaufré's body. Jaufré stirred. He was alive. The smoke billowed, creating a screen between those tied to stakes at the back of the pyre and the friar. The man sharing the stake with Ava opened his eyes. Summoning all of their strength, they got a foot each under Jaufré and levered him off the pyre. Semi-conscious, he rolled down the slope towards the river. Ava looked up to the tree where Esme was hidden and smiled just as a thick cloud of smoke enveloped her.

It took all of Esme's hunting skills to remain in the tree as she saw Ava cough violently, then collapse into unconsciousness. Soon the flames rose high into the sky and engulfed the pyre. Feeling every bit of her body screaming out, Esme squeezed her head with the palms of her hands. She tried to imagine Guilhèm the hunter giving her instructions on what to do next. She looked at the cliffs above the river. He was probably up there watching. 'Look after Jaufré,' she imagined him saying. Jaufré was sprawled on the ground by the river and only a few metres from the base of the pyre. He was motionless. Through the dense, black smoke that swirled around the pyre, Esme glimpsed the friar on his horse. His cloak was raised over his nose and mouth, and his head was turned towards the angry crowd who his constables were holding in place.

Jaufré stirred. With her whole body trembling, Esme slid out of the tree and, crouching low, dashed to a deep hollow just beside him. The cracking and hissing of the enormous fire was deafening. Her hands shook as she pulled her jacket collar up to protect herself from the intense heat. If she could pull Jaufré into the hollow, he might be safe. The hunter could fetch him after dark and take him to his cottage.

'Steady', she heard the hunter's voice in her head. Taking a deep breath, she peeked above the hollow to make sure that the friar and his constables could not see her. She crawled over to Jaufré and shook him. 'Jaufré.' He raised his head slightly but his eyes could not focus. 'Push yourself towards me. There's a hollow just here.' She crouched over him and hooked her arm under his armpit 'Use your good leg,' she pleaded, as she drew on all of her strength to heave him along. 'Help me. Just a little further.'

Jaufré groaned, moved his right leg and gave one big push. With half of his body in the hollow, Esme was able to slide him down the rest of the way. The hollow was damp and cool. Esme put her arms around him and buried her head in his shoulder.

'Stay alert.' Imagining the hunter's command, she forced herself to rise up. All she could see was a wall of flames. She covered her foster father with scrub, brushed away the drag marks on the ground and ran back to her tree.

As the terrible spectacle continued, Esme locked her arms and legs around a thick branch and held on. Unable to bear it any longer, she laid her head on the rough bark and looked at the cliffs above her. There were no birds. She could feel her body becoming numb and her mind dull. Guilhèm would find her and take herself and Jaufré to safety in the cottage in the woods.

Time stood still. Then Esme heard voices. She realised that the roar of the fire had ceased. Stiff, she raised her head. Friar Tiqué approached the smouldering embers with Constables Barca and Del Gurbe beside him. A rush of fear came over her: Jaufré was well hidden but would the friar count the bodies and discover the anomaly?

Something disturbed the friar and he turned back towards the crowd. Through the haze of smoke, Esme could see Raimond walking towards the pyre. Constables shouted at him to stop. The castle soldiers, as silent as the crowd, made no move to stop him.

'Get back!' snarled Constable Del Gurbe.

Raimond walked on down the slope. He stopped in front of the pyre and looked at the unrecognisable bodies in front of him. Slowly, he joined his hands in the traditional way of his people, his fingers intertwined and his thumbs hidden, and held them to his heart.

Behind him, Del Gurbe lifted his lance. Waving the constable away, Friar Tiqué stepped towards Raimond and put a hand on his shoulder: 'Enough, my son. God's will has been done. Go home and follow the word of God with obedience and diligence.'

Raimond slowly turned his head and looked at the friar with his dark-green eyes. A chill ran down Esme's spine as she saw Tiqué recoil. Raimond lowered his gaze and turned back to the pyre. He bowed slightly and returned to his sisters, Matina and Alayda.

Esme could see Tiqué frowning, his brow furrowed and his thin lips pursed, as he watched Raimond disappear into the crowd. She wanted to cry out to her friend to run, escape from Labernoc, get far away from Tiqué and his men while he still could, but she was powerless: she had to remain where she was until it was dark and the constables and soldiers had returned to the castle.

2

The hunter's cottage, Labernoc, October 1236

THE FOLLOWING MORNING, Esme woke, groggy from a long sleep. She pulled back the curtain that concealed her narrow bed from the main room in the hunter's cottage. She blinked as bright sunlight flooded in through the door and small window. What was she doing in bed during the day? A man groaned loudly and she heard Serena respond quietly. Slowly Esme separated her dreams from the reality of yesterday's events. Ava. Jaufré. She slid out of bed, pulled on her woollen tunic and stumbled barefoot into the room.

Two of the chairs by the fire had been pushed aside and Jaufré was there, lying on a bed of thick straw and wool. His eyes were closed but he was agitated, his head moving from side to side. Serena, the hunter's wife, was mopping his brow and talking to him in a soothing voice.

'Come outside, Esme,' Guilhèm's mother, Agnes, whispered to her.

Esme followed the elderly woman. The cottage was set in a clearing surrounded by forest. To the south, craggy outcrops and vertiginous mountains rose high, sheltering the cottage. There was no sign of Guilhèm. Automatically Esme petted Spider, Guilhèm's dog, and sat down at a weatherworn table.

'I'm not hungry, Doña Agnes,' said Esme looking at the bread and cheese on a board in front of her. 'How did I get home? I can't remember.'

'Guilhèm was watching and as soon as it was dark, he got you both. You were in a daze, little one, but you were able to walk. I gave you a potion to help your sleep. Now drink this before you eat.' Agnes poured hot water into a cup and stirred it.

Esme sipped the drink obediently, suspecting it contained one of Agnes' tonics. Slowly memories of yesterday's events became clearer. She choked. Agnes sat beside her and enveloped her in a hug.

'I have to talk to Raimond. He needs to leave Labernoc.' She wriggled out of Agnes' arms. 'I saw the friar looking at him. He's in danger. He doesn't know that Jaufré is alive.' Her voice was rising.

'Rest, little one, rest. Guilhèm is at the lookout watching the movements of the friar and his men. Wait until he returns.'

Esme let out a sob as Agnes drew her into her breast. Rocking her gently, the elderly woman encouraged her to cry. She had known Esme since she was born. Despite losing her mother at birth and being abandoned in a village with no blood relatives, Esme had grown into a merry young woman.

But nothing could have prepared the fifteen-year-old for the shocks of yesterday. Right now, tears were the only release.

Guilhèm appeared from the forest and Spider gambolled over to meet him. 'They are leaving today,' he said without preliminaries. 'They're loading their chests into carts.'

Esme sat up. 'Yesterday, Guilhèm, I don't remember you finding me.'

'By the time the constables left the pyre, you had been in one position for too long, Esme, and you were in a sort of trance. But you did very well. You couldn't have done any more. Now stay with mother. I'm going to see how Jaufré is.' He ducked his head as he went through the cottage door.

'No change,' whispered Serena to her husband. 'We have manipulated his hip back into place as best we can but there is a lot of damage. I've been rubbing Agnes' potions for broken limbs onto it but, Guilhèm, I don't know. The blow to his head may be more serious than it looks. He hasn't said a word and he hasn't opened his eyes.'

Guilhèm placed his hands under Jaufré's head, which was still rocking from side to side, and tried to comfort him. 'You are safe now, old friend. You are safe.'

'Try praying,' Serena whispered.

Guilhèm raised his eyebrows. He was not given to praying but knew the Lord's Prayer, the prayer of his people. 'Our father in Heaven, May your name be hallowed,' he began. He felt Jaufré's head relax a little. He continued the prayer, repeating it twice.

'Easy my friend, easy. Rest.'

Jaufré's head was still. Serena checked his heart. 'This breathing is becoming more normal. You see, husband, as I tell you, your prayers are very strong.'

Agnes shuffled into the room and beckoned Guilhèm to her. 'Esme wants to watch their departure. Have they taken our dead?'

Guilhèm nodded grimly. The friar's constables had returned to the pyre at dawn, smashed the bones of the deceased and shovelled them onto a cart. It was well known that the friars did not allow the local people to bury their dead so their own men made the remains unrecognisable and took them away for dumping in a distant place.

Agnes picked up Esme's jacket from the end of her bed and brought it out to her.

'If you are going with Guilhèm, stay warm. The ground will be wet.'

Leaving the dog behind, Esme followed Guilhèm into the forest. It took them nearly fifteen minutes to make their way through the thick undergrowth and along a dangerous cliff top to the lookout. Concealed by low bushes, they lay on the damp ground. Fifty meters below them was Labernoc, a star-shaped village of about eighty homes. Five roads of varying qualities led away from the village square, one to Labernoc castle, another to the river, a third went south high into the mountains, a fourth went north-east along steep slopes, and the fifth was the main road out of town, which led down to the plain and towards Puivert Castle.

From the castle courtyard they could hear the clanging of metal, neighing of horses and dull thuds of wooden crates being loaded into carts. Outside the gate, mules, already hitched to carts containing large boxes, were grazing on hay as they waited.

'Guilhèm, I have to tell Raimond and Matina and Alayda that their father is still alive.'

Guilhèm glanced at Esme. He had never seen her so anxious. Her olive skin was unnaturally pale, she had dark circles under her eyes and her body was stiff with shock. He did not know how to ease the situation for her. Even when Ava and Jaufré were in the castle cellars, he had been able to distract Esme by taking her on a hunt and by encouraging her to prepare stories to tell Raimond. But these approaches seemed terribly inadequate as they watched the cart containing the big heap of bones being led out of the gate.

'Cover it, for pity's sake,' they heard one of the soldiers cry.

The constables responded rudely; the antagonism between the castle soldiery and the friar's constables had been evident for some time. Two soldiers appeared with a couple of old blankets and, ignoring the taunts of the constables, covered the bones.

'Ava is in there.'

'Don't react, Esme.'

She nodded and pressed her hand to her heart.

There was a barked command from the familiar voice of Tiqué and the courtyard became silent. After a lengthy pause, the sounds started up again and Tiqué rode out through the gate, his peaked cowl now low over his face, his cloak draped on his horse. His party fell in behind him. They paraded slowly through the deserted village and took the north road.

Esme buried her head in her arms when the rearguard,

constables Barca and Del Gurbe on horseback, cleared the village outskirts. It was known that Tiqué was going into the mountains towards Ax-Les-Thermes and possibly beyond. Along the way he would see the castle on Montségur in the distance but it was unlikely that Rome would permit him to detour by the mountain top community. The Roman church considered Montségur to be one of the most dangerous strongholds of Christian heretical practice in the region and, as such, any approach by their men could only be authorised at the highest level.

'I can't watch them anymore,' said Esme, raising her head. Her eyes were filled with tears. 'I must tell Raimond now.'

Guilhèm put a hand on her arm. 'Let me. We've kept ourselves hidden for all of these months. We should keep it that way for a little longer. We don't know how people are going to behave in the village now.'

Esme did not argue. Jaufré's younger brother, Bernard, was now head of the household she had grown up in. Bernard's wife, who believed that Esme had gone to live with her father in Foix, did not want that 'wild young woman' returning to the home of which she was mistress.

'Where are those two going?' Esme asked suddenly.

Two soldiers walked into the square with purpose in their stride. They wore their swords but were not otherwise armed. They took the south-west road that led towards Jaufré and Bernard's house.

'Raimond!' Esme sat up and cried out when they turned into the family's yard. Guilhèm put his hand over Esme's mouth and pulled her to the ground by her waist as one of the soldiers looked around, seeking out the cry. Esme's eyes were wild with panic. 'Go into your heart, Esme, now!' he whispered sharply. Esme continued to struggle. She was too strong and panicked for Guilhèm to carry her away without being noticed. He remembered Serena's comment. Taking a deep breath, he hurried his way through the Lord's Prayer in a low voice. Esme stopped struggling.

'Bring all of your attention to your heart, Esme,' Guilhèm whispered, not letting go of her. 'Remember what we do when we are confronted by a mother boar. And remember that Jaufré is hiding out with my mother and my wife. Ready?'

Esme nodded. He released her.

'I'm sorry, Guilhèm. I won't do that again.'

They looked back at the homestead. The soldiers were standing in the yard, which was formed by two adjoining houses and a large barn. The chickens ran around in their coop and the cow was chewing and watching. Bernard was talking to them; Bernard's fourteen-year-old son, Julian, and Alayda were with him. Raimond and Matina appeared. It was a quiet conversation. Even Alayda was reserved.

The young people went back into the house. Bernard, a man of few words, stood silently with the soldiers. Raimond reappeared carrying a pack. He hugged his sisters and left the yard, walking back through the village between the soldiers. Alayda put her arm around her cousin Julian and wept on his shoulder. Beside them, Matina stared at the ground without moving.

After the short walk from one side of the village to the other, Raimond reached the castle gate. Esme could see the squat, bald-headed figure of the bailiff, Miguel Garcias, waiting for him. His greeting seemed friendly. Raimond went into the castle and, as Esme watched, the heavy wooden gate closed behind them.

3

Labernoc, October 1236

It did not take Guilhèm long to find out what had become of Raimond. He got some information from Matina and Alayda but it was the castle cook, Algaia, who knew what was going on. Algaia was also the town's healer and even while the friar and his men were in town, Guilhèm continued to supply her with herbs and fungi from the forests. The same night that Raimond was taken to the castle, Algaia and Guilhèm met at their secret meeting location.

'Before he left, Friar Tiqué demanded that Raimond be trained as his servant and clerk,' Algaia reported.

'Was it anything to do with Raimond praying in front of the pyre?' Guilhèm asked.

'Who knows how that man's mind works? He already knew about Raimond's scholarship and the quality of his handwriting. I'd heard him say that it was unusual to find such skill and ability in the remote mountains, so he had had his eye on the lad. But perhaps... who knows?'

'How long is he to be kept away from his family?'

'The friar's instructions, which he repeated in front of all of us this morning when he was leaving, was that Raimond is to stay in the castle until Tiqué's return. He won't be allowed to see anyone but, Guilhèm,' Algaia took the hunter's hands, 'tell Esme and the girls that I will look after him. He'll be fed and comfortable. His education is to continue; the bailiff's boys will stay at the coast until Raimond is gone, so he will have the tutor to himself. He is also getting the visiting servant's room above the kitchen to himself. The bailiff will have no visitors while Lady Sibella is so unwell.' Everyone in the village knew that the bailiff's wife had responded to the incarceration in the castle cellars of so many people, including her dear friend, Ava, by drinking quantities of spiced wine throughout the day. 'The poor woman is not coping. Ask your mother to put her in her prayers, Guilhèm.'

Back at the cottage, Guilhèm tried to reassure Esme.

'But why is he locked away? Why can't we see him if he hasn't been arrested?'

Guilhèm had no answers.

'I have to talk to him. I know the room. I climbed up the outside wall to the window of that room loads of times when we played with Miguel's sons.'

'Not yet, Esme, you are not strong enough,' Agnes intervened.

'But he doesn't even know that his father is alive,' Esme argued.

'Esme, pet, you were so shocked by everything yesterday, that your body froze in the tree,' Agnes said gently. 'You're not ready. You could make a serious mistake. Wait for a few days until you are stronger.'

♦ ♦ ♦ ♦ ♦

For seven days, Agnes mothered Esme, held her as she cried, gave her potions and gently encouraged her to look into her heart and accept the situation. At last Agnes agreed to let her go and find Raimond. Alone, Esme waited on the bank behind the back wall of the castle. It was pitch dark and dry but there was no sign of anyone in the room that Algaia had said was Raimond's. Her mind was restless as she looked at the castle wall and wondered at how so much could have changed in such a short time. She had spent many happy hours climbing these walls and playing with Raimond and the bailiff's sons. As they had grown, Raimond had attended classes with the boys while she went hunting with Guilhèm. Now Raimond was in an unknown sort of captivity and his captor was, until a few months ago, a family friend.

And Raimond as a servant to the man who had killed his mother? The idea that Raimond might become a servant to anyone was ludicrous. Serving refreshments, laying out clothes, cleaning shoes, preparing a horse for a journey? Raimond was a scholar and wrote beautifully. The bailiff sometimes asked him to write out documents for him. But Raimond was certainly not a practical person and would make a terrible servant. That he would have to serve Friar Tiqué made Esme feel nauseous.

Esme pulled her jacket around her. The servants' room above the kitchen was at the back of the castle and far away from the family quarters. It had a narrow, barred window, which was six or seven metres off the ground but the castle wall was of rough stone and her small hands and feet fit easily in between the crevices. There was a protruding stone to the right of Raimond's window on which she could perch. The window looked onto a forested hill. There was a track around the back of the castle but it did not lead anywhere and there was no reason for anyone to walk this way.

A candle light appeared in the window. Esme held her breath. Then she saw Raimond's distinctive thick, curly hair. She let out her breath; it hung in the cold air for a few moments. He seemed to be alone. Trying to stay calm, she checked that she was also alone before standing up and making the sound of a bird cheeping as if it had been disturbed in the night. She saw Raimond move to the window. She let out another sound. His candle went out and he came to the window and cheeped. Taking a quick glance around her, she dashed over to the wall and within moments was on the perch and holding the bars at Raimond's narrow window with her right hand.

'Raimond, *besson,*' she whispered, using her childhood name for him.

'*Bessa*! I knew you would come. Be careful!'

'I'm on the ledge. Raimond, do you remember it?'

'I was hoping that it was close enough to the window.'

She laid her arm on the windowsill. He laid his arm on top of hers. 'You're freezing.'

'You are lovely and warm. I wish I could see you.' The thickness of the wall and the angle of the window made it impossible for them to see each other. She blew her breath in Raimond's direction.

There was silence, then they both talked at the same time.

'Me first. *Besson,* your father is alive, Jaufré is safe in Guilhèm's cottage.' She spoke in an urgent whisper. Raimond gasped loudly.

'Shhh. He wasn't dead when the constables put him on the pyre. And they put him on at the back of the platform away from the friar. There was a slope and Ava was able to push him off.'

She sped through the story. She could feel his grip tight on her arm but carried on.

'He's in pain and he's sleeping a lot but Serena and Doña Agnes look after him. He doesn't have a fever but the bones around his hip are badly damaged. He is not talking much.'

'Who else knows he's alive?'

'Only Matina and Alayda. No one else knows, not even Doña Algaia.'

She could hear Raimond smothering a sob. He dropped his head to Esme's hand. She turned her arm so she could touch his cheek. It was damp. She did not know what to say. By now she knew that there was no question of Miguel Garcia defying the friar and releasing Raimond. If he did, Garcia and his family, Raimond and his sisters, and probably Bernard and his family would suffer immediate retribution.

'Your turn,' she said, hoping to cheer him up. 'Tell me about you. Is it true that you are studying all day?'

At her prompting, he told her that the castle tutor, a learned monk who had taught Raimond and the bailiff's sons before the friar arrived, was pleased to have his brightest student under his tutelage once more. 'I'm finding it difficult to concentrate but Brother Renaud keeps telling me to accept my circumstances and use study to find peace. In a way he is right; when I am learning I can forget.'

He trailed off.

'Tell me what you are studying.'

'Latin, mathematics, history and even some of the French language. We are left alone. No one comes near us and Brother Renaud loves to share his knowledge.'

To Esme's relief, he continued to talk about his studies. Raimond was a scholar at heart. Jaufré's family had been scholars with contacts in the powerful houses throughout the lands of Trencavel and Toulouse. In 1209, hearing that a French Crusade was coming in their direction, Jaufré and Bernard's parents had sent them away from their native town of Béziers. Then aged ten and eight years old respectively, they had gone to relatives in Labernoc. Their parents had perished in the slaughter that ensued. In Labernoc, Jaufré, already well-grounded in Latin with a little Aramaic, continued his studies while Bernard concentrated on farming.

'Esme, you know I will have to learn the practices of the Roman church.'

Esme bit her tongue. She did not want to upset Raimond with her true response to that news. 'We're all praying that the friar forgets about you, *Besson,*' she said instead. 'I'd like to pray for something like an avalanche landing on top of his party in the mountains but Doña Agnes won't let me.'

Raimond chuckled. '*Bessa,* she is right! But we can pray he'll forget about me, that is good.'

She noticed that her legs were numb. Holding on to the bars of the window, she shook each leg. 'I'd better go, *besson,* but I can come back tomorrow and the night after. Whenever there is no moon and it is not wet, I'll be here.'

Raimond let his elegant fingers rest on her arm, pressing into her soft skin. Then she felt him kiss her hand. His lips lingered. His breath on her hand seemed to travel throughout her body, warming her. With promises to be there the following night, she climbed down the wall and ran back up the mountain to Guilhèm's cottage.

4

Labernoc, March 1237

THROUGHOUT WINTER, Esme spent every dark, dry night on the perch talking to Raimond. She made a leather strap for her right foot, which she hung from the bars. It allowed her to stay there for extended periods without losing sensation in her legs. Guilhèm warned Esme not to stay too long: 'Raimond won't be able to concentrate during the day if you keep him from his sleep.'

The young pair often became too engrossed in their conversation to remember this advice. Together they talked about their days, his studies, her hunts. She brought love from his sisters, and news from the village and the cottage. Sometimes they talked about Ava and Jaufré and the friar but, with Esme balanced on a stone above a long drop, and Raimond about to spend another night alone, they tended not to dwell on those events.

'The break in your father's hip is not mending properly,' Esme said to Raimond one evening in early March. 'He is beginning to walk a little with the crutch that Guilhèm made for him, but it is so painful that it takes all of his energy. But at least he is trying.' She did not add that Jaufré was increasingly prone to angry outbursts. Sometimes they were directed at Friar Tiqué and the Roman church; at other times he turned his anger on himself and what he called his stupidity in underestimating Rome's determination to destroy anyone who might challenge its power.

'I wish I could see him or at least talk to him.' Raimond caressed Esme's arm. 'I want to find out more about his months here with mother.'

'He won't talk about it. I've tried but…' Jaufré had told Esme that the bailiff had provided them with straw and blankets; Algaia had prepared their food with special herbs to help them. But any more than that, he would not say.

'Make sure father knows I am comfortable and well looked after.'

They sat in silence.

'I had better sleep soon, Esme. A priest who's related to Lady Sibella is arriving tomorrow to test me in Roman ritual.'

'Has Sibella been watching you?'

'I haven't seen her for a while. I've heard the servants whisper that she is in a very bad way but if they take the wine away from her, she screams and shouts. Sometimes I can hear her across the courtyard.'

'Do you remember the time she taught us all one of the courtly dances from her people. She was so pretty and nice.' Sibella came from a noble family near Montpellier. After an initial disappointment in the quality of the company in

Labernoc, she embraced her new life. Ava became a special friend, and Ava and Jaufré were frequent visitors to the castle.

'I pray for her, Esme, and for Lord Miguel.' Raimond said quietly.

That did not surprise Esme; Raimond had always liked praying. 'Have you included the friar in your nightly prayers yet?'

'Only that he forgets about me.'

They stopped talking and, in their silence, blew breath at each other. Sensing his sadness, Esme wanted to massage his hands tenderly. Serena had a way of working her thumb slowly around Guilhèm's coarse hands, caressing and massaging as she went; the love emanating from the simple practice brought peace to every corner of the cottage. Esme wanted to try it on Raimond but blushed at the idea.

Instead she said in a deliberately bright voice, 'Serena is definitely pregnant. She told us all today. Guilhèm doesn't know what to do. He is so excited and nervous. At least I think he is, I've never seen him nervous before.'

Raimond expressed his delight.

'He once said to me that he thought he would never marry or be a father,' Esme continued. 'It was because he is different. But Serena never cared what anyone thought. And now they are having a baby.'

Serena had been working in the kitchen of Puivert Castle when Guilhèm met her. An independent woman, she ignored those who advised her against becoming too close to a man of questionable parentage. Being tall with a light complexion, Guilhèm looked different to most of the people of the district, including his own parents, who were short with darker complexions. It was said that he talked to animals, and that the herbs and fungi he brought back from the forest for the local healer were unusually powerful. But Serena had no fear of the gossips. Even now, a year after moving in with Guilhèm as his wife, she had raised no objections to harbouring an escaped heretic in their home.

'When is the baby due?'

'In the autumn, I think.'

After a while, Raimond stifled a yawn. '*Bessa,* I really had better go to bed. I don't know what this new priest will be like.'

♦ ♦ ♦ ♦ ♦

When Esme had disappeared, Raimond sat cross-legged on his low, comfortable bed to say his prayers before sleeping. Closing his eyes and taking his most sacred object, his personal stone, out of the small pouch around his neck, he intertwined his fingers and prayed. He was very tired. The winter months in the castle had drained him. He was allowed to walk in the courtyard when there was no one around. He had not seen his sisters, although they had stood below his window several times and they had whispered to each other. But he missed them, he missed his parents, he missed being able to sit with Esme by the river, he missed Doña Agnes, Guilhèm and Serena. Only prayer kept him from sinking into despair. Holding his stone between his thumbs, he intertwined his fingers and sought out the warm light in his heart. As he meditated, he sensed the presence of his mother. He allowed the prayer to take him deeper into himself, a place where he was surrounded by light and a profound sense of peace, and where the dark forces in the world did not exist.

The following morning, Algaia went into Raimond's room to wake him. When she looked at him, his kind face surrounded by dark curly hair, she did not want to disturb him. Dismissing a sadness that brought tears to her eyes, she shook his shoulder. 'Maman,' Raimond muttered before opening his eyes and, seeing Algaia and daylight, he leapt out of bed.

The priest was waiting for him in the chapel to commence his exercises and expressed his annoyance when Raimond hurried in adjusting his clothes. The priest set a gruelling pace. The chapel was small with a high ceiling. The chairs and benches were neatly arranged with an aisle down the middle. The plain altar was on a raised step with a massive crucifix dominating it. A narrow window facing east shone light on the bloodied figure of Christ. Like many of his people, Raimond regarded the crucifix as an instrument of torture and death; he could not understand why the Roman church used it as a symbol for veneration.

After the morning sun moved on, the chapel became dark and, to Raimond's mind, sinister. He imagined Tiqué in here after questioning his parents in the dungeons below. Raimond had never been to the dungeons. If the church was so cold, damp and dark, he hated to think about the conditions his parents had suffered during their incarceration. Had the friar insisted that his prisoners plead for salvation in this chapel? Probably not. Tiqué had not wanted to convert his parents. Nothing but their execution would satisfy him. How else could anyone explain his lack of compassion towards Ava, a woman who loved her children dearly and had only shown kindness and support to her neighbours all of her life? He wished he could talk to his tutor about it but it was the one subject that was assiduously avoided.

By the end of the morning, the priest was instructing Raimond on how to carry a crucifix up the aisle of the chapel and present it with a bowed head to the celebrant. Raimond walked slowly up the aisle holding the metal object out in front of him, his arms aching. He reached the altar but the priest was standing on a step so high that Raimond had to strain his shoulders to put the crucifix into his outstretched hands. He was on his way back down the church to repeat the exercise when he felt a wave of exhaustion move over him. Mother, he whispered. Closing his eyes and clutching the crucifix in one hand, he placed his other hand on his heart.

'No! Not here!' cried Sibilla, suddenly appearing at the chapel door. 'You won't do that to us!'

Startled, Raimond opened his eyes and dropped the crucifix.

Wearing her night attire, the bailiff's wife rushed forward to pick it up. 'Heresy! I saw you, and in our house,' she hissed angrily, moving her face close to his. 'Do you want us all to burn?'

Raimond stepped back and opened his mouth to protest. He had not seen her for several weeks and was shocked at her condition. Her face was puffy and red, the whites of her eyes were yellow and her breath was foul. Her carer hurried into the chapel and reached for her. Sibilla dodged the woman's grasp and dug the crucifix into Raimond's cheek, breaking his skin just below his right eye. 'You and your kind will not destroy our family,' she cried, dragging the jagged metal tip down his cheek to his neck. Blood poured out from the deep gouge. As he fell backwards, the carer managed to get hold of the sick woman. Sibilla dropped the crucifix and sagged onto the floor, sobbing. The priest dashed forward, picked up the crucifix and hurried away with it to clean it.

Raimond lay beside Sibella, blood pouring from his wound. He drifted into unconsciousness and saw his mother put her arms out to him and smile. Then tears ran down her cheeks, her hair became straggly, her face gaunt, and ropes strapped her arms to her body. Mother, no! The friar's men were pushing her forward. She was twisting her head, he tried to call out; Alayda's mouth was straining as she tried to shout; Matina opened her mouth but no words came out. Their mother was disappearing into a mist. Raimond tried to run after her but his legs would not move. He cried out.

'Hush, my pet, hush. You are safe,' a woman murmured.

'Where am I?' Slowly Raimond focussed on his surroundings and discovered he was in the kitchen lying on cushions on the ground. The pain in his face was excruciating.

'It's just a cut, Raimond,' said the cook, dabbing at the gash running down one side of his face. 'I'm sure she didn't mean it. She should not have been out of her bed. Stay nice and still, my pet, let me finish cleaning it.'

Images of the fire consuming his mother and the holy people invaded Raimond's mind. He tried to halt the onslaught of grief but the pain was too much for him and he fainted again.

5

April 1237, Labernoc

FOUR WEEKS LATER, Esme and Guilhèm tracked Friar Pierre Tiqué and his party as they made their way slowly towards Puivert. It was now known that Tiqué was on his way to take charge of the friary in Carcassonne city. There were quicker ways from Ax-Les-Thermes to Carcassonne, and this suggested to them that the friar had not forgotten about Raimond. The party had expanded. There were twelve carts, each being pulled by mules and managed by a man. Esme counted twenty-three other men including another friar on horseback and several novices or additional clerks wearing long black cloaks and walking two by two. There were fourteen constables, including Barca and Del Gurbe, who took up the rear on horseback.

'At least they'll be easy to follow,' Esme said. 'They are so slow and so noisy that you could fall asleep under a tree and still find them when you woke up.'

Guilhèm was concerned about Esme's plan to follow

Raimond to Carcassonne. She had not travelled far from Labernoc before and would have no idea how to handle unwanted attention, which she was bound to receive as a young woman alone.

'I'm the daughter of troubadours, it is time I got on the road,' Esme replied when Guilhèm tried to caution her. 'And I'm not abandoning Raimond. He doesn't know how to live in a forest or talk his way into a castle kitchen. He would die out there alone.'

Guilhèm knew Esme's determination well. She might be small and vulnerable, but she was also strong and stubborn. If Tiqué took Raimond, no one would stop her from following. Guilhèm could not let her go alone but he did not want to leave his wife and mother, especially with Jaufré in the cottage.

Serena, however, was the one who made up his mind for him: 'You have to go, beloved. The baby is not due for another five months. Your mother told me that your world is bigger than this forest and sometimes you have to step out into it to do your duty.'

Guilhèm admonished his mother for putting Serena under pressure, but Agnes only smiled and rubbed his cheek softly, 'You are special, Guilhèm. You need to spread your wings. Your wife understands this; she is a wise woman.'

Guilhèm had no qualms about the journey itself. With his mother's encouragement, he had been travelling from a young age. His first long journey by himself had been at the age of seven when he went to Montségur, about half a day's walk from the cottage and not far from where they were sitting now. Getting there had been easy because the castle on the top of the pog was visible from afar. He had spent a long time watching the soldiers on the upper defences and wondering what it might be like to live in 'the castle in the sky,' as Agnes called it. He had become confused on his return journey and had to scramble up a high ridge to locate Puivert Castle in the distance and regain his bearings. It was dark by the time he got home but his mother had only smiled at him in her curious way and given him a large bowl of soup. Since then he had travelled great distances, hunting and exploring and surviving on his wits. He had been to Carcassonne and Toulouse and other large towns in the region but had never stayed long. He found them tense places where people behaved in unpredictable ways. Guilhèm understood animals, knew their instincts and reactions, and respected them. Men, however, acted on fears that bore no relation to the danger around them.

As Tiqué and his party trundled along the main road to Labernoc, Esme and Guilhèm took a short cut along the cliff tops to a lookout. From here they could see the villagers scurry indoors just as Tiqué led his party into view. The constables were vigilant, their lances held at a menacing angle, as the entire party clattered through the deserted marketplace. They reached the castle gates without incident and Tiqué rode into the courtyard to disappear from sight.

♦ ♦ ♦ ♦ ♦

Raimond stood beside his tutor as he waited in a respectful line with Miguel Garcias and the indoor staff in the stone hallway of the castle. He tried not to touch the scar on his face, which was itchy. He had only seen Esme four or five times over the past month. Algaia had kept him in her quarters for days after the incident. Then the moon had been too bright and the sky cloudless, and after that there had been rain. He prayed every night that Tiqué would decide he did not want him after all. Why had God blessed him with such good handwriting? Maybe if he had not been a scholar? Maybe if he failed at his lessons? But Raimond could not do that; his mother had always told them that they had each been born with gifts and they should always do their best.

He heard the sound of horses and the shouted instructions of the soldiers. Keeping his head bent and his eyes on the ground, his curly hair fell over his forehead and cheeks. He heard the nervous voice of the bailiff, Miguel Garcias, greet Friar Pierre Tiqué. Raimond could see the friar take off his cloak and drop it into the waiting arms of a castle servant. He watched the swishing of the friar's habit as he crossed the hall. The hem of his tunic was muddy.

Miguel was apologising for the absence of Sibella, who was confined to her quarters, when Tiqué interrupted. 'My lord, I have had a trying time, the mountains are full of violent ruffians, and I wish to leave tomorrow morning with my new servant. Where is he?'

He stopped in front of Raimond. He smelt of medicinal pomander. The shiny ring with a silver cross on the bezel and a gold oak leaf on either side of it looked out of place on his rough hands.

'Young man, I trust you have worked hard.'

Slowly Raimond raised his head to the taller man. The

coarse face, ruddy from the exertion of the lengthy horseback ride, looked down at him. Raimond watched as Tiqué's face transformed from one of tired efficiency to fury; his brow furrowed, his left eye opened wide, the veins in his temples bulged and red marks appeared on his cheeks. Even his lazy right eye seemed to find muscles to express anger.

'What is this!' came the bellow. The scar, still vividly red, ran from Raimond's left eye to half way down his neck.

The bailiff shuffled his feet.

'Sire, what have you done?' Tiqué swung around to Miguel Garcias. 'This is my servant and I charged you to protect him.'

The bailiff opened his mouth to speak but Tiqué was too angry to wait for an answer: 'I cannot have this man in my household. He looks like he has been in an ale-fuelled brawl. How do you expect me to take him to Rome as my servant? We shall be mocked.'

Miguel stood mute.

Tiqué swung away from the bailiff and strode over to the front door and breathed deeply and noisily.

Raimond's heart beat rapidly with renewed hope.

The friar came back and stood in front of Raimond. He put his finger under his chin and moved his face from side to side. Raimond kept his eyes down.

'I am sorry, Raimond,' said Tiqué eventually. 'I offered you the chance for an education and a worthy life but I simply can't...'

A surge of joy rushed through Raimond. He looked up at the friar, his eyes sparkling.

Tiqué stepped backwards, as if he had been slapped. His

face turned from anger to puzzlement and then to what Raimond later could only describe as curiosity. Tiqué turned to his host: 'I am going to my quarters,' his voice once more firm and authoritative. 'Send refreshments up to me. We will leave at daylight tomorrow morning. Have Raimond ready to accompany me.'

6

Labernoc April 1237

THE FOLLOWING MORNING Guilhèm and Esme were once more on the lookout, but this time they each carried a small pack. Shortly after sunrise, the Inquisition party trundled out of Labernoc Castle. Constables Barca and Del Gurbe emerged first, then Tiqué on his brown horse, followed by the men and carts. Esme spotted Raimond. He was sitting among trunks and other goods in one of the carts with several other servants. He wore a large black cloak and was looking around him.

'I'm here', Esme wanted to cry.

Matina and Alayda waited at the edge of the village to see him. As his cart approached, they put out their hands in a vain attempt to grasp his. Then Alayda cried out.

'What have they done to you?' She pushed past a constable to reach Raimond. The constable grabbed her and threw her to the ground. Alayda leapt up and fought to reach Raimond again. Barca rode up and slid off his horse. Tiqué kept going, paying no attention to the shouting and dull thuds of his men dealing with troublesome peasants.

Raimond watched with horror as Barca punched his feisty sister in the face and kicked her as she fell. As his cart drew him away, he watched Matina hold the semi-conscious Alayda gently. He whispered words of love and reassurance to them long after they were obscured by shrubs along the route.

Guilhèm put his hands on Esme's shoulders and turned her towards him: 'Everything I have taught you about stalking an animal in the forest, remember it now. Be patient, remain very calm. Do not get excited about anything – good or bad. We don't know the world we are going into. Nor do we have any plan other than to stay as close to Raimond as possible. One mistake, one moment of stupidity, one cry of fear, and you could jeopardise your own life and possibly Raimond's too.'

Esme put her hand on her heart. She was very grateful to him for coming with her. She hoped that Raimond could escape as soon as the party reached Carcassonne but Guilhèm had warned her not to speculate. 'I know that Jaufré is saying that Raimond should simply walk away once Tiqué's back is turned. But Tiqué is a dogmatist. If Raimond runs away, he will be declared a heretic. Tiqué might also attack Matina and Alayda. So let's go cautiously.'

The Inquisition party made its way down to the vast dry lake bed below Labernoc. The sun was shining and a gentle breeze blew from the craggy mountains to the east. Puivert Castle with its square tower stood out on the ridge to the north. Esme could see soldiers lounging outside the gate of the castle. In the hamlets below the castle, people moved about, tending their vegetables, minding their animals and watching their children play. It looked peaceful and ordinary but Esme guessed that every adult was aware of the trundling carts and the clopping of hooves in the distance.

Esme and Guilhèm skirted around the edge of the forest and made their way to the top of the escarpment. They could see Tiqué and his party moving down through the wide valley towards the Aude River. From there, Guilhèm knew they would follow the river, which would take them directly to Carcassonne city. He also knew that, being so slow moving, they would have to stop for the night along the way. There were plenty of mountain ridges and forest cover in which they could track the group safely. At times when there was no cover, they hung back but there was no danger of losing them. The group stopped at Alet-les-Bains for the night.

Esme waited until it was dark and ran ahead to place sticks in a heart shape along the track where Raimond might see them from his seat in the cart. The next morning she was pleased when he spotted the second one. He looked up at the trees on the steep slope to the west of the river and Esme moved a branch in a gentle rhythm. With a quick look around him, he put his hand on his heart and smiled slightly.

The party proceeded into a narrow pass. The tree-covered slopes of the hills dropped to the river where, over many centuries, a track wide enough for two carts to pass each other had been fashioned along its western side. Sound travelled easily in this pass so Esme and Guilhèm hung back. They heard one of the friar's men singing a hymn. Others joined in. As the echo carried their voices further, they gained confidence and sang louder, reaching for higher notes with ease. The beautiful sound filled the valley. Suddenly the music turned into howls and yells. Guilhèm and Esme hurried forward. The Inquisition party was under attack. Raimond, the clerks, novice friars and servants were covering their heads with their arms as rocks came hurtling down from the western slope. Tiqué was hit on the arm and spurred his horse forward. The constables were already off their horses and charging through the forest undergrowth towards the assailants. Shouts from the trees indicated that the situation was under control. Esme strained to see if Raimond was injured. He was looking out warily from under his arms and, as the constables called down with their assurances, he sat upright. To Esme's relief, he gave no indication that he had been hit by anything.

Tiqué returned as his constables dragged three boys from the trees and threw them to the ground in front of him. Still nursing his left shoulder, Tiqué demanded an explanation. A lanky red-headed boy of about ten or eleven years stared back at him defiantly. Two smaller boys, also red-headed, whimpered as a constable kept a hard grip on their necks.

'Where do you come from?'

The constable shook the youngest boy, who pointed along the track in the direction Tiqué was heading.

'Tie them up. We'll take them to their parents,' snapped Tiqué, turning to walk on.

Ropes were looped around each of the three boys, tying their arms to their bodies, and they were pushed out in front of Tiqué. As the valley widened, a cluster of houses appeared.

A woman working on a vegetable patch at the edge of the hamlet spotted the boys and rushed forward.

Acknowledging the imposing figure of Friar Tiqué on his horse, she stooped to untie the ropes on the smallest boy. 'I am sorry, Most Reverend. Have our boys have been annoying you?' She was struggling to undo the knot with one hand while wiping the boy's tears with the other. 'They are only young and a bit high-spirited. I am sure they didn't mean… ahhh'

Constable Del Gurbe had leapt off his horse and hit her hard on the side of the head, knocking her to the ground. Several villagers ran forward as more came out of their houses to see what was going on. The constables raised their weapons.

'What are you doing, Reverend? They are women and children' a tall man with red hair and a bushy beard shouted angrily as a constable blocked him with his lance.

A dog barked and tugged at the garment of one of the clerks. The clerk, a slight man, shouted and kicked at it. A little boy ran up to the dog and, in his attempt to restrain the dog, also pulled at the clerk's cloak. The clerk kicked the child.

'Please!' cried an older woman who had rushed to help the injured woman. 'You are men of the church. Have pity.'

Constable Barca lifted his sword and struck the woman. Blood spurted from her shoulder as she collapsed. The red-headed man lunged at a constable but he too was struck by a sword. Several more men went to his aid and a vicious mêlée erupted. Tiqué, still on his horse, backed away. Raimond sank into the protection of the trunks.

The constables gained control. Tiqué signalled to Barca, who issued an order. The constables formed a tight defensive line. At least one woman and two men were dead, and several more were badly injured. The three boys, terrified and still held by the ropes, were huddled together in the open space between the constables and their families.

Tiqué turned his horse back towards the track. 'Constable Barca, we must press on. Deal with this.'

With that Barca raised his sword and slashed the neck of the older boy. As he fell, Barca swung his sword back and slashed the other two boys, wounding one after the other. The three fell into a heap, blood pumping from their bodies. Screams distorted the villagers' faces. Tiqué turned back and scowled in disgust: 'Constable! Deal with this means regroup our party and let us get on the road.'

Her eyes wide with fear, Esme clung to the tree. The cry that had escaped her moments earlier had been inaudible above those of the villagers. Now she held on for her life, desperately trying to keep still and looking to Guilhèm for help. He was staring at a small bird that had landed on the branch in front of him. Only fear of being found stopped her from shouting at him to do something. His concentration on the bird, however, was so peculiar that, despite the savagery only metres away from her, she found herself in its spell.

Guilhèm blinked his eyes and the bird flew away. Esme watched it circle the departing group and land on the head of one of the mules pulling Raimond's cart. It spread its red tail as it hopped onto the animal's rump. The bird remained on the mule, hopping up and down in response to the steady movement of the animal's hind legs. Raimond paid no attention to it. He was trying to control his nausea. 'Watch the birds, my beloved son'. He looked around for the source of the whisper. It was a favourite saying of his mother. Then he spotted the bird, still hopping on the animal's rump. Involuntarily, he glanced in the directions of the trees. A branch swayed gently in the wind. Esme was here. He turned his head back sharply and, feeling his colour rise, looked quickly at the other servants in the cart. Their expressions were blank. He neutralised his own facial expression as he watched the bird fly away.

7

Carcassonne, April 1237

GUILHÈM SAT CROSS-LEGGED with his eyes closed at the edge of a forest to the north of Carcassonne city. Esme was beside him, quiet and still. The scene was striking. Set on top of a hill in low undulating land was an enormous castle. The city walls were at the base of the hill. Within those walls Esme could see the roofs of so many houses that she wondered how anyone could move between them. There was a church inside the wall on the edge of the town. If a friary was attached to it, Raimond might be based there.

Soldiers stationed at the entrance to the town appeared to be taking a relaxed approach to the people who passed through the gate. There were no signs of interrogation or rigorous control; but perhaps only locals came and went and the soldiers knew them all. It was a good sign, however.

Esme glanced at Guilhèm. He was deep in meditation. He sat like that during a hunt when he was listening for the animals. She suspected that he was listening to the town and everyone in it. She closed her eyes to see if she could sense anything but all she could think about were the three red-headed boys. Before the friar arrived at Labernoc, she had begun to master the art of hearing deer through her own heartbeat but it had slipped away as soon as her foster parents were arrested. She had tried again recently but without success; there was too much sadness in her heart for stillness. But if she was to survive in Carcassonne, she would have to find a way to rebuild that skill.

Guilhèm opened his eyes and observed the activity in the distance.

Esme took cheese, bread and dried meat out of her pack and laid it on a small cloth. 'What are we going to do?'

'This is going to take a while, Esme. Be patient,' he said. He took a knife from his waistcoat and cut some meat.

He watched birds and butterflies flit in the warm air, and rested. After a while he sat up straight, closed his eyes and returned to his meditation.

Esme picked at a small hole in the woollen sleeve of her tunic. She opened her sewing pouch and selected a needle and thread to mend it. She had demonstrated an aptitude for sewing when she was young and, over the years, had developed her skills, especially for fine embroidery and darning. When she was eight, her father had visited from Foix and given her the sewing pouch that had belonged to her mother. She thought about her parents as she threaded the needle. She knew the story about her birth and her mother dying moments later. She knew about her father's distress and Ava's agreement to look after her along with her own newborn son, Raimond.

Esme's father did not return to Labernoc for five or six years, by which time Esme had become settled with Ava and Jaufré's family. Her father moved to Foix where he became a successful merchant. He visited Labernoc regularly and often brought her presents. The sewing pouch was a treasured possession. She had added to it since then and hoped to earn her living by sewing in Carcassonne.

Farmers were now leaving the city pushing empty drays. It must have been a market day. She watched them as they made their way back to the hamlets nestled in the landscape. No one came in their direction.

A bee landed on Guilhèm's nose; he did not notice. Esme wondered how Raimond was coping with the horror they had witnessed in the village. At least she could talk to Guilhèm. But Raimond was alone, surrounded by the people who had killed his mother, injured his father and had now committed another atrocity. She knew he would want to pray but praying in the traditional way, his fingers intertwined, his stone between his thumbs, would be dangerous. Even resting his hands on his heart would be risky because it had become associated with heretical practice; it suggested to the Roman priests that these other Christians were looking to their own heart for guidance rather than the Pope and his bishops. Raimond would be allowed to pray aloud to Jesus but not to Mary Magdalene and certainly not to their daughter Sarah. He would have to cross himself and take oaths, both of which went against the teachings of their people.

Esme's breathing became shallow. Not wanting to disturb Guilhèm, she reached into a little pouch that hung around her neck on a golden chain and took out a small, dark-grey stone. She squeezed it in her right hand. This was her personal stone, which a holy woman had helped her to find when she was seven. It was supposed to calm her down. 'Our greatest temple lies inside ourselves,' the woman had said. 'Select a stone, study it and when the time is right, engrave it with an image that is an external representation of your soul.'

She remembered when she had gone to the river with Raimond to choose a stone each. She had selected a stone that was round except for one pointed edge. Raimond found one that was almost a perfect diamond shape. It was a flat stone with smooth surfaces. Three of the sides were straight and of equal length. The fourth was longer and had a jagged edge. When they put their stones together, her pointed edge and his jagged edge interlocked. They had accepted this coincidence without surprise. Esme thought of her stone as a place where she could keep her favourite stories. She etched images of fissures onto it and envisaged her stories going into the stone through the scratches.

One day, when she was ten years old, Esme's father had visited Labernoc and given her a shining grey pearl that her mother had worn. When Esme placed her stone and the pearl side by side, the light in the pearl reflected the fissures on her stone. At that moment she saw her personal stone as a pearl. Five years later, she believed that her outward representation of her soul was a stone pearl that was full of stories.

When she was younger, all of the stories she had gathered were happy ones. In the past year, the stories had been full of cruelty and sadness but, after consulting Guilhèm, she had put these into her stone also. Now she wondered if she should put the story of the three red-headed boys and their families in too. Could the stone pearl hold that many terrible stories? Would they squash her happy stories? Would that change her? She would never forget what had happened in that village but did she want to keep reminding herself? Maybe if she put the memories into the stone, she could clear them from her mind? Esme closed her eyes and held the stone to her heart. Yes, the stories should be in here. If she had the capacity to hold those memories, then so had her stone. She opened her eyes and envisaged the story of the boys and their families going in through a fissure and finding a quiet place to rest.

It was dark when Guilhèm finished his meditation and told her to prepare for a night in the forest. As they wrapped themselves in their jackets and curled into the roots of trees, he explained that he had been listening to the heartbeat of the city. This was a new experience for him; he had never listened to the heartbeat of a large number of people in a cluttered place before. It was taking a long time. He sensed two layers to the city; one prosperous, busy and confident; the other troubled and unhappy. He knew that the people of Carcassonne had suffered at the hands of the Pope's crusaders following a siege in 1209.

'Many people in this town are now hiding who they truly are,' he said to Esme as they settled down for the night. 'They've had twenty-eight years of French rule. Nine of those years were under de Montfort. His rule may have damaged many good-hearted people.'

'Like Miguel Garcias,' said Esme.

'I'm not talking about the lords. It's the ordinary people we have to be wary of. You are used to living in a very spacious environment and knowing everyone around you. Here you will become confused with the crowds and may not be able to tell a friend from an enemy. Stay close to me and, if in doubt, do not speak.'

The following morning, Guilhèm once more sat still with his eyes closed but he did not remain like that for long.

'Prepare to leave on my word. We are about to get help. When we go into Carcassonne you will be my daughter. I will be recently widowed. My name is ... Clement. Yours will be Pixie. We have come to the city to give you a chance of female company as you grow up. And if people think that you are a girl of eleven or twelve years old, don't argue.'

A lively expression came over Esme's face as she rearranged her jacket to hide her feminine figure: 'I can do eleven or twelve very well.'

'Esme, this is not a game.'

Her expression changed. 'I know, Guilhèm, but I don't know how good a liar I am, so I'll have to think like a troubadour or I might give myself away.'

'Just remember the consequences and say a few prayers to help yourself.'

'I know it is serious when you tell me to pray!'

He smiled at her, his brown eyes crinkling up. 'You're able for this or I wouldn't risk it.'

With their bundles ready to hoist on their shoulders, they monitored the approach to the city.

'There he is. That's the man who'll help us,' Guilhèm

jumped up and pointed at a thick-set man who was pushing a cart with several carcasses on it. A large, shiny black dog walked beside him. The man was struggling with the cart on the slope leading to the town gate. Guilhèm and Esme emerged from the forest and walked quickly towards the man. As they approached him from behind, one of the three gutted deer carcasses on the cart began to slide.

Guilhèm moved forward to help. 'They're good carcasses,' he said as he secured the carcass on top of the others and put his shoulder to the cart.

'Thank you, friend,' said the man, puffing with exertion. 'But it has taken so long to get them to the kitchens of the castle that I'm afraid the meat will be no good.

'Cleverly cut, they should still yield many dinners,' said Guilhèm.

'Ah, my hands are too tired to get the best out of them,' the man stopped to rest and, leaning on the side of the cart, looked with interest at Guilhèm's rusty-red waistcoat with its array of hunters' knives slotted neatly into different-sized pockets. 'You're a hunter?'

They looked each other in the eye. A moment of recognition passed between them. It spoke of a shared way of being, a way that was peaceful and tolerant. The man tried to hide his surprise. Few people in Carcassonne dared to look with such familiarity into another's eyes in case it prompted an accusation of heresy. This light-skinned man had no such hesitation. The old hunter wanted to smile and embrace him but only said in a low voice, 'Be careful, friend. I don't want to know what you want here but if you can help me improve the yield from these carcasses, you are welcome to work with me. My name is Nicholaus.'

Guilhèm introduced himself as Clement and Esme as Pixie, and pushed the cart while Esme kept the slippery carcasses from falling off. Nicholaus was greeted by the soldiers at the town gate and, after a chat and the promise of a parcel of meat once his new friend had helped him to cut it, they were waved on. Esme tried not to appear too excited. They were in the town and had not been challenged. Her curiosity took over as they made their way up the cobblestone road towards the castle. The road was hemmed in by low buildings, which Esme guessed were rows of separate homes because at brief intervals there was a door and a window or two before another door. Occasionally there was a gap but these just led to lanes also lined with houses. Looking in through open doors and windows, she saw tables and chairs, and pots and pans. The interiors, she concluded, were the same as those in Labernoc. She wondered how the people living here could breathe; there was very little space for air.

Men and women walked along the roads, greeting each other or sometimes stopping to talk. They were well dressed and their clothes were clean. Many of the women had light colours in their dresses and wore veils on their combed hair. Esme glanced at herself. She knew that her hair sat on top of her head like a bird's nest and her clothes were dark and well-worn. She was glad that she was walking with the hunter; no one expected hunters to look clean and tidy after a night in the forest.

Several people exchanged pleasantries with Nicholaus.

A man who was pushing a cart of wood, stopped to let Nicholaus past. He looked with curiosity at Guilhèm. 'Pons still carousing with the friar's men, I suppose.'

Nicholaus sighed. 'He's too old to give orders to now.'

The man shrugged. 'Ah, errant sons. What can you do?' And he passed on his way.

Nicholaus, Guilhèm and Esme approached the impressive main gates of the castle. Esme tried not to look nervous. The gates were huge compared to Puivert Castle and there were at least ten soldiers guarding them. Her heart sank. How would they ever get past them?

'We don't use the main entrance,' said Nicholaus. 'That's for the seneschal and his officials and for the friar and his men, who live in there too. We go directly to the kitchen courtyard. It's just along here.'

Esme opened her mouth to ask for more information but Guilhèm's sideways glance stopped her. They pushed the cart to the left of the main gate and along the castle walls for some distance. The walls were high and the stones well cut. There were no hand holds, foot holds or convenient ledges. They came to a gate. Two soldiers were on guard. They welcomed Nicholaus noisily. A big sergeant emerged. The men deferred to him.

'And who have we here?' the sergeant asked, looking at Guilhèm and Esme closely.

Nicholaus introduced them saying that if Clement proved to be a good butcher, he was going to employ him as his partner.

'So you've given up on Pons at last?' asked the big man. 'You are wise to do so.'

He waved them on. Esme found herself in a spacious courtyard with trees covered in white spring blossoms at intervals. Long trestle tables were stacked up against the trees. The courtyard was surrounded by high walls on the north, east and south sides. On the west side of the courtyard was a row of doorways. Above it, on the first floor, was a long balcony with arched doors opening onto it. Towering above that again was a high wall that was part of the castle. She could hear voices but there was no sign of anyone.

Leaving the cart outside a closed door, Nicholaus led them up the steps to the first floor and into a long, wide kitchen. The sun came from behind a cloud and light streamed in through the south-facing doors. As Esme's eyes adjusted, she absorbed the scene before her. There were four or five lengthy, wooden tables down the middle of the room with benches on either side. There was a big fire at one end of the room and two small fires, one in the middle and one at the end. Smoke was funnelled away from the fires so the air was surprisingly clear. Several people sat in groups along the tables. They turned to look at them, nodded at Nicholaus, quickly took in Guilhèm and Esme, and returned to their conversations. Esme could see women working near the biggest fire.

A tall woman with grey hair swept on top of her head approached them and greeted Nicholaus with a kiss while looking enquiringly at Esme and Guilhèm. Nicholaus introduced her as his wife, Jacotina, who was in charge of the kitchen. He explained that Clement was going to help him to butcher the meat and suggested that Pixie remain with her. Jacotina welcomed them without hesitation and, as the men left for the ice house below the kitchen, Jacotina invited Esme to sit on a comfortable chair by the fire and have some food. As she settled into the soft chair, Esme suddenly felt exhausted. A cat pushed into the seat beside her and rested its head on her lap. Cuddling the cat, named Mouser, she dozed off thinking of Raimond, who was somewhere on the other side of the great stone wall that divided her from the main castle.

In the early evening, having completed their work, Guilhèm and Nicholaus sat in the kitchen over the main meal of the day chatting amiably to the sergeant who they had met at the gate. Soldiers, servants, blacksmiths and other castle workers filled the tables. As a hunter, Guilhèm found easy acceptance among these people. The conversation revolved around hunting and stories of successes, failures and techniques were exchanged. As the wine flowed, Guilhèm feigned interest while taking in the activity of the staff area with all of his senses. It was a pleasant environment. Everyone was defined by their work. He could see that senior members of staff, whether the sergeant or the head blacksmith or the housekeeper, kept an eye on the general staff. A young man who was drinking too much wine was sent to his sleeping quarters. A soldier who was being aggressively flirtatious with one of the kitchen girls was warned to mind himself. This gathering might otherwise have suggested a village party but was in fact an extension of their working world.

Suddenly Guilhèm noticed the room go quiet and felt Nicholaus stiffen beside him. He shifted in his seat and turned slowly. A tall, light-haired man had come through the door. He shouted greetings, none of which were returned with any enthusiasm. He strutted up to the women at the end of the kitchen, roughly kissed two of them and came down the other side of the table towards Nicholaus. The old hunter looked up and acknowledged his son, Pons, warily.

'I hear you went out with another hunter, old man?'

Reluctantly Nicholaus introduced Guilhèm, who raised a cup in acknowledgement. Pons' face was puffy, his clothes were stained and smelt of stale wine.

Pons leant down and thumped the table with his fist. 'Do you really think you can dismiss me?' His voice was slurred.

'I'm sorry, son, I couldn't wait for you yesterday and went out by myself. I was lucky enough to meet Clement on the way back. He helped me with the butchering.'

'But I still get my cut. That's the deal. He's not getting it,' his slate-grey eyes narrowed as he looked at Guilhèm.

'He's already got it,' said Nicholaus, keeping his voice low. 'And unless you are willing to join me sober and on time, I can no longer work with you.'

'It's my entitlement. You can't give my entitlement to anyone else without the seneschal's permission.'

Nicholaus shook his head to end the conversation. He had finally run out of patience with his son. Nicholaus liked this newcomer and his small daughter. Clement was an exceptionally skilled butcher and appeared to know a lot about hunting. With him as his companion, the older man could continue to earn a living for some time yet.

Without warning Pons launched himself across the table at his father and knocked him backwards. Instinctively Guilhèm reached out for Nicholaus to stop him from falling while the sergeant and several soldiers grabbed Pons and pulled him back to his side of the table.

'It's my entitlement, old man,' Pons shouted from beneath the arms that held him. 'Give it to this stranger and you'll be sorry.'

Still shouting, Pons was pushed out of the kitchen and down the steps to the courtyard. 'Go back to the friar's men,' one of the soldiers called after him. 'They'll make you welcome.'

Nicholaus turned to Guilhèm. 'I apologise for my son, Clement. A friar arrived a couple of days ago. Pons has been drinking with his constables ever since.'

'He's trouble with or without the constables,' said Jacotina, sitting down beside the men.

Guilhèm was glad when someone started to sing.

8

Carcassonne, April–June 1237

Nicholaus and Jacotina eased Guilhèm and Esme's entry into Carcassonne. Despite his son's opposition, Nicholaus offered Guilhèm a job. The couple also insisted that Guilhèm and Esme take one of the three spacious rooms in their home near the castle walls. When they assured Guilhèm that this was originally Jacotina's house and that he was not taking Pons' space, Guilhèm welcomed the offer. It was an easy matter to get bedding for himself and Esme.

Guilhèm's butchering skills enabled him to extract more meat from each carcass than Jacotina expected. So, with Nicholaus's collusion, he distributed some of the excess as small gifts to the sergeant and the castle guard. Jacotina gave Esme work in the kitchen, found her sewing jobs for extra income, and fussed over her as if she were her own daughter.

Esme was fascinated by the town and many of the townspeople enjoyed feeding the curiosity of the hunter's scruffy child.

Accompanied by Nicholaus's black dog, Lopp, she walked around freely, confident that none of Tiqué's men had seen her in Labernoc. She chatted to the Carcassonne castle servants, the soldiers on every gate, the market stall holders, the women who sat outside their houses and anyone who admired Lopp. She asked them about foods, fabrics, oils, tools and other items she had never seen before, and admired the colours and stitching on women's clothes. She knew not to ask anyone personal questions but she was surprised at how many people offered her information about themselves. She heard about their families, their lives in Carcassonne, gossip about neighbours and, of most interest to her, about life under Simon de Montfort and the crusaders from some of the older people. 'It is your gift,' said Guilhèm, repeating an observation made by his mother about Esme. 'People like to talk to you and they feel comfortable sharing a little of their story with you. But remember to put the information straight into your stone and don't repeat it. It will be safe there.'

She was also gathering plenty of practical information about the city. She learnt that Tiqué was living in special quarters within the main castle; his administrators, servants and other friars lived in the same area while the constables had a camp in the dry moat by the castle. Tiqué seldom left the confines of the castle but strolled around the inner courtyard talking to important people. It was whispered to Esme on more than one occasion that everyone, including the seneschal, was wary of the friar, whose reputation had preceded him.

While Esme enjoyed her interactions with the people of Carcassonne, she felt the absence of Raimond all the more keenly. She could tell Guilhèm about her day but it was not the same as sharing it with Raimond. She saw him periodically, in a procession of friars, administrators and servants that walked between the castle and the church near the town gate. There was no pattern to the timing of these processions but they were never at mealtimes. After she heard someone say, 'Rome's men are on their way to the church again', she would drop what she was doing and position herself for their return trip. The procession usually skirted around the edge of the marketplace, went up a short lane and turned into the main path to the castle gates. With Lopp for company, Esme would leave a heart made of twigs, or a little pile of leaves with a feather on top by the side of their route. She would watch from the shadows of a laneway to see Raimond's secret smile when he spotted them. But not being able to talk to him was frustrating. She wished she could have even a few moments with him.

Guilhèm meditated each morning and started by focusing his attention on his wife. Each time he sensed that she was peaceful and enjoying her pregnancy. More importantly, his mother was also calm. He knew that if he picked up any anxiety from Agnes, it was time to go home. But everything at the cottage felt good.

Then he listened to the city of Carcassonne. His skills at listening to the city were developing well and he could sense a shift in the mood of the city. From the beginning of May, he discerned a dark mist hovering over Carcassonne. Each day it became a little thicker and moved a little closer. He could not see how it was manifesting in the city because daily life appeared to be continuing as normal. But Guilhèm remained wary.

♦ ♦ ♦ ♦ ♦

At the end of May, six weeks after they had arrived in Carcassonne, there was a surge of activity in the city as several friars with clerks, servants and constables arrived to take up residence in the castle. The atmosphere in the town changed immediately. It was presumed that there was to be another Inquisition.

'It won't be in the city itself,' Nicholaus confided to Guilhèm. 'If Tiqué wanted an Inquisition here, the gates would have been closed by now. It's probable that they are going to use this as their base and go to outlying villages and hamlets.'

Guilhèm chose to stay in Carcassonne but told Esme to stay on constant alert. 'Keep your belongings together and if I say we are leaving, come with me without argument.'

A few days later, on a hot afternoon, Esme sat in the marketplace with Lopp. A procession from the friary walked along the edge of the marketplace towards the church. None of the newly arrived friars looked as commanding as Tiqué but they walked in a tight group, as if the people of Carcassonne were their natural enemy. Raimond was not there.

She was resting her chin on the dog's shiny coat when, a few minutes later, she saw Raimond running towards the church carrying a document. He was alone. She jumped up.

'Would you like some cherries, Pixie?' asked a stall holder nearby. 'I'm closing up now; it's too hot to stay here.'

Hiding her agitation, she took the cherries with thanks and planned the little signs she would place on the ground for Raimond's return journey. Just then, two friars came out of the church and hurried back towards the castle. Raimond followed them, walking at a normal pace. Esme walked into a side road; then, with Lopp at her heels, she ran as fast as she could around the backs of houses and up a narrow lane that intersected with the main route. When she reached the main road to the castle, she stopped, breathless. The shutters of the houses were closed to the afternoon heat and people remained indoors. Only the flies buzzed about. Kneeling down, she nuzzled Lopp while keeping her eye on the road. The two friars scuttled past deep in conversation. A few moments later, Raimond came by.

'Lopp,' she called softly as she let the dog go.

Raimond slowed down and looked around him. Esme called the dog's name again. Raimond stopped and turned to her. His eyes lit up. Esme's heart turned over and her cheeks went bright red. She looked up and down the road. The friars had already vanished around the corner to the castle gate. No one else was visible. 'It's all clear,' she whispered. Raimond stepped into the laneway and bent down to stroke Lopp's shining coat. Esme crouched down on the other side of the dog.

'Esme, you look so well... Oh it is so good to see you,' he gripped her arm, which lay on Lopp's back.

Uncharacteristically flustered, Esme could only squeeze his arm with her other hand. She had imagined this moment so many times but was stuck for words. She could not say that he was looking well. His head was shaved but for a dark tonsure, which made him look older. His face was pale and dominated by the angry red scar; it must have been very deep to leave such a mark three months after the assault.

'One of the friars gave me an oil to help with the scarring,' he said following her eye. 'It will ease in time.'

Esme wanted to kiss the scar but she kissed the dog instead. 'This is Lopp.'

'Where are you staying? Are you safe?'

They spoke rapidly and in a jumble as they tried to catch up with each other's lives since they had last spoken. She told him about her new identity, Guilhèm working for Nicholaus, her new friends in the castle kitchen and her conversations with soldiers and traders.

'I'm impressed,' laughed Raimond. 'They really think you're a child called Pixie and they are petting you and feeding you!'

She laughed with him. 'I work as well, helping in the kitchens and do some sewing. But *besson*, I have so much to tell you. I miss having you to talk to. Guilhèm is very patient but it's not the same as telling you. But how are you? What's it like in there?'

Esme watched him as he spoke quietly, his green eyes glistening with unshed tears. He told her that life with the friars was tolerable and that most of the friars, including the latest arrivals, were friendly to him. There was plenty of time to pray and to study, both of which suited him. His ability to absorb Latin was noted and his script admired. 'When the friars heard about my parents, they just said that I was unlucky to be born to heretics and would now be saved.'

Esme snorted loudly. 'Oh Raimond it is so good to talk to you again.' He was looking at her as he had always done; she imagined they were back in the forest together sharing the excitement of some activity from the day.

'*Bessa*, if we ever get separated, if Tiqué ever takes me to Rome, will you make sure that your father in Foix always knows where you are. When I escape, I won't go to Labernoc just in case I'm followed there. I've been thinking about this. I have to wait until the moment is right. I remember your father from his visits; I'll find him. Please, just let him know where you are so I can find you.'

'Why, what's going on?' Fear crept into her voice.

'Tiqué is ambitious. He is using me to get ahead.'

'How can he do that?'

'I write up all of his important documents. He is very proud of my work. Also,' Raimond hesitated. 'I found out that he was the son of a heretical father and I think he wants to show his masters that I too can be a good friar.'

'But that means he will take you to Rome!'

'That's why, just in case, you must make sure your father knows where you are.'

Esme agreed. They looked at their hands on the back of Lopp, who was standing quietly.

'Esme, you've probably noticed that there are more friars arriving.' He explained that the recent arrivals would soon be going into the villages and hamlets around Carcassonne to arrest people who had been named as heretics.

'Can we warn them?'

'I don't know who they are. He keeps that list to himself.

Tiqué wants to impress Rome with this Inquisition. What he really wants to do is an Inquisition at Montségur. He's heard they have sacred documents from the time of Jesus.'

'The people on Montségur will just look at him from the top of the mountain and tell him to go away.'

'*Bessa,* I have so much more to tell you but I'll have to go. Please be careful.'

'Wait for the rest of them; then pretend you stayed on in the church.'

He held her look without responding. After some moments, she dropped her eyes, blushing. 'I miss you,' he said quietly.

Esme looked at their intertwined arms. 'When is this going to end, Raimond? When will we be free?' She squeezed his hand, struggling to contain her tears.

'I get so sad sometimes, Esme. My mother, she was so good and kind… It's hard to pray in our way here. We pray a lot but it's always aloud and together. I don't get any time to listen to my heart.'

They heard voices in the distance.

'They're coming. I must go,' he stood up to leave. With a quick glance up and down the street, Raimond pulled Esme up and hugged her. 'My wonderful *bessa,*' he whispered and pulled away.

Flushed by the unexpected intimacy, Esme gabbled something about watching out for Mouser, the kitchen cat. 'I keep sending her to you with messages.'

He laughed and told her that a fat cat often sat in a tree in the courtyard near his window. 'Sometimes I think she is you because of the way she waves the branches.'

'I haven't worked out how to turn myself into a cat yet!'

Still laughing, Raimond stepped out into the street and with one look at her, walked purposefully towards the castle gate. Lopp ran with him. At the gate, he stopped: 'Back Lopp, back.'

Soldiers watched in amusement as Raimond tried to persuade the excitable dog to go home. One of the soldiers came over to help. Raimond hurried into the castle. When the soldier released Lopp, the dog bounded back to Esme. She cuddled the dog and looked up. Nicholaus's son, Pons, was standing with the soldiers staring at her.

9

Carcassonne, June 1237

A DAY OR TWO LATER, a rumour that Rome was going to suspend the Inquisition travelled rapidly through the castle staff and out to the marketplace. Even taking into account exaggeration and speculation, it became known that Pope Gregory IX was reconsidering Rome's approach to attacking Christian dissenters. Word had it that influential nobles had been complaining about the behaviour of some inquisitors. 'Maybe he has finally worked out that extreme violence doesn't sit well with the teachings of Christ,' Nicholaus said to Guilhèm one evening.

There was an excitement around Carcassonne as every new messenger to the castle was looked upon with interest. The castle household staff kept their ears open and, in the absence of anything to report, embellished whatever titbit they heard to promote the idea that the Inquisition was indeed coming to an end. But then in mid-June, the constables brought in a group of people accused of heresy. The prisoners, all tied to a long rope, walked slowly from the distant hills to the north-east, through the town gates and up the narrow road to the castle. Esme lingered in a lane as they went past. There were seven accused. Five of them, two women and three men, looked like ordinary village folk. They were well dressed and well fed, but clearly worn out by their march through the heat of the day and very frightened. In contrast, the other two prisoners were thin, poorly dressed and deep in prayer. She looked closely at the men in prayer to see if she recognised either of them as travellers who may have come to Labernoc. But they were strangers to her. She slipped away before anyone might see her tears.

The prisoners were taken to the castle and placed in the dungeons. It was not long before the same friars and constables left the town again, this time going in a different direction. Esme wanted to run ahead and warn the villages on their path but it would have been a futile and dangerous effort. Some of the people who would be arrested would be unaware that their names were on Friar Tiqué's list. A few might believe that they had right on their side, just as Jaufré had done, and would try to argue their way out of the situation. Some would hopefully have fled by now.

The atmosphere in Carcassonne and among the castle staff changed perceptibly as the days got warmer and the numbers of prisoners rose. All speculation about the suspension of the Inquisition ceased. The tension was most pronounced in the kitchen courtyard during the evening meal with so many people gathering to eat, drink and talk. Except when it was raining, everyone ate outside. Esme was employed to serve during busy times. Before the arrests, the courtyard had been lively and Esme had found some enjoyment in the singing and banter, which might continue until well after dark. After the arrests, however, the soldiers drank far more than usual, the singing veered from raucous to melancholy, and the banter had a sharp edge to it. Spats erupted between the soldiers and the constables but so far these had been controlled.

One evening, late in June, Guilhèm sat at a table near the steps up to the kitchen and watched Esme as she ran up and down the steps serving food. She was in a reasonable mood. Earlier Raimond had smiled when he spotted a heart she had placed along the track. Guilhèm ate slowly and listened to the soldiers' conversations. Nicholaus arrived and sat beside him as Esme placed a dish of boar stew on the table.

Dusk fell and the full moon appeared above the courtyard wall. It was going to be a bright night. Nearly every table was occupied with soldiers, constables and castle staff.

Five constables entered the courtyard through the door that led directly from the main castle courtyard. Their colleagues made space at one of the tables. The constables kept their voices down; they knew that the castle staff were hostile to them but they preferred the food in the kitchen to that served at their camp, and Jacotina welcomed anyone who was entitled to eat here. They were polite to the kitchen girl who told them what was being served that night. Guilhèm, who had finished eating, whittled arrow heads and watched.

The soldiers at the table nearest the constables were arguing among themselves. As their voices rose, there was some jostling, wine was spilt, and a fight broke out. The rest of the courtyard became silent and waited. The sergeant and some other soldiers intervened before the fight spread. Everyone settled into an uneasy peace again.

'It was the same the last time Rome's prisoners were held in the dungeons here,' Nicholaus said to Guilhèm. 'The soldiers hate locking them up, especially the women. They end up arguing among themselves but what they really want to do is to fight the constables.'

A jug of hippocras was passed down Guilhèm's table. He took a little and continued to work on his arrows. The moon, now high in the sky, lit up the courtyard. The air was balmy. A table of soldiers began to sing. Others, including several constables, joined in. Guilhèm watched Esme chatting to some of the castle guard. They were teasing her about something; there was a lot of laughter. He was relieved; laughter was good for her.

When they were finished serving, Jacotina, Esme and Tanzi, one of the young women who worked in the kitchen, sat at Guilhèm's table. Tanzi put her arm around him and kissed him on the cheek. 'I love the way you never get involved in any of the arguments, Clement. You're a very nice man.'

'Oh to be young again,' laughed Nicholaus.

'Old man, you are still charming,' soothed the girl, blowing him a kiss.

'Old man, nothing,' snorted Jacotina.

Tanzi flirted and fussed over Guilhèm, pouring him a measure of the spiced wine. He lifted his cup and put it to his nose: 'A drink that comes from the heart of our land,' he said taking a sip.

Tanzi sighed: 'Oh Clement, you are truly a troubadour.'

Pons came into the courtyard with Del Gurbe and Barca. They were drunk. Pons staggered over to Tanzi and threw his arm over her, grabbing at her breast.

'Get off me, Pons.'

'You're a dirty old whore,' slurred Pons, still groping at her. Del Gurbe and Barca leered their encouragement.

Tanzi shook Pons off her while Nicholaus urged him to go away.

'Am I not good enough for you now that you are giving all of my money to the mountain man here?' demanded Pons, reaching towards Tanzi again.

Tanzi pushed in against Guilhèm for protection. By now Pons and his two braying companions had the attention of the entire courtyard. The sergeant was moving towards the table.

'Give her one!' shouted one drunken constable.

'And then pass her on to me,' leered another.

'Get your own, you lazy bastards,' Pons laughed as he fell forward and rammed his hand down Tanzi's dress.

Tanzi screeched. Guilhèm tried to stand up but his movement was restricted by the long bench. Nicholaus slid out the other end of the bench and grabbed his son's shoulder.

'Enough now, son. Go and sleep it off.'

Pons tried to punch him but Nicholaus deflected his fist. Del Gurbe and Barca, portly and drunk, made a move towards Nicholaus. Once more, the sergeant and his men intervened and surrounded the constables. The sergeant had authority over the friar's constables in the castle courtyard and let it be known.

Pons was too drunk to bother with authority. 'I am no

longer your son,' he shouted at Nicholaus. 'I have no father. You are welcome to the mountain man. But I am still entitled to my share of the hunt money.' He swung a punch at Nicholaus, which was blocked by a soldier. Del Gurbe and Barca lashed out at the soldiers surrounding them. The soldiers fought back, prompting constables to join the fight in support of their comrades. The fighting escalated.

Guilhèm manoeuvred Tanzi out of harm's way and, reaching for Esme, steered her away from the fighting. 'Go,' he said in a low voice. 'I'll see you back at the house.'

Her knees shaking, Esme ran from the courtyard followed by Lopp. The shouts of the fighting men faded into the background as she made her way to the west wall of the city. Just as she was feeling calmer, she heard barked commands and the sound of horses' hooves on the cobble stones coming from the direction of the city gate. She went to look. Two constables on horseback were leading a new group of eight prisoners, walking two by two, each with one hand tied to a single rope that ran down the middle of the group. Behind them were two young friars on horseback. Esme thought that they looked embarrassed. Six constables surrounded the captives.

A woman with long fair hair walked barefoot at the front of the group. She reminded Esme of Ava, her foster mother. Catching Esme's eye, the woman pointed to her chapped lips with her free hand. The drinking trough was nearby; wooden cups used in the warm weather by town folk and travellers were strewn about it. Esme filled a cup with water. Closely watching the constables, she sidled over towards the woman to await an opportunity to offer her the water. At that moment

Lopp barked loudly and charged at a dog that was walking alongside the procession. The dogs fought, tumbling into the constables who tried vainly to separate them. Esme stepped forward and gave the fair-haired woman the cup of water. The woman held it up to the mouth of the elderly man who was tied to the rope beside her, letting him drink first. When he had finished, she tipped her head back to take a drink. Esme noticed a distinctive birthmark on her neck: it looked like a butterfly. The woman handed the cup back and smiled at Esme: 'Thank you,' she said softly. Esme went home and, for the first time since arriving in Carcassonne, sobbed herself to sleep.

10

Carcassonne, July 1237

GUILHÈM'S INSTINCT WAS to get out of Carcassonne immediately. His great desire was to go home to his wife, even for a few days, but he could not leave Esme unattended. He could feel Pons' antagonism towards him growing. If he left, Pons might turn on Esme and she would have trouble withstanding him. The menacing mist he saw in his morning meditations was now sweeping through Carcassonne and it was easy to see evidence of it. Few people sat around in the evening warmth to chat with their neighbours. Constables and friars were avoided. The dungeons of the castle were deep, yet, in the silence of the night, the cries coming from beneath the huge stone building were clearly heard. Even the mid-summer sun in the cloudless sky did not seem to shine so brightly on the cobbled streets.

Guilhèm was also growing very concerned about Raimond. Until recently, he had found it easy to sense Raimond's heart in the quiet of the morning. Since the arrival of the last group of prisoners, he had lost all contact with the younger man. Esme had seen Raimond several times in processions and thought that he looked strained. His walk was heavy and he frowned a lot. He was no longer seeing the symbols she left out for him. Under these circumstances, Guilhèm could not leave either Esme or Raimond.

In the middle of July Guilhèm was with Esme in the market square. As the traders were packing up, Guilhèm chatted with them while he waited for the procession to the church. He wanted to assess Raimond's condition for himself. He was beginning to feel conspicuous when the procession appeared. His heart lurched when he saw Raimond: his face was grey, his broad shoulders slumped and there was none of his usual vibrancy in the way he walked. Raimond looked up and, seeing Guilhèm, clapped his hand on his heart as if he did not care whether anyone noticed him or not. Guilhèm was shocked. This was not Raimond; none of his character, his inner calmness, his fortitude was evident. Something had happened to him. With the dungeons full of the friars' prisoners, he did not want to think about what that might be. The procession continued down the short track to the open space in front of the church. There they would pause to light a candle before entering the church two by two behind an upheld crucifix.

Guilhèm was turning to walk away when a scream rose from the direction of the church. It was closely followed by shouting, more screaming and the panicked neighing of horses. Guilhèm pulled Esme to him as several people ran through the marketplace shouting out.

'Call the guard.'

'We're being attacked!'

Holding onto Esme, Guilhèm moved towards the church, staying close to the houses. Flames shot into the sky and thick smoke spread through the laneways. He suspected that the hay at the stables near the church was alight. Soldiers rushed towards the fighting.

Esme was frantic. 'Raimond! I have to help him!'

With a firm grip on her shoulder, Guilhèm guided her towards the opening to the church square. Smoke swirled through the square and, with their eyes stinging, they could see little, but the sounds of crashing swords and the cries of men were unmistakable.

The smoke cleared for a moment. 'It's the villagers, Guilhèm,' said Esme. 'From where the boys were killed...'

'Murderers! Murderers!' A tall man with curly red hair and a beard yelled as he tried to swing his sword even as he was being pounced on by several soldiers. His comrades, several with red hair, attacked the soldiers. The fighting was vicious.

More soldiers came onto the scene. The attackers were outnumbered. Esme and Guilhèm looked around for Raimond but the swirling dark smoke made it difficult to see. It cleared again and they saw a several men including Raimond scramble up from behind a low wall and scatter. Raimond ran through a gap in the houses. Familiar with every lane in Carcassonne, Guilhèm and Esme rushed through the warren of narrow streets and met Raimond coming towards them. There was a friar behind him with blood streaming down his head and into his eyes.

Guilhèm pulled Raimond into the alley. The bloodied friar stumbled past them.

Raimond struggled to get out of Guilhèm's grip, crying 'No! Let me go!'

'It's us, Raimond, it's us,' cried Esme trying to keep her voice low.

'No! I must return.'

Guilhèm looked closely at Raimond and felt a sharp jolt. The whites of the younger man's eyes were yellow and his pupils dull. Guilhèm's mind was racing; he would get Raimond out of Carcassonne immediately and deal with the consequences later. He crouched down in front of Raimond and held his arms firmly. In the background, he could hear the shouts of soldiers.

'Raimond, look at me,' he said in a voice that was just loud enough to be heard above the din. 'Look at me,' Reluctantly Raimond obeyed him. 'It is me, Guilhèm, and you are safe. But we must leave now. Raimond, we must leave, now!'

'Leave me alone,' Raimond tried unsuccessfully to shake off Guilhèm's grip.

'Raimond, stay looking at me. You are one of us. It is time to come home.'

'We have to go, come on, Raimond, please,' Esme begged.

'Raimond,' Guilhèm ignored Esme and continued in his commanding voice, 'Come home with us, back to the forest, to the birds, to the trees, to your father, and your sisters. Come back to the people who love you.'

'I can't,' Raimond whispered, his green eyes softening for a moment. 'I can't leave. Forget me. The boy you knew no longer lives.'

Guilhèm's grip loosened slightly. Raimond slipped out of his hands and ran back to the castle.

11

Carcassonne, July 1237

Carcassonne was locked down. No one was allowed in or out. The constables were rostered on guard duty with the castle soldiers. The once-friendly atmosphere at the town gates evaporated. A friar, a clerk and a servant had been killed and others badly injured. Most of the attackers were dead and those who survived would be executed in the coming days. As they were led to the dungeons, the survivors had shouted out the reason for the attack and Tiqué's role in it. By evening, lurid versions of the slaughter of three innocent boys and their mothers were circulating through the town.

Guilhèm insisted that he and Esme should go to the castle courtyard for their evening meal. 'Now is the time to act like you have never acted before. If we are to get out of here alive, we have to behave as if this is all a bit of a nuisance.'

Esme stayed close to Guilhèm with Mouser sitting on the bench beside her. The evening weather was unseasonably cool and she was wrapped in her jacket. The tables filled rapidly.

Castle soldiers made a lot of noise; the constables, at a separate table, were exceptionally quiet. Among their number was a small hooded man who Guilhèm had spotted several times before. He always sat with his back to the castle staff but would sometimes turn his head and move his hood slightly so he could see who was talking. He never drank wine and he ate little. Guilhèm had no doubt but that he was a spy for Friar Tiqué.

As the evening wore on, the castle soldiers became morose and quietened down. The noise level at the constables' table rose a little but no one was looking for a fight. Nicholaus started to sing. Jacotina, finished her work for the day, sat down and looked at him with fondness as he started another song. Some of the soldiers and the constables joined in. There was melancholy in the songs.

Esme was whispering to the cat. 'Oh Mouser, why did he not come with us? We could have got away.'

'Food! Drink! Come on, women of the kitchen, we're hungry!' Pons crashed into the courtyard with constables Del Gurbe and Barca, and three women. They had been drinking heavily as usual. They shouted loud greetings but got no response.

Esme buried her face in Mouser's soft fur and let her hair fall over her eyes.

'You'll smother that cat, love,' shouted Barca.

'Leave her alone,' ordered Jacotina.

'Ah, what's her problem? It's just a bit of fun,' retorted Barca.

'Yes, what is her problem? Why doesn't she want to come and have a bit of fun with us?' slurred Pons, who had commanded space for himself at an adjacent bench and was helping himself to wine; beside him, a young woman with long black hair and bloodshot eyes was drooling in his ear.

'Oi girl, come and have a drink to celebrate! We destroyed the invaders,' called Del Gurbe, who was annoyed that he had missed the fight outside the church.

'Yes, why don't you?' drawled Pons. 'Oh you say you are only a girl. But are you really? I've seen signs of womanhood lurking underneath your jacket.' He gestured rudely with his hands. 'I think you and your so-called father are not who you say you are.' The girl was now stroking him under the table; the front of her dress had fallen down. 'How do we know you were not involved in the attack this afternoon?'

The courtyard went quiet. The constables and the castle soldiers kept their heads down but their bodies twitched, alert. Nicholaus stood up, gathered some leftover food on a plate and placed it in front of his son: 'Pons, not tonight, it's been a hard day for everyone. Please, eat something,' he said quietly.

'Why not tonight, old man? You've been bewitched by the hunter. I just want to know who he is and whether he was behind the attack today.' He belched loudly and raised his voice. 'Or is he a heretic trying to cause a rebellion? Ha! You ask him that.'

There were audible gasps in the long room. Del Gurbe and Barca straightened up. Even the girl stopped her caresses.

Esme lifted her head, shock on her face.

'Ah stop, Pons, you've upset the little one. Leave it now,' said Jacotina, going over to Esme and wrapping her arms protectively around her.

Nicholaus put his hand on Pons' shoulder: 'Son, please.

Why don't you go and sleep it off.'

'Take your hand off me,' Pons slapped him away. 'You're an old heretic. You've always been a heretic. You think you can charm everyone here because you're the big hunter but they all know, and if they don't I'm telling them now. My father is a heretic!' he waved his mug of wine in the air as he shouted down the table.

Nicholaus's face went white. Nobody moved. Guilhèm broke the stillness by standing up and embracing Nicholaus. 'My friend, this is a sad end to another sad day;' he turned to Jacotina. 'I think it best if I take Pixie off to rest now.' He lowered his voice.

He lifted Esme into his arms. Being a tall, well-built man, he was able to position Esme on his shoulder so she curled up like a child. They left the courtyard.

'You're letting them go?' Pons shouted at the sergeant of the castle guard, who was sitting with his men. 'I've just called them heretics and you're letting them walk out of here? Hey, Jacques, Eric,' he addressed Del Gurbe and Barca. 'You're in charge now. Arrest them. They're heretics and so is my father and my father's whore.'

Barca assessed the situation. The constables were outnumbered by the soldiers and this sergeant outranked him in the courtyard. 'Settle yourself down and have a drink, Pons. They are not going anywhere. We can sort this out tomorrow.'

The short constable with the hood stood up and crept out of the kitchen leaving his uneaten dinner on the table. The remaining constables and castle soldiers did nothing; they were tired and off duty, and in the kitchen of the generous woman who fed them with meat provided by the hunter and his companion. They would leave this to the friars.

12

Carcassonne, July 1237

RAIMOND PACED UP AND DOWN on a small roof terrace, which opened out of the ante-room to Tiqué's office. Geraldus, the hooded constable who had taken it upon himself to spy for the friar in the kitchen courtyard, had scurried into the office a few moments ago. He was so excited that, without checking to see if anyone else was present, he declared that the castle was full of heretics and he had an informer. Tiqué ordered Raimond to take a break from his clerical duties and the heavy door was closed before Geraldus spoke again.

There was a bench by a low wall on the terrace, but Raimond was too agitated to sit down. Were Esme and Guilhèm still in Carcassonne? Had they left after he refused to go with them? His mind was racing. He wished he could go for a run in the mountains or plunge into a cold river. He smiled involuntarily. When did he last run up a mountain or dive into a cold river? Really, he preferred to walk when Esme ran, or to wait until the rivers were warm when Esme leapt into icy water. Esme often teased him about that. He wiped away tears with a rough gesture.

He dropped down on the bench. He wished he could pray but after the work he had been obliged to do over the past few weeks, even prayer had abandoned him. He tried to summon up images of his mother or of Esme but they had been destroyed too. He pressed his hands to his ears and shook his head. Oh Esme, please do not be in Carcassonne. A spasm of deep sadness wracked his body. Life without Esme? He clutched his head as he tried to fight tears but he felt so empty that he did not care who heard him.

The kitchen cat pushed her way through the door and out into the little garden. 'Mouser!' The cat jumped up onto his lap and pressed her head against his heart. He remembered the blessing his parents used to give him when they tucked him into bed. 'You are your heart Raimond,' they would say to him, and touch his heart. They did the same to his sisters and Esme: 'You are your heart Matina', 'You are your heart Esme', and 'You are your heart Alayda,' although Alayda was probably already asleep. 'You are your own hearts, you are all love and you are all loved. Be of good character, children, and always do right by others. With love, you will know no fear and feel no shame.'

'Oh mother, Esme!' he called out.

Suddenly Mouser jumped off his lap, digging her claws into his legs momentarily.

He looked up. A tall dishevelled man stinking of wine stood above him.

'Where's the friar's room?' he demanded.

Raimond pointing to Tiqué's quarters.

Pons remained where he was. 'First the dog and now the kitchen cat. I know who you are now. You all arrived at the same time.'

Raimond felt a blush rise in his face. He recognised this man; he could see the constables' camp from his dormitory window and had often seen this man drinking there with Del Gurbe and Barca.

Stepping onto the terrace, Pons jabbed a finger towards Raimond: 'If the friar doesn't burn your little friend and her greedy father first, then I'll get them myself.'

He turned and disappeared into Tiqué's room.

13

Carcassonne, July 1237

At dawn the following morning, Guilhèm and Esme waited silently for Nicholaus' return, their few belongings wrapped around their bodies under their clothes. The door opened and Nicholaus came in.

'Rolfe de Turre is on duty,' he said, referring to the big sergeant. 'He says the city gates should open today; the seneschal believes the attack the other day was an isolated incident. So you can go hunting with Esme.'

'Come with us, Nicholaus. The seneschal will be obliged to follow up Pons accusations; the friar will make sure of that. We can make an excuse for taking Jacotina out to the woods and find you a safe place.'

Nicholaus took Guilhèm's hands. 'Thank you, dear friend, thank you. But I have talked to my beloved. We are staying. Pons is my son and if he is to bring heartache, I would prefer that it was to me. And I can't persuade Jacotina to go to safety.' He dropped his head and drew Guilhèm's hands to his forehead. Guilhèm embraced the kindly man.

'Lovely Pixie,' he turned to Esme and, with strained jollity in his voice, gave her a hug, raising her feet off the ground. 'Will you take good care of Lopp for me?'

'Lopp? No, he is yours. You can't live without him.'

'We'll take him,' said Guilhèm.

Esme looked at Guilhèm and back to Nicholaus. She went pale. 'When everything is safe again, I will bring Lopp back to you.'

Jacotina appeared silently from their bedroom. Her eyes were red and swollen. She hugged them both.

'You must go now, before the officials wake up,' said Nicholaus, as Jacotina put her arms around him. 'This is your chance. Go now with our love.'

Esme's sorrow was replaced by a sense of panic rising in her throat as she stepped into the street. The sky was cloudless and the air was cool but it promised to be a warm day. There were a few people about and, with her heart pounding and her legs feeling like jelly, she walked alongside Guilhèm. They stepped into the main street and walked down towards the city gates. As soon as they got around this bend, they would have thirty metres to assess the situation at the gates. Equally, the guards at the gate would have thirty metres in which their approach could be studied.

'Ready?' asked Guilhèm as the came to the bend.

She nodded nervously and kept pace with him.

The scene at the gate was calm. The big wooden gates were closed but the small door in one gate was open. Two guards stood on duty by the gates. Several more soldiers and two constables in big cloaks were standing by the smouldering fire nearby. The constables' backs were to the street but she did not recognise either from this angle. Esme glanced involuntarily at Guilhèm. His face was calm and resolute. Esme resisted the urge to take his hand. She breathed in heavily trying to absorb some of his strength. She felt his hand brush against her arm, steadying her.

The big frame of Sergeant Rolfe de Turre appeared in the sharp light of the open door. He filled the small doorway. It occurred to Esme that if the sergeant remained in the doorway, no one could squeeze past him. The thought put a smile on her face as she pushed her legs forward. The soldiers at the gates nodded a greeting; a couple of the soldiers by the fire gave them a friendly wave but stayed where they were. All of the soldiers had, at one stage or another, benefited from Guilhèm's generosity with offcuts.

'Good morning,' said the sergeant softly, his eyes quickly making note of the whereabouts of the constables. 'We expect to be told officially today to reopen the gates so we'll be glad to have the larders refilled after the lock down.'

'That is good,' replied Guilhèm, matching the sergeant's volume. 'Supplies are running low and Jacotina is anxious to...'

'Where are they going?' came a sharp demand.

Guilhèm put his hand on Esme's shoulder and manoeuvred her past the sergeant and out the small door. Then, he turned around.

'Sergeant de Turre,' an armed constable moved in close to Guilhèm. 'Where are these people going? The city is locked down. Who gave this man and his child permission to leave?'

The sergeant stepped in from the doorway, forcing the constable back and leaving way for Guilhèm to step outside.

'Life has to go on. The hunter has to hunt – unless you want to eat nothing but vegetables,' said de Turre evenly.

The constable tried to restrain Guilhèm but the sergeant was in the way. The other constable approached, his cloak thrown back revealing his sword hanging off his belt.

'The city is locked down. Our men were killed. These people could be assassins.'

'This is our hunter and his little daughter,' said the sergeant dismissively. 'He has been hunting for us for a long time, long before you all appeared here. You have your assassins. Go back to the fire and warm yourselves.'

The constable scratched his head. It was true, the assassins were locked up. There was nothing to suggest that the hunter had anything to do with the fight. He yawned. He had been on duty for over twelve hours and was ready for sleep.

'How long are you going for?' he made one more attempt to assert his authority. 'And what about the child? She's not a hunter. She should stay.'

'We'll be gone a few hours, maybe a bit longer,' said Guilhèm, who remained in the constables' view. Esme was already half way down the hill. 'But it depends on the boar.'

'Of course it does,' responded the sergeant letting out a big belly laugh. 'When did a boar ever do what you wanted it to do? I remember a hunt I did in those mountains. The animal had us running for days.' As he guided the constables back towards the fire, another soldier began his story about a long hunt. The sergeant kept the conversation going until the constables joined in. By now, he was sure Guilhèm and Esme were well out of sight.

Once they reached the cover of the trees by the river, Guilhèm set a blistering pace. He did not want to give Esme time to change her mind about leaving Carcassonne. Nor did he want to give Tiqué time to order a round-up of all of those named by Pons on the previous evening. In theory the friar would have to wait for clearance from the seneschal before he could arrest anyone in Carcassonne but if he was chasing publically denounced heretics, he might make a move any time.

As he hurried along, only his concern about Raimond and his friends in Carcassonne tempered his relief at being free of the city and on his way home. Nicholaus and Jacotina. Two good, kind people who had looked after himself and Esme so well without asking any questions. And now he had brought misery down upon them. Where did a person like Pons come from? How did the son of a good man become so angry?

'I neglected him when he was a child,' he remembered Nicholaus explaining to him. 'When his mother died, he was thirteen and I encouraged him to come on the hunt with me. I made the mistake of splitting the take equally. I thought it would make a man of him. He worked with me for a few years but even then he was lazy. He began to hang around with the soldiers and to skip one hunt after another. Like a fool I continued to split the earnings. When the soldiers got tired of him, he found drinking friends among the constables and that was it.'

Did Nicholaus' absence during Pons' childhood turn the boy the wrong way? Guilhèm was sure that Pons' bad character went deeper than anything Nicholaus might have influenced. But he vowed to be there for Serena and his own son; he would not neglect his child, nor would he tolerate laziness. He smiled to himself; no son of Serena's could possibly be lazy or difficult. And the child, who would arrive in a few short months, might even be a daughter. He felt a rush of love and picked up the pace. Very soon he would be in the soft and loving arms of his pregnant wife.

Esme, numb from the events of the past few days, kept up with him and by late afternoon they glimpsed Puivert Castle in the distance. They were exhausted from the exertion but the sight of familiar mountains for the first time in over three months gave them a final burst of energy. They skirted the plain quickly, pushing away conflicting emotions surrounding this return journey, and hurried up the hill towards Labernoc.

14

Labernoc, July 1237

HER LEGS WERE SHAKING from exhaustion when Esme reached Guilhèm's home. Serena was at the doorway of the cottage taking the evening sun. Heavily pregnant, she walked out to meet them, a big smile on her face. She hugged Guilhèm with a deep sigh of happiness. 'I knew you were on your way,' she whispered. Separating slightly, they touched each other's face. Guilhèm bent down and put his ear to Serena's belly.

Esme walked on into the cottage with Lopp by her side. Guilhèm's mother, Agnes, was in her usual chair by the fire. She looked up and, seeing Esme, put her arms out to her. Esme buried her head in Agnes' breast and wept.

Jaufré, who had been dozing on his long seat by the fire, woke up and grunted. It took him some moments to work out who had arrived. 'Esme? Is that you?' He sat up painfully. 'At last, my dear. Well done. Come on here my boy and give your father a hug. Where is he? Where's Raimond?'

‘Oh, Jaufré, it was no good,’ sobbed Esme, sliding out of Agnes’s arms and crouching down to hug Jaufré. ‘We tried but he wouldn’t come. It is so dangerous…’

‘Wouldn’t come? What do you mean? Why isn’t he with you?’ Jaufré sat forward with a jerk, stifling a cry of pain.

Esme tried to explain.

‘Don’t tell me all of that. I know cities. I was born in one. Now I will have to go and get him myself. Get me my crutch.’ He struggled to stand up.

Hearing Jaufré’s voice rise, Guilhèm extracted himself from the warm bliss of his wife’s arms and hurried into the cottage. He directed Esme back to Agnes’ embrace and sat down beside the distressed man.

Jaufré turned his anger on Guilhèm, accusing him of letting him down and abandoning his son. Guilhèm responded gently. Although Jaufré eventually calmed down, he refused to accept that Guilhèm and Esme had good reason to leave Raimond behind. He muttered incomprehensively while Serena laid out a light meal of smoked pork, cabbage, walnuts and wheat bread. Exhausted, Esme struggled to eat and, as soon as she could excuse herself, went to sleep in her small alcove with Lopp at her feet. Jaufré was demanding details when Agnes intervened.

‘Hush, Jaufré,’ Agnes leant towards him. ‘We can find out more tomorrow. Let Guilhèm finish his meal and go to bed’ she nodded pointedly to her son and daughter-in-law as she passed Jaufré a cup of spiced wine.

The following day was fresh and sunny. Esme sat on a log outside the door and looked at the familiar landscape. She could hear Agnes and Jaufré talking inside. Her mind was blank.

'Esme!' Alayda appeared from the forest to the east and ran over to hug her foster sister. She was followed by her cousin, Julian, and Spider, Guilhèm's dog. 'When did you get back? Where's Raimond?'

Esme tried to greet them both but had a lump in her throat.

'Raimond?' called Alayda, walking into the cottage.

'Alayda, Julian,' Guilhèm took over. Talking quietly, he brought them to the pile of wood that they had chopped in recent days. Together they stacked the wood as Guilhèm explained what had happened.

'We can't just leave him there,' Alayda said, heaving a log onto the top of the pile with a bang. 'We have to do something.'

Jaufré hobbled out. 'I thought I heard you, daughter. Come and help me. They left Raimond behind. I have to go to Carcassonne to get your brother myself. You can come with me.'

Esme sank her head into her hands. Up in this peaceful mountain refuge, Jaufré and Alayda could criticise her but how could they have done any better in a city with high stone walls, powerful security and a routine where town life carried on while good people were walked into dungeons by priests of the Roman church? She had lived here all of her life. Jaufré and Ava had taken her in when she was a newborn baby and they were the only family she had ever known. Maybe it was time to go and live with her father in Foix. Sadness enveloped her.

Serena appeared from behind and put her arm around Esme's shoulders. 'Esme, don't worry about Jaufré; he won't be able to go to Carcassonne for some time. The pain makes him talk like that. But you must rest for a while. You have done enough for the moment.'

Esme laid her head on Serena's shoulder and closed her eyes, tears seeping through her eyelids.

15

Labernoc, October 1237

Serena and Guilhèm's baby was born in the middle of October into the steady hands of Agnes. The birth of the girl was straightforward and Serena recovered quickly. She was named Bonassias after Serena's mother. Matina came up to the cottage with Alayda and Julian to see Bonnie, as the baby was called. Tall and once beautiful, Matina had become frail and nervous. She missed her mother terribly, and her dreams of being a wife and a mother and a homemaker had evaporated. Even though word had come through that the Pope had suspended the Inquisition, few men would risk marrying the daughter of condemned heretics.

Serena and Matina sat outside the cottage in the autumnal sunshine talking companionably. Matina cradled Bonnie, singing quietly to her. Leaving them together, Serena sought out Esme who was sitting on a log in the forest, staring into space.

'You didn't go with Guilhèm last night?'

Esme shrugged and moved up the log to give Serena a comfortable spot to sit on.

'You've been home for three months now, Esme. You are behaving as if you are ill.'

Esme did not answer immediately. She had found it very difficult to settle back into the rhythm of a life she had once loved so much. She hunted with Guilhèm now and then, helped Agnes and Serena around the house, exercised with Jaufré, and spent time with Raimond's sisters and cousin, but all she could think about was a grey-faced Raimond choosing the violent priest over her.

'I can't believe that I left him in Carcassonne by himself,' she said into the silence. 'I should have stayed close to him.'

Serena studied the young woman, who was sitting with her arms folded tightly, her eyes unseeing and her forehead curled into a painful frown. 'You love him, don't you? And not as a brother or a twin?'

Her silence confirmed what Serena had suspected. She wiped the tears from Esme's face with a cloth she was carrying for the baby.

'I can't give up on him, Serena. I know he chose to stay with the friar but I'm sure something terrible has happened to him. He looked so different. If I could just talk to him again, I know he would be himself again.'

♦ ♦ ♦ ♦ ♦

Several nights later, as the family sat by the fire in the cottage, Serena suggested that Esme do some sewing.

'No, I can't concentrate long enough to do any,' she said shortly.

'Don't be rude,' snapped Jaufré. 'You are sitting around here night after night sulking. It's about time you did something with yourself.'

'Like what?' demanded Esme. 'Go back to Carcassonne and present myself to Friar Tiqué and his constables?'

'Don't speak to me like that.'

'What do you want me to say? Why don't you believe that I tried everything and I'm as upset as you are?'

'No one is as upset as I am. How could they be? He is my son, it is my family, my wife,' Jaufré raised his voice as a painful spasm gripped him. 'My responsibility. All mine. How could I have been so stupid?'

Bonnie woke up and started to cry. Agnes tried to hush Jaufré as Serena cradled the baby. It was a while before the household settled down.

Later in bed with Bonnie now sleeping peacefully in the cot beside them, Serena wrapped her arms around Guilhèm. 'Beloved, we cannot go on like this, not with Bonnie being so disturbed by the shouting,' she said. 'It is hard enough to keep Jaufré calm without Esme giving him an excuse to lose his temper. And she is going to make herself ill with misery. Perhaps you would take her out on a long hunt. We'll be able to manage while you're gone.'

Guilhèm needed some persuading. While the idea of a hunt over several days appealed to him, he was reluctant to leave his wife and daughter for longer than a few hours.

'Go on, it will do you both good,' said Serena. 'Get a nice

couple of deer for Puivert Castle. They'll be glad of it and we'll be glad of the money and the offcuts.'

The following day, with a little more persuasion from his wife, Guilhèm and Esme set off with Lopp at their heels. It was a perfect autumn day with little cloud, a fresh breeze and warm sunshine. Serena packed plenty of food and insisted that they take their time. Holding Bonnie in her arms, she waved them off from the cottage door, a contented smile on her face. If anyone could help Esme to recover herself, it was Guilhèm. 'Your father is a wonderful man,' she whispered into her sleeping baby's ear.

Guilhèm turned to wave once they reached the trees. He paused to take in the scene, the cottage with the smoke, his wife at the door holding their beautiful baby, his mother sitting on the bench in the sun. He blew them a kiss and turned back into the forest.

Guilhèm set a brisk pace at first, stopping periodically to let Esme listen to the sounds around them. Lopp, an experienced hunting dog, stayed close by. Several times Guilhèm picked up the heartbeat of a deer but chose to wait until Esme was sufficiently aware of her surroundings. They travelled west, across open ridges and back into the forest. They stopped for a night in a clearing where they had a perfect view of the pog of Montségur with its castle and community on top. As dusk fell, they watched silently as lights in the castle windows were lit and, shortly afterwards, extinguished. Soon only the glow of small fires along the defence lines could be seen as the watch prepared for the long night.

On the second day, as they went up a high mountain to the

south, Esme's mood began to shift. When she threw herself on the ground, puffing loudly and laughing with exhaustion, Guilhèm decided that they had gone far enough. They started back and the real hunt began. Esme's senses were more alive than they had ever been. She forgot about Raimond and her troubles as she listened to the forest. Steadying herself, she tried to pick up the heartbeat of a deer or a boar. She saw signs of these animals and knew they were nearby. They could have chased one down with ease but Guilhèm was giving her time to hunt by listening to her heart. Suddenly the rhythm of her heart changed. It was a tiny change but noticeable. She turned her body to the left. The tiny sensation vanished. She turned to the right, it started again. Showing no excitement, she pointed to Guilhèm. He smiled. Esme was back. Slowly, steadily, they stalked the deer and, just as night was falling, they caught and slaughtered the animal.

'Guilhèm, I really felt it. I knew which direction to go in. I could feel its heartbeat,' exclaimed Esme.

Guilhèm laughed: 'Well done, little one, you are learning.'

Together they prepared the meat, Guilhèm butchering, Esme packing it in bags she was carrying, throwing some of the waste to Lopp and burying the rest. The moon was bright in the sky when they finished and they used the light to begin their journey back to the cottage.

'Thank you, Guilhèm,' said Esme as they crossed an open stretch of ground. 'I feel much better. I don't know what to do for Raimond but I can see that making myself ill is not helpful.'

'We'll think of something. Esme. If the stories are correct

and Rome has ended the Inquisition, it will be safe for us to look for him. The world is a big place but a man like Tiqué doesn't disappear. Sooner or later we will hear news of him and when we do, we'll find Raimond.'

Dark clouds drifted up from the south-west and soon the light from the moon was extinguished. They were not far from the cottage but with the weight of the meat on their shoulders it would still take another two hours to reach it. And, without moonlight, the cliffs made it dangerous to continue. They decided to wait until dawn.

When the pale light appeared from the east, Esme was curled up at the root of a tree, asleep with Lopp at her feet. Guilhèm looked at Puivert Castle in the distance. He listened to the forest and smiled with pleasure as he thought of Serena and Bonnie.

Suddenly he shivered. Lopp stood up, his nose in the air and his tail wagging. Guilhèm leapt up and looked around. His heart was pounding. Wolves? A boar? Lopp barked.

'Is something wrong?' Esme stirred.

'Serena! The cottage! Esme, come on. Run! No, leave that, leave everything!' He was shouting now as he ran in great strides towards home, Lopp just ahead of him.

Esme jumped up, picked up her knife and ran after him. They charged through the forest, ignoring brambles that pulled at their ankles and branches that slapped their faces. Within forty minutes, they burst into the clearing around the cottage. There was no sign of anyone at the back of the house. They ran around to the front. Jaufré was lying on his side in the open doorway, his eyes dazed and blood trickling round his neck. Guilhèm reached him first.

'I couldn't protect them... a friar... too many... couldn't...'

Guilhèm slipped past him while Esme crouched down to help Jaufré. She put her hand on the back of his head and found the wound. At that moment Guilhèm let out an unearthly roar.

Frightened, Esme kept one hand on Jaufré while she leant into the cottage. As her eyes adjusted, she saw Agnes slumped by the fire. Guilhèm had gone into his bedroom. Telling Jaufré to hold on while she got a bandage, she went to Agnes, who was groaning, blood oozing from a deep shoulder wound. A gurgling sound came from the back of her throat. Grabbing a sheet, Esme tried to stem the flow of blood. With her left hand, Agnes grabbed Esme. 'He must... Montségur bloodline...'

'Guilhèm, your mother...' Esme cried.

It was dark in his bedroom but Esme could see Guilhèm holding Serena and Bonnie. 'No!' Esme stifled her voice. She listened for a baby's cry but only Guilhèm's desolate moan filled the room.

A noise from Jaufré stirred Esme. Leaving the sheet on Agnes' wound, she laid the elderly woman down and closed her eyes. Shaking, she found another cloth and some cushions for Jaufré.

'A friar... constables...' Jaufré muttered as Esme tended his wound, which was not deep. 'Where were you? There were too many. I couldn't fight by myself.'

Only now aware of the danger, Esme looked around. Lopp was standing by the track in the forest, his tongue out and his tail wagging. Friars, constables? There was neither sight nor sound of anyone. Were they still about?

'Have they gone?' she whispered urgently.

Jaufré nodded, placing his hand on the back of his head. 'Yes, but not long before you arrived.'

Esme thought quickly. There was only one track between Labernoc and the cottage. If the attackers had left, she might see them from the top of the long cliff. She ordered Lopp back to the cottage and ran through the trees to look. The track to the village went around the base of this cliff. Local knowledge was necessary to find it, which is why few people came up this way.

She heard voices below her. Cautiously she lay on the ground and looked down. A friar and four constables were walking down a steep path towards a Labernoc castle soldier, who was holding five horses. She immediately recognised Del Gurbe and Barca. Feeling instantly nauseous, she clasped her hand over her mouth. She looked again at the group. A young constable, unknown to Esme, was very distressed, his voice travelling in the still air.

'You never told me we were to kill women and a baby,' he looked up at the friar.

'You drew the first blood,' snorted Barca. 'Killing that old man before we could interrogate him.'

'He jumped out at me with a knife,' wailed the young constable.

'He was 90 years old and a cripple. Jumped out at you – huh!'

'But the women and a baby,' the constable sounded like he was on the verge of tears. 'You don't even know it was the right house.'

'The bailiff knew who we were talking about,' said Barca. 'It was the right house.'

'But why the ....'

'One more word and you'll go the same way,' The friar grabbed the man by his tunic and shook him. At that the friar's hood slid off, revealing matted light-coloured hair, which was instantly recognisable to Esme. It was Pons.

'Saddle up,' snapped Barca, as they reached the soldier.

'We have to walk down. It's too steep to ride,' said the soldier, walking away from them.

The men followed the soldier into the forest. At that moment, Guilhèm appeared and, lying beside her, saw the last of the constables disappear. He was covered in blood.

'Are they both... Serena and Bonnie?'

Guilhèm, his face distorted in grief, nodded.

'It's Pons, with Del Gurbe and Barca,' she forced herself to speak.

Guilhèm pressed his face into the ground. After some moments, he looked back into the forest, where slight movement of the trees indicated the group's progress. There had been a lot of rain recently and the ground would be slippery.

Shaking his head, he whispered, 'May God's will be done.' He jumped up and ran along the cliff. Esme followed him. They went into a dip and up another cliff, this one with a perfect view of the road from Labernoc down to the valley. They reached there just as the soldier returned to the castle and Pons and his party continued through the village, which was already busy. Esme saw Alayda watching them from behind a post. She guessed the younger woman would recognise two of the constables and would go straight up to the cottage to check on Agnes, Serena and Bonnie. She dared not think about Aladya's reaction to the scene she would encounter.

Guilhèm was watching Pons and his group as they left the village and made their way down the track to the plain below Puivert Castle. As the track widened, Pons let out a whoop and spurred his horse into a gallop. The others followed and together they raced at speed out onto the plain. Esme glanced at Guilhèm. He was staring at Pons. Suddenly Pons' horse lost its footing and stumbled, hurling the rider to the ground. The young constable, unable to control his horse, continued to gallop towards Pons. His horse became entangled in the flailing Pons as its rider fell to the ground.

Guilhèm remained where he was as Barca confirmed that Pons was dead. The young constable had broken his leg or ankle. Guilhèm rested his face on the ground once more. 'God's will,' he said before rising slowly and walking back in the direction of the cottage. Del Gurbe and Barca strapped their dead companion to his horse and helped the injured man up on his. They continued slowly on their journey.

Alayda and Julian reached the cottage a short while later. Esme could not speak. If she had not asked Guilhèm to come to Carcassonne with her, this would never have happened. The one peaceful place in the world, the one place that the Romans had not destroyed, the one place where everyone was happy, Doña Agnes, little Bonnie and lovely Serena, it had been shattered and Esme felt that she had brought this terrible fate to their doorstep.

In the background, she heard Jaufré, now upright and alert, tell Alayda and Julian what had happened. She heard the cries of Alayda and the low sobbing of Guilhèm. Julian found a shovel and, with Alayda, went to the edge of the clearing and began to dig a deep grave. Esme helped them. As the sun passed noon, Guilhèm was gently coaxed by Julian to wrap his mother, wife and child in blankets and together they carried them to their graves. With their faces cleaned of blood, they looked peaceful. Guilhèm snipped a lock from each of their heads and wrapped them up with Agnes and Serena's personal stones. He laid their bodies in the deep grave.

Kneeling by the open grave, he struggled to pray aloud. No words would come out. Julian began to say the Lord's Prayer. Alayda, Jaufré and Esme joined him.

They sat there until dusk.

'Thank you, my friends,' Guilhèm put his hands on Alayda and Julian's shoulders. 'Go home and please don't tell anyone anything for a while, if you can.'

Esme started to cry, choking on her tears. Alayda and Julian stared at Guilhèm.

'Please go. I will fill in the grave.' He picked up the shovel. Esme went to pick up the other shovel but Guilhèm sent her away.

As the moon rose, Guilhèm got on with his solitary task while Esme cleaned the cottage as best she could.

Interlude, Foix January 1316

WILLIAM BÉLIBASTE STOPPED talking, pressed his hands to his heart and bowed his head.

'I knew none of that, Aunt Esme,' Stéphanie said quietly, wiping a tear from her cheek. 'I had heard of Raimond of course, and Matina and Alayda, I remember the name of Guilhèm, but I didn't know... Aunt Esme?'

Stéphanie stood up to look closely at her elderly great aunt. Esme's eyes were closed and she was still. As Stéphanie bent down to see if she was breathing, Esme opened her eyes.

Stéphanie wet Esme's lips with water and offered her a sip from a cup.

Esme acknowledged her with a look. *I was lost in the story.*

'Shall I continue?' William asked. He had plenty of time before dawn and wanted Stéphanie to hear the whole story in Esme's presence.

Esme nodded again. The stone was still resting in her right palm. *Please do. William, you see the story so clearly. The magic of the stone... I never knew it was so powerful.* She touched it with the fingers of her left hand. Through her failing eyes, she saw mist rising out of it. *Oh there is my father, and Andreva. And even Arnold. I'd forgotten about him!*

'Shall I talk about your time in Foix?' William asked.

Esme was looking at the mist and smiling. *A little, enough for Stéphanie to know about our family in Foix. She can find out the rest herself.*

William adjusted his position, sat up straight and rested his hands on the arms of the chair, his palms facing towards Esme's stone.

'Where was I?'

Stéphanie checked that Esme was comfortable and sat back in her chair.

William closed his eyes and opened them again. He looked at the stone in Esme's hands.

Part 2

16

Foix, October 1237

The morning after Guilhèm buried his family, he took a small pack and left for the mountains to the south-west. Esme and Jaufré went slowly to Foix to find Esme's father. Alayda and Julian helped them for some of the way and they got short lifts on passing carts. Eventually the square towers of Foix castle came into view. Exhausted from the trip and Jaufré's poor humour, Esme approached it cautiously. The town was built around the imposing castle and set on the confluence of two rivers, the larger of which separated them from the town. Esme observed the soldiers guarding the bridge over the river. They seemed relaxed. Behind them the town looked calm and prosperous. The morning market was closing up and people stood about talking to each other in the sun, their baskets full.

Esme and Jaufré stepped onto the wooden bridge, aware that they were being watched. The water rushed several feet below them, sweeping away the smell of fresh goat droppings on the bridge. Esme squeezed Jaufré's arm involuntarily.

'What's wrong?' he said, with irritation.

'Just steering you around the waste, Jaufré,' she whispered nervously.

'Stop fussing! It never did anyone any harm.'

A soldier stepped out.

With her heart in her stomach, Esme explained that they had travelled from afar to visit the bone-knitter of Foix.

'I can speak for myself,' snapped Jaufré.

'Ah another patient for our famous healer!' he said with a sympathetic look at Esme. He waved them on.

Using descriptions given by her father during his periodic visits to Labernoc, Esme found his house with ease. It was a substantial building with numerous shuttered windows and one large, glazed window. Smoke came out of a cavity in the wall. The house was set in a small field with several outhouses. Wood was stacked up to one side, a tethered horse could be seen chewing on hay nearby, and a large well-tended vegetable garden was visible to the rear of the house.

Esme knocked on the door with some trepidation. It was opened by a servant who looked them up and down and directed them to the back of the house where they would receive food.

'Tell Philippe it is ...' Jaufré spoke up.

'Please tell Philippe that we are family,' interrupted Esme hastily.

At that moment, Philippe appeared at the man's shoulder and peered closely.

'Esme! My dear, it is you! I've been expecting you. I am

so relieved!' he flung open the door and threw out his arms to her. He looked at Jaufré. 'It can't be' his voice dropped to a whisper. Instructing his servant to prepare hot water and refreshments, he ushered them into the room with the glazed window. His delight and relief at seeing Esme was tempered at his shock at seeing Jaufré. He had visited Labernoc while Esme was in Carcassonne and had talked to Matina and Alayda, but they had not told him that their father had survived.

Andreva, Philippe's wife, welcomed Esme with delight. She was a tall, elegant woman of twenty-seven years who made no secret of her yearning for a child. 'My husband's own daughter, I am so happy to meet you at last. And you are so beautiful,' she exclaimed. 'Or I am sure you are beautiful but we must clean you up and get you some lovely clothes.'

Esme was given her own small room on the upper floor of the house and, under Andreva's direction, it was furnished with hooks and shelves for her belongings. An outhouse was converted and made comfortable for Jaufré with a fireplace, a bed and chairs for visitors. The bone-knitter began working on him immediately. It was a slow process and his loud outbursts were attributed by neighbours to the pain associated with the bone-knitter's work. Esme did what she could to calm him but often ran out of patience. Only a convivial drink with Philippe was sure to relax him.

Meanwhile, Andreva persuaded Esme to smarten up so that she looked a little more like the only daughter of one of Foix's more successful merchants. Her skin was polished, her hair combed and reluctantly she agreed to wear plain dresses in fine wool. Yet while Esme liked her warm-hearted stepmother and appreciated her efforts, her heart was not in it. She often donned her forest clothes and retreated to the high mountain ridge overlooking Foix from the east. She had found a deep rocky outcrop there where time stood still. She usually took food so she could stay for a few days at a stretch. Sitting on a dry bed of twigs and leaves, Esme would listen to her heartbeat and think about Raimond and Guilhèm, and Ava, Agnes, Serena and Bonnie and wonder where they all were now. Sometimes she imagined Ava or Agnes holding her, or Serena with Bonnie in her arms stroking her hair and her heart would beat softly. Then she would think of Raimond and the pounding would start again. She could not wipe away the memory of the look in his eyes that last day she had seen him.

One day in spring, six months after she had arrived in Foix, she was sitting in the outcrop looking at the blossoms on the trees and contemplating new life. She noticed her heart start to beat in a peculiar way. Before she could work out what was different, the face of Guilhèm appeared at the front of outcrop.

'Esme, are you in here?' he called softly.

'Guilhèm!' She jumped from behind a low shrub and threw herself in his arms. 'Where have you been?' He looked thin and worn-out, and his eyes were terribly sad.

He sat down beside her. 'Your father guessed where I would find you.'

'I never told him where I was going.'

'He used to come to this outcrop himself when his own sorrow became too much to bear. It is a very special place; your instinct is good.'

They sat silently for a while.

'Food?' Without waiting for an answer, she laid soft bread, two different types of cheeses, nuts and olives on a cloth.

Guilhèm smiled: 'You are always well prepared, dear Esme.'

'Where have you been?' she asked, as they ate companionably.

Guilhèm told her that after he had left Labernoc, he had gone up the mountains to the south of Montségur and had made camp in a forest. Only instinct had kept him alive during winter. He was on the point of closing his eyes forever when an elder from Montségur appeared before him.

'Was he real or a vision?'

He chuckled. 'Ah, Esme, only you.'

'But you could have been having visions if you were lying down to die.'

'He was real, although I don't know how he found me or even how he made it up the mountain to where I was camping. He is quite old so you are right; his appearance was a mystery.'

The elder, a man named Leyas, stayed with Guilhèm for three days and nights talking to him about Serena, Bonnie and Agnes. He invited Guilhèm to come with him to Montségur and spend a little time there surrounded by people who devoted their lives to prayer.

'There was something about him that was very persuasive, so I went with him. I am getting a lot of help from the community on Montségur. They are just as my mother said they would be.'

'So you heard me passing on the message from Doña Agnes! I thought you hadn't heard.'

'Thank you for that message. I've learnt some ... um... strange things about myself. But I can't fully understand them myself so you will have to hold your boundless curiosity until I am ready to tell you.'

Guilhèm left a few hours later and, to Esme's surprise, he did not give her any advice.

♦ ♦ ♦ ♦ ♦

Yet the visit from Guilhèm had lightened Esme's heart. She returned to the house with a new sense of purpose and a determination to embrace the life Philippe and Andreva were offering. Throughout the summer, she worked with Andreva to transform her own appearance. Her long dark hair was brushed until it was shiny and pinned into a fashionable style each day. Her face and hands were fresh and clear, and she allowed Andreva to emphasise her eyes, cheek bones and lips with colour. She learnt how to carry herself in expensive dresses, to dance, to behave at elegant parties, to engage in light conversation and to remain impeccably groomed for an entire evening. With Andreva's guidance, she selected some exotic accessories from Philippe's more exclusive stock. Her stepmother's warm nature and her enthusiasm for beauty and elegance were infectious and, by the end of the summer, Esme was going to bed happy and exhausted each night.

In the darkness of the night, she still felt the weight in her heart but now, as she fell asleep, she imagined the mothers, Agnes, Ava and Serena, wishing her good night. She also sensed another mother with them, a small woman with dark hair, olive skin and almond-shaped eyes. The woman seemed to hang back and Esme did not invite her closer. She did, however, ask all four women to sing to Raimond as he was going to sleep too.

Her most satisfying evenings were spent late at night talking with her father. She noticed that Andreva left them alone to talk and was grateful. She desperately wanted to find out about the small woman who she guessed was her mother but did not know how to open that conversation. Instead she pressed Philippe for stories about his early life, about his parents, and the growth of his business. Philippe had no hesitation in talking about that time, even though much of it had been shaped by war. He had been born in Toulouse in 1199 to a successful merchant family at a time of tolerance and prosperity in the city. He had two older brothers and his arrival had been a surprise to his parents. The Crusade had commenced in 1209 and Toulouse, being one of the more powerful cities in the region, became a target. His brothers died in the fighting and the family's fortunes collapsed. In 1215, his parents had given him what money they had left and insisted he leave Toulouse before Simon de Montfort and his army arrived.

'It was not easy leaving my parents,' he said to Esme, who was sitting on a comfortable chair by the fire holding her stone in her cupped hands. 'The wars had ruined their health and my brothers' families were struggling to survive. But my parents knew that I would probably die in the fighting and wanted one of their sons to be able to help the extended family as soon as de Montfort and Rome's men left. My parents died of disease during the siege in 1218, the one where de Montfort was finally killed.'

Philippe explained how he had travelled east and found it easy to get on with people, even if most of them did not speak Occitan. For some years, he bought cheap commonplace items in one location and sold them as exotic merchandise in another. 'After de Montfort's death, I was able to go back to Toulouse and help my brothers' families, but I did not want to stay there. I liked the vibrancy of the eastern markets.'

It was in the autumn, a year after Esme had first arrived in Foix, when Philippe was finally ready to talk to his daughter about meeting Emersenda, her mother. Emersenda was with a troubadour company and they instantly fell in love. He persuaded the company to take him with them even though he had no performance ability. 'I tried singing and telling stories in verse but failed at both,' he chuckled at the memory of Emersenda's mock despair at his attempts. Instead, he helped them with practical things, with costume, money and contacts. And while he was travelling with them, he extended his trading network.

'We travelled to Puivert several times and it was there we met Jaufré and Ava. Emersenda and I stayed with them in Labernoc for a break before catching up with the rest of the troupe again. Then, one day, when Emersenda was pregnant with you, she became very tired all of a sudden. We were not far from Puivert so we went straight up to Labernoc.'

Philippe stopped talking and looked at the fire.

'You've probably heard the story many times,' said Philippe. He did not look at Esme for a response. 'Ava was pregnant with Raimond. It was the end of September and he was due any day. You were not due until November. Then Ava went into labour and, without warning, Emersenda went into labour too. The village healer rushed over. More women arrived. Jaufré and I were told to leave. We heard the cries… Jaufré said it was normal. It didn't sound normal to me.'

He caught his breath and drained his glass of spiced wine.

'You were beautiful; a tiny little thing. So was Raimond. Two women brought you out for a moment to show us, then brought you back to your mothers. Emersenda… I could hear her, she sounded in pain. Women ran out and fetched things, cloths, water, and ran back. No one looked at me. Then there was silence. I knew.'

His voice caught in the back of his throat.

'I saw her laid out, looking very beautiful, very peaceful. You were on Ava's breast with Raimond. You looked so natural there. I couldn't take you away. I couldn't stay either.' He swallowed. 'And the healer said that you could not go anywhere for a while because you were too small. So I left.' He looked up at Esme. 'Can you forgive me?'

Esme was startled. 'I didn't… I don't…Father, there is nothing to forgive.'

'But I did not return for you for nearly six years. And I did not insist you come here.'

'You are here for me when I need you most.'

♦ ♦ ♦ ♦ ♦

Philippe's late night conversation with Esme about her birth and her mother changed the mood in the house. Each night, Esme imagined her mother joining Ava, Agnes and Serena in wishing her goodnight. She even tried to address her mother directly, but the woman just enveloped her with such a sensation of love that Esme dropped off to sleep instantly.

At the same time, the relationship between Philippe and Andreva shifted perceptibly. They seemed closer as they shared loving glances and caressed each other if they thought no one was looking. It made Esme a little uncomfortable but she was glad for them.

Guilhèm visited Foix periodically. Each time he looked a little stronger. He stayed in Jaufré's house so he could bring some comfort to the older man. Jaufré's hip was mending well. It had been a slow and painful process and, a year after he arrived, he was able to hobble around on crutches for extended stretches each day. Philippe usually joined Guilhèm and Jaufré for a chat late into the night. Esme occasionally sat with them but she found Jaufré's moods difficult to bear; she was also feeling a little guilty that she had not made any attempt to visit Matina and Alayda since she had moved to Foix. It was only a couple of day's walk away for her but she could not face going back yet.

Guilhèm was pleased to see Esme blossom into a beautiful young woman. He could see that she loved her father and enjoyed Andreva's company, and he was glad that she was being given the option of a comfortable and stable life. But when he was leaving, she would put on her forest clothes and walk some of the way towards Montségur with him. Inevitably she would ask him to ask the holy people to pray for Raimond but she never discussed Raimond otherwise. Watching her walk back towards Foix, Guilhèm could see her pain sitting like a cloak on her shoulders. There was little he could do for her at present except pray.

17

Foix, 1239

Shortly after one of Guilhèm's visits, Esme went to a gathering with Philippe and Andreva. It was a warm night in late spring and the evening was in honour of a family that had just moved from Toulouse. It was a crowded event. During the course of the evening Esme was drawn to a group in the centre of which was a man playing a lute and singing. Shorter than most of the people there, she strained to see who was singing. A gap appeared in the crowd and she beheld a handsome man, slim, wavy black hair, a square jaw and brown eyes brimming with passion. When he turned his eyes to her and sang of love for a beautiful woman, she felt she would melt. He smiled flirtatiously. Esme blushed from head to toe. The gap closed again and she scurried out to a veranda to cool down.

'I thought I was dreaming when I saw you,' a voice came from behind her. 'But it seems that you are real.'

Esme's heart flipped over. As she turned slowly, she tried to remember Andreva's instructions on how to flirt but her mind was blank. He was looking at her with smiling eyes. He introduced himself as Arnold and explained that he had just arrived in Foix with his family from Toulouse.

'Because you had a liaison with a trobairitz,' said Esme without guile. 'Everyone heard about it before you arrived.'

Arnold threw his head back and laughed. 'You might be the only honest person I have ever met! How marvellous! How do you fit in here?'

Still trying to remember the rules of flirtation, Esme gave him the standard line about having lived for many years with her late mother's family by the coast and living with her father for the past 18 months.

'Ah now I know who you are. It was said you were a beauty and yes, you are. Of course there are plenty of beautiful women.' He shrugged and reached for Esme's hand. 'But you, you have more than beauty. Lady Esme, you are enchanting!'

He kissed her hand and, with a smile, walked away.

Several days later, they met again. This time Esme stayed close while he sang of a beautiful woman with almond-shaped eyes. Esme blushed, oblivious to the ladies of Foix nudging each other. Arnold's mother made her way to Andreva and, after a brief discussion, the two women gave each other their approval that Arnold might woo Esme.

And woo he did, with enthusiasm. The summer flew by and Arnold's devotion to Esme became more ardent than ever. He declared his adoration for her in song and was attentive and amusing. He encouraged her to sing but after a little while, they both agreed that singing was not where her talents lay.

'How about storytelling, sweet Esme?' he asked her as they strolled along the empty marketplace beside the abbey.

Esme demurred. 'I like telling stories but I don't want to sing them or make them rhyme.'

'Then we will have to invent a whole new way of storytelling. With your beauty and your eloquence and your warmth – oh Esme, I can see you holding a hall of courtiers in rapture, rapture!'

Esme laughed as Arnold threw his arms about, describing her many virtues that would turn her into a famous storyteller. 'You create intimacy in a moment. Everyone would insist on sharing their stories with you. The simple and the powerful. And when you address your audience, well! Strong, forthright, courageous, everything that is needed. Yes. Esme the storyteller!'

They walked around the corner towards the river. Esme glanced at the abbey and the thought flashed through her mind that this was probably where the friars would stay if there were still an Inquisition.

'Esme, my love, you're shivering.' Arnold whipped off his cloak and laid it on her shoulders.

'I like hearing other people's stories but I don't know if I could tell them to an audience.' She had not told Arnold about her stone pearl scratched with fissures for stories. Such practices were now too closely associated with heresy and she did not know yet where he stood on such matters.

Arnold studied her. 'Look at this beautiful visage, these mysterious eyes, these smiling lips, this intelligent brow. Yes, yes, yes, everyone will want to listen to you, if only to be allowed to look at you while you are speaking. Oh wondrous Esme,' he raised his hands in the air. 'Tell the world its story.'

Esme laughed. Sometimes it was hard to take Arnold seriously.

But at an occasion in early autumn, Arnold's mother sidled up to Andreva. 'It is now time for my husband to talk to your husband,' she said to Andreva in a low voice. 'They are a good match, and I speak for myself and my husband. They are both wealthy but we want more for our son. We want a sensible, strong young woman with a good head for business. He is too distracted by his music and verse. With the right woman he will take his place as a merchant of Foix. Esme is a sensible young woman. She is healthy with good teeth and good skin. We can tolerate her well.'

Andreva hid her surprise and amusement at the woman's intense speech. After all she was right in her assessment of Esme, and had confirmed Andreva's own assessment of Arnold. She promised to talk to Philippe. She was keen to see her dear step-daughter successfully married. She knew about Raimond and there was no doubt in her mind that Esme had loved Raimond. But if Philippe could find love for a second time, maybe Esme could too.

Philippe was gratified to see the sadness finally lift off his daughter but he had misgivings about Arnold's character. However the matter would have to be resolved soon or Esme's reputation would be damaged. He promised Andreva he would talk to her but before he did, the decision was taken out of his hands.

♦ ♦ ♦ ♦ ♦

On a warm autumn evening, the Count of Foix held a lavish party. It was attended by the nobles and important merchants of the town. Like many of the women of Foix, Esme and Andreva went up the steep slope to the castle sitting side-saddle on horseback so they arrived fresh and cool. As usual, Arnold rushed out to greet Esme on her arrival and took her straight to the dance floor. Happy, they danced until, laughing and flushed, they went out to a balcony for air. Arnold's mother watched them with a satisfied look on her face.

Inside the hall, an exhausted messenger pushed his way through the dancers. A murmur ran through the crowd, the musicians stopped playing. The messenger talked rapidly to the Count, answered a few questions, then bowed and retired. The powerful men of the town, including Philippe, gathered around the Count. On a signal from an official, the musicians resumed playing. Andreva watched from a distance. She could see from the expressions on the faces of men close to the Count that the news, whatever it was, was not good. She could also see that Philippe's face was deliberately bland, a sure sign to her that there was something wrong.

A whisper left the inner group. 'An inquisitor is coming to Foix.'

The noise level rose as the news travelled around the crowd without discretion.

Outside on the balcony Arnold and Esme were talking intimately. He took her hands and looked deeply into her eyes.

'Dear, beautiful Esme, I love you so much. May I visit your father?'

'You can visit my father anytime,' she whispered. 'You don't need my permission.'

'Oh, Esme, you know what I mean. I want to visit him,

visit him to talk about you and about our future.'

A woman walked out onto the balcony, talking loudly over her shoulder to a companion: 'His name is Tiqué. He's from Carcassonne or thereabouts. They say he will be here in a week or two.'

Esme's eyes opened wide and she looked at the newcomers. 'Tiqué?' she exclaimed in a low voice. 'Friar Tiqué, is coming here?'

'Esme?' Arnold looked at her with great puzzlement.

Esme pulled her hands out of Arnold's and confronted the woman. 'Did you say that Friar Tiqué is coming here?'

The woman nodded and was about to speak but Esme had already bolted into the hall to find her father. Bemused, Arnold followed her. Andreva, seeking Esme out, stepped in front of her. 'Calm down, Esme,' she whispered, squeezing her arm. 'Remember where you are.'

Arnold stood beside Andreva so he could see into Esme's eyes. 'My beautiful woman. What is wrong? What has happened? You look so...' Arnold struggled to find the right word. 'Oh Esme, my beautiful muse, where have you gone?'

18

Foix, October 1239

Dressed once more in her old clothes, Esme went into the forest above Foix with Lopp to await the arrival of the friar's party. She settled back against a rock to wait. The hours passed. Without warning, her heart began to thump. She noted it with an inward shrug, a fox, a deer, a boar perhaps. The thumping continued and was getting louder. She thought she recognised the rhythm. Slowly, it dawned on her that it was not the rhythm of an animal but the old, familiar rhythm of Raimond's heartbeat! She sat up straight and whispered his name. Her heart thumped even louder. In the distance, she picked up the sound of horses and men's boots on a stone track. She strained her eyes. In the distance, coming from the north, was a procession. There were men on horseback, men walking and several carts being pulled along by mules. They were moving slowly. As they got closer, she recognised the unmistakable figure of Tiqué sitting upright on his brown horse, his cowl perched on the top of his head, his cloak fanning out over the back of the animal. Frantically she searched for Raimond.

Two constables rode in front of Tiqué. Behind this trio were six more constables and eight men in the cloaks of the Order of Preachers, all on foot. Was Raimond among them? They had their hoods up so she could not even tell whether they were friars, clerks or other administrators as their travelling clothes were similar from this distance. They were followed by four carts with equipment and several young servants. She scanned the carts; Raimond was not there. Two more constables on horseback took up the rear. She felt a jolt: constables Del Gurbe and Barca!

The sun burst through the clouds and one of the cloaked men turned his head upwards. His hood fell back. It was Raimond! Esme wanted to cry out to him. It really was Raimond. He was alive. He was safe. And he was in Foix. She studied him. He looked older and more manly than when she had seen him last. His cloak sat very well on his broad shoulders. His head was still shaved to the tonsure. He walked energetically, his head slightly bowed once more and his hands folded in front of him. He was talking earnestly to a friar walking beside him. Something about his contentment made her uncomfortable. But at least he was here.

She rushed back to her father's house and found him with Guilhèm in Jaufré's house. 'Father, I've seen him! Guilhèm, Raimond's here! He has come with Tiqué.'

'Hush,' Guilhèm whispered as he stood up and hugged her.

It was too late. Jaufré banged his stick on the ground: 'He's here already. That friar is here! Why didn't you tell me? Take me to him. I want to see him, face to face!'

Esme hurriedly closed the door.

'Jaufré, it is better that you leave immediately.' There was urgency in Philippe's low voice.

'You told me he wouldn't be here for a while. But he's here now. I won't go. I want him to see me.' Jaufré was trying to stand up. 'I want him to know that he did not win. He has taken my wife but he will give me back my son. I will have my family together again.'

Philippe urged him to drop his voice. The bone-knitter had done a skilful job and Jaufré was able to walk at a slow, steady pace for considerable distances on flat ground. Prolonged walking still caused him stiffness and pain. But his uneven temper was a serious problem, especially in a town on edge.

Philippe said quietly to Esme, 'Montségur has agreed to give Jaufré and his family immediate refuge.'

'Montségur?' Esme was surprised. Montségur was very protective of its privacy. No one was allowed up there without an invitation. A garrison of knights and men-at-arms made sure of that.

'I consulted the elders Luisana and Leyas and they meditated on it.' The mention of the elders seemed to calm Jaufré momentarily. Guilhèm continued to talk in a low voice, deliberately using the elders' names. 'Jaufré, Luisana and Leyas have said that you and your family would be very welcome if you wish to find immediate refuge. Help will be provided to find a haven once this threat has passed. Jaufré, a short while ago, you said that you would take up Luisana and Leyas' offer immediately.' He laid his hand on his shoulder.

'Guilhèm, do you promise me that your friends on Montségur will allow Raimond in, even if he has become a friar?' Jaufré's voice was calm.

'The community on Montségur will welcome Raimond especially, Jaufré. But they have asked that you go there immediately. We need to leave tomorrow morning.' He looked at Philippe for help.

'Yes indeed, my old friend, you must leave at dawn. José, a good knight, will help you with your journey. We will bring your daughters and Raimond to you.'

'I'm not leaving until I see the friar. I want to look him in the eye. I want him to see me.'

Esme spoke: 'Please Jaufré, please go to Montségur. You have to go. I will bring Raimond to you.'

'You failed last time,' snapped Jaufré. 'Why should I leave it to you now?'

'Perhaps if you get your daughters,' Philippe suggested. 'Then Guilhèm and I could help to release Raimond.'

The arguments went around and around. Esme stopped listening. There was nothing she could say to Jaufré that would make any difference when he was in a mood like that. She was thinking about Raimond.

Guilhèm and Philippe eventually negotiated a deal with Jaufré. He would drop his demand to confront Tiqué in exchange for going to Labernoc and fetching his daughters, Matina and Alayda. Neither Philippe nor Guilhèm was happy about the plan but at least it would get Jaufré out of Foix before it was too late.

Very early the following morning, Guilhèm, Jaufré and

José, a knight paid for by Philippe, prepared to leave. With Jaufré being so weak, it would take them at least four days to reach Labernoc. They hoped Jaufré would give up along the way and go directly to Montségur, which was not far off their route. Esme was to follow them and go into the village to fetch Matina and Alayda. Of all of them, her presence would raise the fewest questions.

'If you hurry, you will only take a day or a day and a half to get to Labernoc,' Guilhèm gave her instructions as they prepared for departure. 'Leave on the third morning and we will see you before we reach the village. And Esme,' he looked at her with a warning in his eyes, 'stay away from Raimond. Once Jaufré is safe, we will find a way to help him.'

As they turned to leave, Philippe embraced Jaufré. 'My old friend, I hope to see you in happier times. Here,' he stepped back and pulled a dagger from the pouch hanging from his belt. 'Take this with you and protect our daughters.'

19

Foix, October 1239

ESME SPENT THE NEXT TWO DAYS strolling around town with Andreva and trying to hide her agitation. On the second day, many people came out even though it threatened to rain. They talked in loud voices about the weather, the quality of the seasonal vegetables and the supply of wood. The sight of a member of the friar's retinue caused momentary interruptions before conversations continued with renewed vigour. Esme's eyes darted everywhere. Where was he? How would he react when he saw her dressed in her finery? Raimond had never seen her dressed in such elegant clothes.

Andreva gripped her arm. 'Esme, your distraction is far too obvious. You must learn to disguise your feelings. Come along, it starting to rain.'

The streets were clearing when Esme saw Tiqué and Raimond walking by the river together. She unhooked Andreva's arm and said she was staying for a while.

Andreva argued.

'Please, Andreva, let me stay. I need time to think. You go home or you'll get wet.'

Andreva shook her head in bemusement and turned for home.

Further drops of rain fell. There was a thunderclap. Esme took shelter behind a pillar. Raimond and Tiqué hurried through the marketplace, towards the abbey. Suddenly Lopp, who was walking behind Esme, took off. He chased Tiqué, snapping at his cloak. Tiqué kicked out at him but that only encouraged the dog to jump up at the friar.

'Raimond, stop that dog. Hold on to it.'

Raimond managed to get a grip on Lopp. Tiqué carried on; he turned a corner and disappeared. Raimond stood up slowly and regarded the dog with puzzlement. 'Lopp?'

'Raimond,' Esme whispered from the canopy. 'Raimond, here.'

Raimond looked around but could not see anyone.

'Raimond, *besson*, here, behind the pillar.'

Raimond turned his head so quickly that his hood fell down. In seconds his bald head was glistening as rain poured down his face. 'Esme, is that you?' he whispered.

Esme stuck her head out from behind the pillar. 'In here, *besson.*'

With a quick look over his shoulder, Raimond stepped out of the rain and came face to face with Esme. Her veil was sodden and her hair was plastered to her head, the colour that Andreva had painted delicately onto her face was dripping away.

'Esme, what are you doing here? Have you been following me?' He looked her up and down. Her light blue dress, now soaking wet, clung to her skin and he was momentarily distracted by her small breasts, which were rising and falling as she breathed rapidly. He frowned and looked away.

'No. I am living here with my father. Raimond, have they made you a friar?'

He rubbed the bald part of his head. 'Soon. Are you safe?'

'Yes, yes, I am. But you? You are not a friar yet? Oh Raimond, I am so relieved.' She took a step towards him, holding out her hands.

He stepped back and raised his hands. 'No Esme, no, stay away. The church is my family now.' He told her that he was serving Tiqué as his scribe and, he added with a change in his tone, he was accorded many of the rights of a novice friar with plenty of time for prayer and permission to attend tutorials on the scriptures. As he spoke, Esme searched for the familiar sparkle in his eyes. He avoided her gaze. He looked mature and confident and seemed so much older than her. He would make a believable friar.

'You are wet and cold, Esme. You should go home now and dry yourself.'

'I've been wetter and colder,' she snapped, disliking his tone.

Raimond head jerked backwards and furrowed his brow as he studied her. Then his face softened and he smiled. 'Esme, so much time has passed since our life in the mountains.'

Esme waited for the smile to reach his eyes. It did not.

Two men ran past in the rain and Raimond quickly drew his head up and said crisply, 'It's been nice to see you again, Esme. I'm pleased you are well but I have to go now.'

'Raimond, no, you can't go yet,' Esme grabbed his arm.

'I must; I have duties and prayers to attend to,' he tried to pull his arm away from her.

'No, Raimond, not after all this time,' Esme held on to him, her heart breaking. 'There is so much to say. Your father and Guilhèm and his family.'

Looking at her hands on his arm, Raimond asked perfunctorily, 'Well, how are they all? Father? My sisters? Guilhèm?'

Quickly she told him that his father's hip was much better but that Guilhèm's family had been killed by the friar's men, 'those people who are now your companions', she said deliberately.

Raimond's face drained of colour. 'Killed? By the friar's men?' He searched her face for the truth in what she was saying. There was horror in his eyes. Esme let go of his arm and explained in a few succinct sentences what had happened.

'Guilhèm is living with the community on Montségur. They are helping him. He is finding peace with the holy people there.'

Raimond dropped his head into one hand. 'Agnes, Serena and their baby. Their little baby.'

'She was called Bonnie. Oh Raimond, she was so beautiful and so small with tiny hands and feet. She could cry when she was hungry but Serena was always there. And Agnes, she was… And Guilhèm'

Raimond looked up, his confidence and crisp maturity vanished. 'I can't believe… Esme. Is this true? Are you saying this to trick me?'

'Raimond, you can't stay with people who do things like

this. It was those two fat constables who did it, and a man dressed as a friar. He was the son of the hunter who had helped us in Carcassonne. Why don't you come with me? You don't need to remain with these people. I wasn't to tell you yet, but we have been invited to take refuge on Montségur too. All of us, you, your father, your sisters, me. In fact, your father has just gone to Labernoc to get Matina and Alayda. Guilhèm was going to come back for you but why don't you come with me now. It's only a few hours from here and no one will know where you have gone.'

Raimond furrowed his brow: 'Esme, you shouldn't tell me those things, I don't want to know. I have a different life now. I'm going to be a priest and I can't have anything more to do with you or my family. Don't tell me anything about them. It's much better that way, really.'

Esme reacted angrily: 'How can you say it's better? We're your family. You belong with us and our people, not with those murderers.' She reached into the pouch hanging around her neck and took out her stone. 'I bet you still have your stone. Here's mine. Where's yours?' She looked at him challengingly. 'Show me that the true Raimond is still here.'

'I can still be true to myself and be a friar.'

'Well show me. Let me see your stone.'

Compelled, Raimond reached into a pouch that was hidden under his belt and, after some fumbling, took out his own stone. He held it towards her on the palm of his hand. Esme placed it alongside her stone on her outstretched hand, the jagged edges fitting perfectly together.

'I'm sorry that I can't be what you want me to be but you

must let me do the best with who I am now.' He reached to take back his stone but she snatched it with her other hand and pressed her stone into his outstretched hand.

'You can't be true to yourself if you are living with murderers! We'll swap back stones when you leave them. I'll be waiting for you on Montségur.'

'No! Esme, no, you can't swap stones. That's wrong.'

'I just have *besson,'* she put his stone in her pouch and pulled the cord tight. 'Mind my stone and I'll mind yours.' She turned and ran down towards the river through the driving rain without a backward glance.

20

Foix, October 1239

RAIMOND COULD NOT THINK CLEARLY. The news about Guilhèm's family ran around his head; were they really dead or was she just saying that? She had never been a liar but could he really say that he knew her now? She was wearing a dress and raised shoes. The Esme of the forest would never have worn such clothes. He smiled. She had been so wet. He could imagine her walking into a fine house and not noticing the horrified stares from well-dressed and coiffed people. She was still Esme even with those fancy clothes.

As he walked slowly to his quarters, he felt strange, as if he were not walking in his own body. He could not feel his legs or his feet. He knew it was because Esme had taken his stone. Occasionally, over the past two and a half years, he had thought about throwing it away but it was small enough to keep in his belt. Now he could feel that there was a part of him missing.

Were the holy people right, he wondered? Does the stone really represent my soul? The Roman church says that God is far beyond us but maybe there is some truth in what the holy people taught us as children, that man's greatest temple lies inside ourselves.

He pushed Esme's stone into his belt. 'Oh Esme, what have you done?' he muttered. His hands shook as he realised that he was about to carry the representation of Esme's soul into Tiqué's world.

Alone in the dormitory, Raimond hung up his wet clothes and put on a dry undershirt. He remembered the touch of Esme's hands on his arm. He pulled his belt very tight around his waist but loosened it when he could feel her stone against his body. Childhood memories flooded back. Their fun and laughter; their secret places in the forest; their private conversations; their attempts to talk to the birds and the animals like Guilhèm did. He smiled again. Wet and cold! When had Esme ever worried about being wet and cold? No wonder she had snapped at him. She had looked beautiful with her hair plastered to the side of her face, her dress clinging to her, her skin glistening from the rain on her décolletage. He smothered a laugh. Esme in a dress? Philippe must be having a big influence on her. She looked like a woman, a woman any man would be happy to marry.

'Go away, *bessa*, please, go away,' he pleaded silently. 'You are my past. There is no way back.'

He adjusted his tunic. He was committed to becoming a friar and would be happy spending his life in prayer and reading scriptures. He had met many good, kindly friars who reminded him of the devout people who used to visit his parents' house in Labernoc. There was, of course, the inquisitorial aspect of the work to which the order was committed but it had stopped two years ago and every day he prayed that it would never be reinstated.

He knelt down to rub his damp shoes. Unexpectedly a vision of his mother appeared. She was smiling at him, her arms outstretched in expectation of an embrace. Raimond stumbled backwards and sat on the ground. His mother reached to one side and picked up a goblet. Unable to move, Raimond closed his eyes. He imagined his mother pouring a cascade of golden light over his head. It ran through his body. He felt peaceful. His head was empty of thoughts. With his eyes still closed, he turned his face to his mother and smiled. She embraced him. He tilted his head forward and imagined he was nestled in her breast. All of the tension in his body melted away.

A church bell rang out but all he heard was 'love'.

The bell rang again, this time hitting a discordant note. Raimond leapt up, jamming his feet into his wet shoes. 'Mother please... please, go away! I'm late for prayers.' Dressed, he wrapped his hands in the sleeves of his tunic, bowed his head and hurried downstairs to join the household for evening prayers. The chapel was dark and cold. A large wooden crucifix dominated the dismal space. There were only twelve people there, friars, servants and officials. The constables had long ago made it clear that evening prayer was not for them.

Friar Pierre Tiqué looked up from his prayer book as Raimond knelt down. He bowed his head and clearly enunciated each word of his prayers. Twice he glanced in Tiqué's direction and, to his dismay, caught the friar looking at him, his lips pursed and his brow furrowed. Raimond could feel himself flush and bowed his head low.

When prayers were finished, he hurried off with Simon, a young servant who Tiqué had taken from his relatives. Simon's parents, condemned heretics, had been executed just before the Inquisition had been suspended. Aged twelve, Simon was a nervous boy but Raimond had been looking after him, training him in his tasks. As usual, they were preparing refreshments for the friar in the abbey kitchen when, unexpectedly, Tiqué appeared. Raimond felt himself flush from head to toe. Tiqué never came to the kitchen.

'Did you catch a chill, Raimond? You look unwell.' The friar approached him.

Raimond's heart was pounding. All he could think about was Esme's stone in his belt.

'Perhaps you should go and rest. We can send for the herbalist if…'

Raimond looked up at him to assure him that he was quite well.

Tiqué's head jerked backwards. 'Raimond?' he compelled the younger man to look at him. 'There it is. I can see it. Definitely heresy.' He gripped Raimond's chin and moved his head around. Raimond tried to neutralise his face but he knew he was in trouble. Tiqué reacted like this when he suspected he had found a heretic.

'Raimond, I believe you betrayed my trust. I don't understand how and it may be unwitting on your part but we must find out. Come along, boy,' he addressed Simon over his shoulder without releasing Raimond's jaw. 'We have work to do.'

Raimond tried to argue but Tiqué tightened his grip on his jaw. Still holding him, Tiqué forced Raimond out of the kitchen, along a cold corridor and down some steps. He took a blazing torch from a bracket on a wall. They reached a door, which Tiqué kicked open and thrust Raimond into a cold, dark and musty space. The torch threw out a dim light revealing a rack, a fire grate with a small stack of wood and iron implements stacked beside it, a cistern of stagnant water, and several dusty desks.

On Tiqué's order, Raimond stood helplessly by the desk he would normally have occupied in such circumstances. What was Tiqué doing? Had he seen him talking to Esme? He tried to block thoughts of her because he did not want to bring her into this horrible situation. Instead he thought of Sarah, the daughter of Jesus and Mary Magdalene, and begged her to put a cloak of protection around him. He prayed to Mother Mary and asked her for help. Then for the first time in a long time he said The Lord's Prayer in Occitan, repeating its gentle cadences over and over again.

As the torches spread a dull yellow glow around the dark stone room, Tiqué drummed his fingers on the table. 'Look at me!' said Tiqué.

Raimond raised his eyes.

Tiqué studied him, shaking his head every now and then. Raimond knew that he was having one of his internal conversations with himself. His left eye was round and staring, his right eye half closed but that was the one that was scanning him closely.

'Raimond, you have been a good servant to me but I see

the light of the heretic in you.' Tiqué's tone was efficient. 'You may not be aware of it. You may be possessed by something in the air around here. We know that Foix has a history of harbouring heretics. But you will agree with me that it must be routed out. If it is unintentional, if you have indeed been possessed, we shall exorcise it from you and carry on as before. You know what you must do.' He waved his arms in the direction of the rack.

Raimond hesitated. Tiqué sounded mild. Was he really asking him to submit to an interrogation?

'Clothes off, on the rack!' Tiqué barked. 'Delay and you will suffer unnecessary punishment.'

Dazed, Raimond took off his tunic making sure to wrap up his belt with the secret pouch in it. He removed his other clothing and stood there, shivering on the damp, stone floor.

'Well, here we are at the second degree of interrogation,' said Tiqué. He turned to Simon, 'Boy, do you know what the second degree is?'

Simon shook his head, his eyes fixed on the floor. He had never attended an interrogation.

'Tell him,' Tiqué turned back to Raimond.

'The prayer,' whispered Raimond.

'Which prayer?

'The Ave Maria, Most Reverend.'

'The Ave Maria and what?'

'The Ave Maria and, and…'

Tiqué moved his face close to Raimond's: 'The Ave Maria and what?'

'The Ave Maria, and… and… fire or water.'

Tiqué forced Simon to repeat the instructions. It took a while before the terrified twelve-year-old eventually got it right.

'Now boy, I leave the choice to you. Tell me: which should we start with first? Fire or water?'

Still standing by the rack, Raimond knew that Simon was trying to work out which was the milder of the two punishments. He wished Tiqué would ask him what he wanted. His mother appeared in his imagination; she was looking at him with great love and saying 'Do not fear'. Then he heard Simon stammer 'Water'; his bowels opened.

'I suppose it helps that the demon in you knows exactly what to expect,' said Tiqué softly. 'Hopefully this interrogation will be short and efficient. I know we would both prefer that.'

On Tiqué's command, Raimond climbed onto the rack and spread himself out. He knew that any hesitation would make matters worse. He flinched as Tiqué chained his arms and legs to the corner posts.

Without saying a word, Tiqué picked up a funnel, scooped a large jug of water and, placing the tip of the funnel in Raimond's mouth, instructed Simon to commence the Ave Maria. Tiqué then started to pour water into Raimond's mouth through the funnel while Simon stammered through the sacred prayer. Raimond writhed on the rack, drowning. Simon reached the end of the prayer and Tiqué, holding the jug up and waiting until Raimond had finished coughing and gasping for air, said, 'Now boy, say the prayer properly. By not saying it properly, you have added to Raimond's time. Say it as if you were saying it in church. Now, go!'

Simon started again, trying not to stammer but going more slowly as Tiqué poured more water into the funnel and Raimond was drowning again. He could choke no more, his head was about to explode. His mother's face appeared again. He fainted.

He came around on the cold floor, and coughed up some of the foul water. He tried to remember where he was. He saw his naked body. His ankles and wrists were sore. He caught a glimpse of a fire blazing in the corner and remembered.

Before another word was spoken, Tiqué pierced Raimond in the left shoulder-blade with a burning rod. Raimond screamed, banging his hand repeatedly on the floor.

'Oh no! Please, no, no!'

He fainted again. Tiqué threw water on him.

Still gagging and now weeping from pain, Raimond frantically tried to work out what he could tell Tiqué without betraying Esme. 'Everything! I'll tell you everything,' he cried repeatedly. At the back of his mind he knew how feeble that sounded; it was what all victims of Tiqué's interrogations said even if they had nothing to say. But Raimond knew too well that when Tiqué got to this stage of an interrogation, he would keep going until the victim was broken down and would say anything. He felt himself drifting away from his body. The pain receded. He could no longer feel the cold floor. He asked himself why had he stayed with the friar? He had had plenty of opportunities to leave. He could have found work anonymously in one of the castles between here and Rome. Tiqué would have looked for him but he should have taken the risk. But no, he had chosen to remain part of this terror. Maybe he deserved this suffering.

‘Please talk, Raimond, please do,’ pleaded Simon.

Pain seared through his shoulder. Crying out, he opened his eyes and saw a puddle of urine gather around Simon’s feet. He must try and think. Was it Esme that Tiqué was after? Esme said his father had been in Foix for a while; maybe someone had recognised Jaufré and betrayed him to the friar. Would Tiqué stop if he told him that his father was still alive? Was that what he was wanted?

Tiqué prodded Raimond’s ribs with the burning poker. Raimond yelled again. Tiqué ordered him to return to the rack.

With difficulty, Raimond pulled himself onto the rack hoping he would die of fright. He knew some victims die of fright. Usually, however, they were older; Tiqué was too experienced a torturer to allow a young man to die in this way. He prayed to God to take him. Then he saw Esme’s face. ‘Tell him the truth,’ she seemed to say. ‘Trust me, trust yourself. Holy God is looking after us, you can never betray me. Remember what your mother said; you are loved and love.’

‘I can’t!’

Tiqué pulled over a stool and sat beside him. Slowly Raimond became more aware of his surroundings. He could sense Tiqué’s face near him. He could smell the medicinal pomander from his clothes.

‘Now, Raimond, I think it is time to talk. Look at me and tell me what is going on. The demon has got hold of you. You can be saved from it. Confess to me, Raimond, my friend. Redemption is possible. Let it all out. I will cleanse your soul.’ Tiqué spoke in a soft, soothing tone.

'I didn't know she was in Foix. I didn't plan to see her. Really. Now she's gone away. I...'

Raimond fainted again. He floated away from earth. His mother was there, glowing like an angel. There was Agnes and Serena and other people, including a woman who looked like Esme. The image fractured. He came to when Tiqué dabbed cold water on his face.

'Raimond, 'she', who is she? Where did you see her? Is she a heretic?'

'No! She is my friend. I can't betray her.'

Tiqué sighed. 'The demon was still hiding.' He put down the bucket and walked around to pick up Raimond's right hand: 'I am so sorry to do this and I won't destroy your talent. You write so very well, you know. But we must get to the bottom of this, for your sake. Simon, bring me a knife.'

'Please no, I'll tell you anything!'

'Yes, you will, and the next time without any hesitation,' said Tiqué, slowly sharpening a knife on a leather. He leant forward and picked up Raimond's index finger, held it firmly, then slowly cut the soft pad off the top of it. Raimond felt himself scream. In the distance, he heard the friar's voice. 'Do you realise how I risked my career to protect you, Raimond? Rome does not want children of heretics in their midst but I took a risk to save you from the pyre.' He cut off the pad of his next finger. Raimond fainted. When he came around, Tiqué was still talking. 'I said I would prove that the sins of the father need not be borne by the son. Lavaur, 1211. They always said I was the exception until you came along.' He cut off the pad of the next finger. 'The demon can possess the father. The heretical father condemns his wife to the life of a fallen woman. But must the father also destroy the son?' He moved to the fourth finger. 'No, I maintain not, not if the son is true and obedient to the holy authority of Rome.' He cut Raimond's finger viciously. 'And you are not going to prove me wrong.'

Raimond fainted again. He came to with icy-cold water on his face and in so much pain that he did not know which part of his body it was coming from. He turned his head and from the corner of his eye could see that his hand was a mass of blood. He blacked out again.

When he recovered consciousness, he was on the floor and alone. He heard a mouse scuttle across the floor. His right hand was so bloody and painful that he still could not work out what Tiqué had done. The burns on his body were throbbing. He let out a cry; it echoed in the eerie room.

'Esme, Esme what shall I do?'

'Where is my stone?' she seemed to say.

He looked over to where his clothes were in a little pile. He wanted to reach for her stone, but feared that Tiqué might walk in. A little light appeared in the corner of the room.

'Tell him everything, *besson*' he heard Esme say. 'Just tell him the whole lot and have faith that we can work with it.'

'*Bessa*, how did you get in here? You're so clever.' He tried to lift his right hand and cried out. He put out his left hand, there was no one there. 'Where are you?' he groaned.

He heard her childhood giggle. He smiled despite his pain. At the back of his mind, he worked out that he was drifting in and out of consciousness; that was the usual response at this stage. A couple of hours' respite would probably make him ready for the next installment. He wished that Tiqué would ask him a question but knew that he would not; the friar always got far more information by not asking questions. He tried to remember what he had said but all he could remember was betraying Esme.

Raimond was semi-conscious when Tiqué and Simon returned. As he tried to focus on the room once more, he realised for the first time that the clerk, constables and others who normally attended an interrogation were absent. Tiqué was breaching the strict guidelines for interrogations. Raimond was now very afraid; if Tiqué had broken the rules, which he was usually so fussy about, how much further could he go?

'Let's get straight on with it,' Tiqué said briskly. 'This is very upsetting for all of us and I want it to be over as quickly as possible.'

Raimond was unable to move. Simon helped Raimond to stand up. Tiqué reached out and, putting an arm under Raimond's naked armpit, hoisted him roughly onto the rack. Gingerly, his hands shaking, Simon picked up Raimond's pale muscular legs and loosely put a chain around each ankle.

Tiqué moved over to the fire and placed several pokers in the flames, Raimond saw Esme in his mind's eye: 'Tell him everything,' she whispered.

Raimond's eyes filled with love.

Just at that moment, Tiqué looked at him. 'There it is,' the friar cried in a high-pitched voice. 'Now Raimond, you will tell me the whole truth or you will die.'

He lifted the poker and pressed it against the sole of Raimond's left foot.

Raimond screamed.

Tiqué stuck the poker back in the fire.

'No! Everything, everything. Esme, my father, everything. Please!'

Tiqué ignored him. He pulled another iron from the fire and pressed it against the same foot, this time along his heel. The smell of burning flesh filled the room. Tiqué poured cold water on Raimond to revive him and, without a word, got another poker out and pushed it into the ball of his foot.

Tiqué threw more water on Raimond's face. The water was fresh this time.

'Now you can talk,' said Tiqué, standing close and straining to hear him.

'Esme in Foix. My father. He's gone to Labernoc for sisters. Going to Montségur.'

'Your father?'

Raimond drifted off. In his unconscious state, his mother appeared. He put his hands out to her and felt a great peace rush through him. For that moment, he was a happy child in Labernoc once more.

He came to, sitting up in a chair with a rough, wool cloth thrown over his shoulders. He looked down at his foot. The skin at the top was red and blistered and the sides of his foot were distorted. He felt stabs of pain through his right hand. Tiqué was sitting by him with a strange look on his face. Simon poured water on Raimond's foot.

Tiqué leant forward 'Tell me about your father.'

'Father. With Esme.'

Through the haze of pain he saw shock and puzzlement in

Tiqué's face. There was a lengthy pause before the friar asked how this was possible. As Simon poured more water on his foot, Raimond stumbled through all that he knew about his father's escape and his plan to go to Labernoc. He fainted again.

Raimond came around in his own cot. Simon was wrapping a cloth with a thick poultice around his foot. His hand had already been wrapped. His clothes were in a pile beside him.

'We're leaving in the morning,' Simon whispered. 'I'm sorry, I'm really, really sorry.'

'No… Simon … no fault…'

'He has a mule for you. I've cleaned down your clothes a little bit. And I've got soft cloth to put under you. Wrap it to your stomach because I heard him tell a soldier to lie you on the saddle. And the pouch is still with your belt. Don't tell Friar Tiqué I told you.'

Early the following morning, Raimond was carried down to a pack horse by a soldier and gently laid over the saddle. The soldier could feel the cloth around his stomach but, as the young man was barely alive, he said nothing. Raimond flopped on the wide saddle and lost consciousness. The soldier secured him to the horse so that he would not slip off. Raimond spent most of the trip over the next day and a half in a state of semi-consciousness holding hands with Esme.

21

Labernoc, October 1239

IT TOOK GUILHÈM, Jaufré and the knight, José, three days to reach the mountain ridges near Puivert. By now Jaufré was in pain and leaning heavily on his crutch. He had been able to sit on José's horse for short stretches and this helped them to make progress. Guilhèm's sense of unease was growing; he was tempted to abandon Jaufré and fetch Matina and Alayda by himself. However, he forced himself to respect the older man's wishes.

Esme, with Lopp, caught up with them on the morning of the fourth day. The sun was rising to the east and lighting up the familiar mountains around Puivert Castle. She had set a fast pace from Foix but, with no moonlight to help her, she had chosen not to walk during the night. Guilhèm watched her closely as she ran up to them. There was something different about her but, as they were nearing the village, he did not have time to talk to her. They walked through the trees on the steep lower slopes of the craggy mountains leading to

Labernoc. Waiting for Jaufré to catch up, Esme leant against an old broad-leaved tree; she fingered the leaves, which were turning golden brown, and felt the texture of the trunk against her body. Memories of her childhood with Raimond in these forests made her smile. She tapped his stone and shivered. Her smile vanished; she refused to accept that he really had changed.

The party arrived at a vantage point where they could observe the entire village from the safety of the forest. They could see the rambling farm buildings where Raimond's sisters, Matina and Alayda, lived with Jaufré's brother, Bernard, and his family. As they watched, Alayda came out of the house followed by her cousin, Julian, and Guilhèm's old dog, Spider. Oblivious to the drizzle, the two of them practiced stick fighting in the yard outside the barn. Jaufré's younger daughter, now sixteen, was tall and muscular. Alayda's cousin, Julian, was six months younger and heavily-built. Esme watched as he dodged Alayda's stick and threw his considerable weight at her, flattening her. Matina stood in the doorway. Moments later the three returned to the house.

Jaufré sat down and rested his head against a tree: 'My daughters, my beloved daughters, there they are,' he muttered over and over as he watched them.

Quietly Guilhèm told Esme to go and tell her foster sisters to gather a few belongings and join them here in the forest. She ran down the hill and slipped in through the open door of the barn to wait until one of them should appear. It was a while before Alayda and Julian re-emerged. Alayda was talking noisily about how she wanted to improve her sword fighting skills. Esme was about to call to her when Spider gambolled into the barn and barked. Alayda followed him. Esme could see her muscles tense as she scanned the gloom.

'Alayda, it's me, Esme.'

Alayda looked over towards the whisper.

'Keep talking, be normal,' instructed Esme.

Alayda recovered quickly and continued to give orders to Julian on a sword movement as she moved closer to Esme until they could hug. Esme, shorter than Alayda, was swamped by the younger woman. Julian gave her a clumsy hug.

Esme explained what was going on and sent Alayda to get Matina. After she left, Julian looked shyly at Esme. She smiled at him encouragingly; the last time she had seen him was the day they buried Guilhèm's family. 'If you are really all leaving, can I come too please? I can't leave her, you know.'

Esme felt a knot in her throat. Alayda and Julian's bond was as close as her bond had been with Raimond but what would Julian's parents feel about him leaving for a life with people branded as heretics? Bernard was determined to keep his family safe from the Inquisition; he took whatever oath the Roman friars wanted him to take, spoke little and got on with his work.

Matina came in and embraced Esme. She was as tall as Alayda but shockingly thin. As Esme outlined the plan, a figure appeared at the barn door; it was Jaufré. He was alone, his frail body held up by his crutch.

'Father!' Matina yelped.

Alayda slapped her hand over her sister's mouth. 'Hush, Matina! Father, what are you doing here?' Alayda was whispering. 'You can't be seen. Oh please go, it's so dangerous.'

'Not until I've seen my brother. Your uncle does know that I'm alive? You did tell him, didn't you?'

Matina nodded but remained mute.

'Can you get your uncle quickly?' Esme whispered, 'and some of your belongings. We must go while everyone is indoors.'

Alayda grabbed her sister's arm and pulled her out of the barn.

From their vantage point in the forest, Guilhèm had controlled his frustration with some difficulty. Jaufré had refused to listen to reason. He insisted that as head of the family, it was up to him to tell his brother that his daughters were returning to live with him. Physical restraint being out of the question, Guilhèm had to let him go.

The rain eased off. Several people came out of their houses. The gates of the bailiff's castle opened and soldiers lounged in the entrance. Guilhèm saw Alayda run to the house with Matina following. In an effort to remain calm, he said to José: 'There's a young woman with the potential to equal any of those you have fought alongside. She has a warrior's determination. Her sister, however, is more delicate and I think the past years have been hard on her. She will probably need help on the way to Montségur.'

They watched Alayda lead Jaufré's brother, Bernard, to the barn. A few minutes later, Matina followed them with several small bundles held closely to her chest.

Suddenly José nudged Guilhèm and pointed to the north of the village. Four men on horseback were approaching; one of them was pulling a pack horse behind him. As they drew closer, they could see that the man at the front was a friar and the other three horseman were constables.

'Tiqué!' exclaimed Guilhèm. 'With Del Gurbe and Barca.'

When they entered the square, Constables Del Gurbe and Barca turned towards the bailiff's castle. Tiqué and the fourth constable went to Bernard's home. Guilhèm spotted a slumped figure on the pack horse behind them; 'Is that Raimond?'

José squinted. 'It's a man and he's alive.'

Guilhèm instructed José to get ready to leave the area. 'I'm going down there but once they join forces with the bailiff's soldiers, we'll be outnumbered. Don't follow me into the village. Take whoever gets out of there straight to Montségur.'

In the barn, Jaufré was trying to hug his brother: 'Thank you for looking after my children, dear Bernard. I am taking them back now. We are setting up a new home and I will contact you when that is done.'

'You'd better get moving,' Bernard mumbled, holding him off.

Esme took two of Matina's bundles and, as she peered out through the barn door, she came face to face with a horse. She raised her eyes and found Tiqué staring back at her.

The constable jumped off his horse. Tiqué remained where he was and looked past Esme, who had frozen in horror.

Jaufré stepped into the light: 'Pierre Tiqué!'

Tiqué looked down at the bent old man with the wisps of grey hair who was balancing himself on a stick. After studying him for a long moment, he raised his eyebrows.

'Jaufré of Labernoc, can it be you? I am surprised. I sensed that Raimond was telling the truth but found it hard to believe.' Tiqué spoke quietly.

'Give me back my son! He doesn't belong in your church!' Jaufré moved closer to him, his face becoming red; his voice strong and full of anger. 'Give me back my son and stay away from my family.'

At that moment Alayda spotted Raimond. Screeching out his name, she rushed towards him. The constable grabbed her and held her back.

Tiqué ignored Alayda. 'I don't know how you escaped the fire, Heretic Jaufré, but you were condemned for all eternity on that day. By refusing to die, you have contaminated your son. Now, not only will you die, but you will take your family – all of your family with you.'

As he turned his head to see Del Gurbe and Barca leading the bailiff and his soldiers down the road, Jaufré lunged at Tiqué's horse with unexpected force. Caught by surprise, Tiqué lost his grip on the rein and slid off the horse, landing on his feet. He grabbed at Jaufré's shoulder. In a rapid movement, Jaufré pulled out Philippe's dagger and jabbed it into Tiqué's heart.

Tiqué's eyes and mouth opened wide and he fell backwards to the ground. The constable let go of Alayda and drove his sword through Jaufré's back. Jaufré fell on top of Tiqué, the two men lay on the wet ground, staring into each other's eyes.

Alayda cried out and pulled their father off the friar. Blood spurted from his throat. He looked at his younger daughter and died. Matina dropped to her knees. 'Father, dear father, no, please stay with us.' She tried to wipe the blood that pumped through his mouth.

Alayda knelt down and closed his eyes. 'He's gone, Matina, he's gone.' She glanced behind her to where Tiqué was lying, his eyes staring lifelessly at the sky. 'And he's taken the friar with him.'

Esme was with Raimond just as Guilhèm strode up. Together they lifted him to the ground where Esme cradled his head. Raimond's eyes were slightly open.

'Esme,' he breathed, and closed his eyes.

It began to rain heavily but the villagers remained where they were. Miguel Garcias arrived on the scene, his soldiers and constables Del Gurbe and Barca walking a little distance behind him. Garcias looked at the body of his old friend lying on the ground with the inquisitor. He could not believe that Jaufré had survived the pyre and that he had not heard about it. But here he was, two years later, and barely recognisable. 'My friend,' he whispered. 'What terrible fate has become of us.'

As the constable was giving a rapid account of what had happened, Barca and Del Gurbe arrived on the scene. Barca reacted furiously. Raising his lance, he turned towards Miguel: 'Arrest them, arrest them all!'

Miguel turned to issue orders to his soldiers but, as he did so, caught Guilhèm's eye. The hunter was looking at him steadily. Miguel paused and bowed his head. As Barca shouted further demands, Miguel held up his hand to stop him. Turning back, he said, 'This is a very difficult situation, constable. Friar Tiqué is dead, and the man who killed him is also dead. There is nothing left to do.' He looked at the three constables in turn. 'Men, my soldiers will help you to carry Friar Tiqué back to the castle; you will be able to embalm him for burial at a place of your choosing.'

'And the killer's family?' demanded Barca, squaring up to Miguel. 'Friar Tiqué was on his way to find them. They are all heretics. You must arrest them!'

Shaking his head, Miguel summoned his own soldiers and instructed them to carry Tiqué back to the castle. As his men moved forward, Del Gurbe and Barca reached for their swords. Miguel gestured to his soldiers, who put their hands to their swords.

Del Gurbe stared hard at Miguel: 'I warn you, sire, if you let this heretic family go, you will be leaving yourself open to a charge of heresy.'

The bailiff looked down at Guilhèm, who continued to look at him. Two years ago, he, Miguel, had allowed himself to be bullied into revealing the location of Guilhèm's home to these brutal constables. Two women and a baby were murdered as a result. Enough was enough.

He turned back to Del Gurbe: 'Constables, I am in charge here. I am sorry for the loss of your good friar. Prepare his body for his final journey and I will write a full report for the authorities.' His words were placatory but his tone was firm. 'My servants will provide you with food and shelter until you are ready to leave. Bernard,' he dropped his voice. 'Please look after the body of your brother and Guilhèm, take Raimond and the women and go, go now!'

Alayda gripped Matina's arm and urged her to stand up.

'I can't leave him,' she whispered.

'Matina, we have to go,' Alayda glanced up. Miguel was looking at them both, a frown on his face.

Reluctantly Matina reached into her father's belt and retrieved the two stones, his own and Ava's, which she knew he kept there. When in Miguel's prison cells, Jaufré had bribed a soldier to take the two stones to Matina.

'I will ask a holy person to place them somewhere together,' she said, as she kissed him on his forehead and stood up.

Miguel approached Guilhèm: 'I am so sorry, my friend, so very sorry.'

Guilhèm took his hands in both of his. Then he turned to Tiqué's horse and threw the saddle and other belongings on the ground.

'That's the Reverend's horse!' shouted Del Gurbe.

'Let him take it,' snapped Miguel.

Bernard went back into the house. Moments later, he returned carrying a woollen rug and a blanket. Without a word, he stood by Tiqué's horse and waited until Guilhèm had settled himself on it. He handed Guilhèm the bedding and, with Alayda's help, lifted the unconscious Raimond up to him. Wrapping Raimond in the rug, Guilhèm, who was considerably taller than Raimond, used the blanket to strap him to the front of his body. With Esme and Lopp walking beside him, he slowly rode Tiqué's horse out of the village.

Alayda knelt down to kiss her father for the last time. 'Thank you, father, I love you.' She gathered up her belongings: 'Julian, we're going with Guilhèm. Come with us, please. Take Matina's arm and help her.'

Bernard put a restraining hand on Julian's shoulder.

'Father, I must go with her, she needs me.'

Bernard nodded and squeezed his shoulder.

'There will be no escape,' snarled Barca as he and Del Gurbe watched the family disappear into the forest beyond Labernoc.

22

Montségur, October 1239

Guilhèm rode ahead with Raimond. Esme followed with Matina, Alayda and Julian, choosing forest tracks rather than open ground in case the bailiff changed his mind. Matina struggled on the steep slopes but José assisted her, sitting her on his horse on occasion. It was a sombre group and a walk which should have taken half a day took a full day with an overnight stop. As darkness fell, they found a shallow cave. Alayda lit a fire and Matina took bread, cheese, fruit and dried meat out of her pack. They talked in quiet voices about Jaufré, Esme filling them in on his past two years. When Matina and Esme lay down to sleep, José put his cloak over them and took up a position at the entrance to the cave to keep watch until dawn.

Guilhèm was waiting by a dense copse of trees when they arrived on the ridge below Montségur castle. 'Raimond is alive and in very good hands.'

Esme looked at the steep path up to the castle of Montségur.

If she ran, she would make it to the top in twenty-five minutes.

Guilhèm put his hand on her shoulder and pointed to a control point about half way up the pog. A man was approaching a group of soldiers with a heavily laden mule. 'There's a villager making a delivery at the mule stop. When he's gone, we'll go.'

Esme climbed a tree to wait. Wrapping her arms around a trunk, she watched the man with the mule come down the mountain. Soldiers carried the baskets of goods on their backs up to the castle. Esme had seen the castle from the distance many times before and knew its reputation as an impregnable fortress. It was only now that she could see why. The pog rose 170 metres above the ridge with vertiginous limestone cliffs on three sides. The south-western slope, the one she was looking at now, was the only accessible route to the top and even this looked narrow and steep. In sections, there was a sheer drop to the side of the track; anyone who fell could tumble over boulders and scrub for up to 40 metres before coming to a halt.

When the man and the mule disappeared to the west, Guilhèm led the group across open ground to the base of the track. He stopped at a ditch and bowed his head, explaining that this was an invisible gateway to the mountain.

'Montségur is a very special place, far more special than you can imagine,' he said as each bowed their head in respect.

They walked up the steep track, traversing open ground for about thirty metres. When the track entered the forest, it wound its way through the trees in sharp bends. Esme could hear song birds chirping. The damp leaves made the track slippery, but embedded rock and logs gave her feet something to grip. There was dense scrub under the trees on either side of the track. Twenty metres later, the track emerged from the trees and rose sharply through low scrub. At this point it was only wide enough for one person to walk comfortably, although José kept an arm out for Matina. When they reached the mule stop, a soldier stood up to greet them. Guilhèm introduced them all and, in response, the soldier drew a cup of water from a storage tank and presented it to Matina. She took a sip and passed it on. The two dogs were panting in anticipation. Another soldier put a dish of water on the ground in front of Lopp and Spider. They lapped it noisily.

'Water is scarce and hard to store on the mountain,' he told Esme. 'This is a true welcome to you.'

Setting a slow, steady pace, a soldier escorted the small group for the remainder of the steep climb. There were several lines of defence. The first was a wooden stockade and the remaining were thick walls of stone. Soldiers positioned along each line watched them.

They reached the castle fifty minutes after crossing the ditch. Two children playing near the large entrance gate in the high castle wall ran out to pet Lopp. Along the castle wall men and women worked silently in vegetable patches. A woman sharpening a knife on a stone exchanged a greeting with Guilhèm and smiled at the rest of them. The gate of the castle opened into a courtyard, which was quiet although there were people working here. On the right-hand side were stables, a forge and several closed doors. Esme could see two more floors above that.

'It looks small,' said their escort, 'but nearly 350 people live here at the moment.' He explained that there were more than 70 men in the garrison, and nearly 120 men and women who had taken the Consolamentum, the one sacrament of their people. These consoled people had come from distant lands to pray together on Montségur. Garrison families, elderly widows and artisans made up the rest of the community.

The soldier guided them to a door to the left and ushered them into a small, elegant hall, leaving the dogs outside. The hall opened into a spacious room. The wooden shutters of a large south-facing window were open. In the distance, mountain peaks shimmered in the sun. The room was furnished with chairs and richly woven cushions. A young woman welcomed them and introduced herself as Esclarmonde de Pereille, a daughter of the castle's owners. She was wearing a green dress with intricate gold embroidery. Her long, dark hair was plaited and draped over her left shoulder. She had colourful slippers on her feet. Esme bowed in respect. Matina, Alayda and Julian followed her lead.

A woman walked in. She was dressed in fine wool and her thick white hair was swept into a loose bun on top of her head. Esme was immediately taken by the air of magnificence that exuded from this tall, handsome woman. She had met powerful people in Foix but never one with so much presence. Beside the woman was a frail, elderly man dressed in dark robes. He beamed at Guilhèm, the laughter lines around his eyes creasing up. Guilhèm greeted them both with affection. Again the visitors bowed in respect.

Welcoming them warmly, the woman introduced herself as Luisana. She explained that she had lived here ever since the castle became a centre for prayer over thirty years earlier. 'It has been my pleasure to welcome all visitors on behalf of the de Pereille family and our small community.'

She introduced Bishop Guilhabert de Castres. Esme's brow shot up. This was the man who had debated with Domingo de Guzman, the founder of Order of Preachers, Tiqué's people. Jaufré had often spoken of the bishop with hushed awe. The debate had even predated the Crusade of Simon de Montfort. She had no idea that Guilhabert de Castres was still alive.

The bishop approached her with a merry smile on his face. She blushed. 'Guilhèm has told me that you gather stories. I hope I have a little time left to tell you some of my stories from a very, very long life,' he cradled her hands in the traditional way of their people. She immediately felt the peace that always surrounded the men and women who devoted their lives to prayer. She wanted to rest in his warm and gentle embrace. Hesitantly she asked if she could see Raimond.

'Esclarmonde will consult the healer and see if this is possible,' Luisana's voice was soothing. 'We have a house for you. Perhaps put your belongings there and go and join our residential guests for their main meal. It is just about to be served. The food will revive you.'

Esclarmonde led them to a house on the north side of the castle. It consisted of two rooms, one surprisingly spacious and the other, a small ante-room for cooking. Beds of straw with woollen blankets had been piled there, and a little wood had been supplied. Dropping their bundles, they followed Esclarmonde to the communal dining hall where a woman was preparing a meal for eighteen. Matina's spontaneous offer to help was gratefully accepted. Esclarmonde took José, Alayda and Julian to meet a senior member of the garrison, leaving Esme to pace the room.

The diners, mostly elderly women, arrived. Esme forced herself to sit and eat a little of the stew served up. Eventually Esclarmonde brought her back to the main house, through the hall and into a small, bright room. The community's healer, a woman of about forty years wearing a long white apron, studied Esme, her deep blue eyes in her long, thin face scanning the scruffy young woman in front of her.

'Take her away,' the healer said to Esclarmonde sharply: 'She is anxious and dirty. I'm not letting her near my patient.'

With delicate persuasion, Esclarmonde convinced the healer, named Rixanda, to allow Esme to approach Raimond for a few moments. He was lying on a high, narrow bed. A brown-coloured poultice covered his right hand; his left foot was covered in a paste under gauze. Rixanda lifted the gauze to apply more of the paste. Esme gasped; the sole of his foot was a mess of deep black wounds and large yellow and red blisters.

'Leave!' commanded Rixanda in a low voice.

Outside Esclarmonde reassured Esme that it was not as bad as it looked: 'The burns did not expose the bone. But fever is a real danger so the next few days will be critical.'

'I just need to be with him for a moment,' Esme begged.

'Later,' Esclarmonde was firm.

'I need to give him back his stone. We swapped them in Foix.'

'You did what?'

Embarrassed, Esme repeated herself. Esclarmonde expressed

her very great surprise: 'Esme, you must have been told that your personal stones cannot be swapped without the explicit blessing of an elder.'

Tears welled up in Esme's eyes as Esclarmonde led her back to the room. After a quick word with the healer, Esme took back her stone, which had been placed beside Raimond's head, and put Raimond's own stone there instead. She desperately wanted to talk to Raimond, to remind him of her love but the healer pushed her out and closed the door behind her.

23

Montségur, December 1239

As RAIMOND WAS TOO ILL to travel anywhere for some time, the new arrivals were encouraged to stay on Montségur for the foreseeable future. The rhythm of life on the pog was monastic. At the heart of the community were the consoled men and women who devoted their lives to prayer. Several times a day, from early morning to late at night, about 120 people gathered to pray for hours at a stretch. In between the periods of prayer, they undertook the duties needed to sustain the community. They were from many lands and spoke different languages. They had taken the Consolamentum and did not eat the products of animals nor have intimate relationships; their entire being was given over to helping humankind through prayer and example. When a message came through that someone in the region was dying, two of them would leave the mountain to help the person reach a state of purity by giving them the Consolamentum. When Esme was young, she had called them 'holy people'. As she grew up, she learnt that they did not prefer this term as it set them apart from everyone else. Yet she could not help but think of them as special; while they rejoiced in life and the earth and the animals and everyone they met, they did not seem to be of this world. They prayed for the friars and their constables as fervently as they prayed for all around them.

The garrison, which protected the community, was small but professional, exceptionally well-armed and, through a network of spies, fully informed about military and political activities in the region. The knight José, who chose to stay on for the present, was welcomed into the senior ranks of the defenders. Alayda's request to join the garrison was rejected. So, with characteristic determination, she set about proving her worth by carrying goods from the mule stop, and helping with the water and wood supplies. As the men came to admire her strength and stamina, they invited her to participate in military exercises with swords, bows and arrows, and other weapons. Julian remained by Alayda's side. He was often called upon to assist with heavy tasks. Alayda, who had heard her cousin being teased about his bulky size since early childhood, was pleased that his value should be recognised by this elite army.

Matina was welcomed as a new cook in the communal kitchen for the elderly. Unlike those who lived here to pray, the widows had not taken the Consolamentum and therefore ate meat and other animal products. Matina, who had been taught how to make rich stews of rabbit, mutton, deer and boar by her mother, took great care over the preparation of the dinners and was heartened by the appreciative response. She also spent time in creating a pleasant home in the house assigned to the family. Dry matted grass covered the floor, extending halfway up the low, stone walls and kept them warm even in the coldest weather. Matina fussed over the cleanliness of the home, and tidied after Alayda and Julian and Esme without complaint. She kept a bed for Raimond for when he might be well enough to join them. At ease for the first time in many years, a sparkle returned to her eye and her skin developed a healthy glow. Several of the single garrison members were drawn to her but the kind and attentive José had already won her heart.

Esme was the only one of the party who could not fit in. There was no call for her sewing skills as there were plenty of people here to sew and there was no demand for her elaborate embroidery. There were enough experienced hunters among the defenders and none asked for her help. Any hope that Rixanda might draw on her ability to gather medicinal herbs and fungi was dashed by her poor relationship with the healer. She pledged money for her keep, which she would get from her father. It was only a day's return trip to Foix but she was reluctant to leave Montségur while Raimond was still so unwell. But she helped Matina in the communal kitchen and waited for news of Raimond. Rixanda would not let Esme into the healing room but at least she knew that he was out of danger.

Just as the winter snows began to fall, Guilhèm went to one of the caves used by the Montségur community for intensive prayer. He planned to stay there until spring. Before he left, he visited Foix and returned with the news that Andreva was pregnant. While Esme was very pleased for her father and

Andreva, she was more concerned about their safety after the events in Labernoc.

'Your father is confident that no connection has been made between his household and Tiqué,' he reassured her.

'But don't they know about Jaufré? That he killed Tiqué?'

Guilhèm shook his head. 'Of course there is talk about Tiqué's death but all anyone says is that it had something to do with a heretic on his staff. As far as Philippe's neighbours are concerned, Jaufré had his hip fixed by their bone-knitter and he has gone back to wherever he came from.'

After Guilhèm left, Esme felt very alone. As winter drew on, she missed his support. She missed her father and his lively conversations. She missed Arnold and his laughter and his poetry and his delight in her. And she missed Andreva and her chatter about clothes and parties. But most of all she missed Raimond.

24

Montségur, March 1240

THREE MONTHS LATER, Guilhèm emerged from the darkness of the deep cave. It was early dawn as he walked down the mountain track, his senses alive to the vibrancy of the crisp morning air. Enjoying the feeling of his muscles working in his legs, he picked up the pace and strode along the river bank. He smiled broadly as he sat on a rock on the south side of the river. The sun would soon rise above the high mountain ridge and he wanted to experience its brilliant light. He took his boots off and bathed his feet in the freezing water. Steep mountains with high cliffs and craggy outcrops rose on both sides of the valley. Bursts of white blossom could be seen on the lower trees on the southern slopes. If he sat here for a month, he could watch the blossom creep up the mountain until the upper trees were white and the lower ones were light green.

'Heaven,' he breathed as he lay back.

The sun peeked over the top of the mountains. He closed his eyes and placed a leaf over each eye. He had spent the previous days in an outer cave so he could monitor day and night through a crack in the rocks. However, after so long in complete darkness, his eyes were still not ready for strong sunlight. He lay there observing the contrast of the stillness of a black cave and the liveliness of the riverside. Insects buzzed and clicked, leaves rustled, the melting snow water flowed unceasingly over the river rocks, the scent of spring growth floated in the air. As the sun rose, his skin began to warm. The temperature in the cave had been very cold but after a period, his body had adjusted. Now he was enjoying what it felt like to let the sun warm his skin.

A black bird flew overhead. Guilhèm sat up and greeted it. The bird swooped down low. 'This beautiful earth,' Guilhèm spoke to the bird; 'How wonderful it is to be able to see it from above.' The bird grabbed a small fish and flew off.

As he watched it go, an image of Serena holding Bonnie appeared in the bright light. He smiled at them. Tears fell but his smile remained. Two winters had passed since his family had been killed.

'Beloved Serena, I learnt great things in the cave. Most of the time I was by myself but sometimes an elder would arrive.' He told her about the men and women who had visited him to pray with him and teach him about the great mysteries.

He laughed lightly: 'Often I didn't know whether my teacher was real or not. Some brought food so maybe they were real. But who knows?'

He imagined her smiling with him and whispering to Bonnie. Serena always loved the way he communicated with animals so she would not be surprised that he could communicate with spirits.

'I had extraordinary visions. At times I could see images of symbols above me.'

With his hands, he drew the symbols he had seen repeatedly. An elder had told him that some of these symbols were initiation symbols used by their people in the Consolamentum. 'You will not receive the Consolamentum in the ordinary way,' the elder had said. 'The rigorous life asked of those who are given the Consolamentum in the usual way may not serve your work in this lifetime. But be aware that you have received a powerful initiation and must always obey Universal Laws.' When Guilhèm queried what work the elder was referring to, and what he meant about the Universal Laws, the elder assured him that all would be revealed over time. 'But meanwhile, treat your initiation as a sacred gift and the symbols you are being given as sacred tools to be used to heal.'

Guilhèm looked up into the light to tell Serena and Bonnie more about his experiences but they had gone. He sighed. The world he had entered in the cave was blissful in its stillness. The world out here was beautiful but it was also very sad.

He remained by the river for several days, adjusting to the sensation of the natural world. He foraged for food, lit a small fire at night and talked to the black bird, who returned frequently. Serena and Bonnie appeared several times, as did his mother, Agnes, but as each day passed, their images became less distinct.

Soon it was time to return to Montségur.

25

Montségur, March 1240

GUILHÈM APPROACHED THE POG from the west with a sense of anticipation. He was looking forward to discussing his experience in the cave with the elders and with Guilhabert. As he looked at the cluster of buildings, he felt a great love for Montségur and its community. He stood in the ditch at the base of the pog and bowed deeply.

Guilhèm was past the wooden stockade when he spied a small figure sitting on a rocky outcrop. It was Esme and she was watching him come up the mountain. She made no move to greet him until he was beside her and there was none of her usual enthusiasm in her hug.

'Is it Raimond?'

She nodded sadly.

'Oh Esme, I'm so, so sorry.'

Esme wriggled out of his grasp and sat down again, resting her head in her hands.

'Guilhèm, he just won't talk to me. His wounds are healing.

But he doesn't want to see me.' Slowly she explained that Raimond would sit by an open window on a sunny day and stare at the sky or fall asleep. The healer, Rixanda, allowed Matina to sit with him but would only allow Esme in if she was accompanied by Esclarmonde, the daughter of the castle's owners. And even when Esme was there, Raimond would not talk to her.

Guilhèm closed his eyes and said a brief prayer of thanks that Raimond had survived the winter. After a moment of consideration, he instructed Esme to wash and tidy herself while he went to the healing room. There he found Rixanda with Esclarmonde. Raimond was sitting at the far side of the room, staring through a small window in the west wall of the castle. Acknowledging the two women, Guilhèm approached Raimond. Raimond looked at him and mumbled something. The same dull expression Guilhèm had seen in Esme's eyes was also evident in Raimond's eyes. His dark hair had grown back but his face was thin and pale. His right hand twitched; his fingers looked like they had healed over but the skin was tight. The left foot was on a stool with the toes pointing upwards. He tried to move it.

'Let me help.' Guilhèm pulled up a chair and tenderly took the injured foot on his lap.

'I have to keep my foot moving or else it's going to curl upwards.'

As Guilhèm massaged the damaged foot, Raimond dozed off. Rixanda surrounded him with cushions and covered him with an extra blanket. She beckoned Guilhèm and Esclarmonde into the hall and closed the door.

'I'm concerned about him,' she said. 'He seems to have little interest in helping himself.' She explained that the fingers on his right hand would always be sensitive but were otherwise healed. The burns on his body were now scars that should cause no discomfort. His foot, however, still required work.

'There is no reason why he should not be able to use that foot in the long term; it will probably be uncomfortable for him to put his full weight on it but with the aid of a stick and some padding in his boot, he will be able to get around. But if he doesn't do the exercises, the muscles will seize up and walking will be very difficult.'

They discussed options. Guilhèm described a yellow fungus that had helped him as a child.

'I know the one you mean,' nodded Rixanda. 'It is potent but if it improves his energy, it's worth a try.' She said it could be found in a particular forest to the south-east of the pog.

Guilhèm offered to postpone his work with the elders and go immediately to find some.

'Take Esme with you,' said Esclarmonde. 'It would do her good to get off Montségur.'

Guilhèm shuddered involuntarily at the memory of the last time someone had suggested that he take Esme to the forest. He closed his eyes and let the peace he had known in the cave settle him. Then he went to find Esme.

26

Montségur, March 1240

Guilhèm and Esme, with Lopp behind them, went down the pog, across the river and east up a steep hill into the forest. They stopped on a knoll where they had a perfect view of Montségur. Esme took food from her small pack. Guilhèm studied the bread and the cheese and ate both slowly, savouring the scent, the texture and the taste. Esme watched with curiosity; he looked remarkably healthy for someone who had lived in a cave for a whole winter.

When they finished eating, Guilhèm closed his eyes and sat upright for a while. Clouds drifted by and the air was still. Relieved to be with Guilhèm as he meditated once more, Esme listened to the crickets and the birds and the wind in the leaves, and watched a yellow butterfly with black dots flit around them. Her mind meandered. Unexpectedly she thought about her mother, and wondered what she might have been like. Philippe said that her mother's smile could light up the darkest cottage. She had a lovely singing voice, and sang lullabies to Esme before she was born. Esme loved lullabies; she might try singing some to Raimond.

Her heart began to pound and she flushed with a familiar guilt.

'Ah there it is,' said Guilhèm into the silent air. He opened his eyes and turned to her. 'Now, Esme, what are you not telling me?'

She fiddled with a blade of long grass and took a while to answer. 'Guilhèm, it was my fault that Tiqué attacked Raimond. Tiqué must have seen us talking and then tortured him to find out who I was. If I hadn't told him the plan about going to Labernoc, Jaufré would still be alive.'

Slowly Guilhèm got the full story of Esme's meeting with Raimond in Foix.

'So you told him what we were doing and then swapped your stones.' Guilhèm breathed deeply. 'Esme, Tiqué did not need to see you talking to him to be suspicious. Carrying someone else's stone would have changed Raimond. Tiqué would have been highly sensitive to changes in people.'

'Is it not possible that he just saw us?'

Guilhèm drew her attention to a pair of ravens drifting on the thermals. She lifted her head as one bird soared upwards, followed moments later by the other.

Guilhèm asked Esme to take out her stone. 'Tell me about it, starting with the day you selected it. Go back to that time, remember it, and when you have it, tell me about it. There is no rush.'

Esme rolled the stone from one hand to the other, quickly at first, then more slowly until she let it rest. In her mind she went back to the day when two consoled people, a man and a woman, came to Labernoc to bless a dying man. She was about seven years old at the time. The consoled people stayed with Ava and Jaufré, talking, praying, resting, eating and singing. On the third day, Ava asked the woman, named Rossa, if she would help Esme and Raimond to find a personal stone each.

Guilhèm made several symbols with his hands over Esme's stone and then flicked his fingers into the air. The sun came out from behind a cloud and lit up Montségur. He asked her to continue. Although she knew that Guilhèm was familiar with the story, Esme described the day she found her stone and discovered that Raimond's stone matched hers along the jagged edge. Rossa, she said, told them that their stone was an outward representation of their souls on earth and should be honoured as such. They were to etch a picture of their own soul on their stone. When Esme protested about how difficult that would be, Rossa assured them that as they got older and stronger, they would be able to manage.

'She said that as we scraped away at the image on our stone, we would be cleaning our own souls and discarding that which was no longer relevant.'

Again Guilhèm made symbols. Esme wanted to leap forward to the day she received her mother's pearl and knew that her stone and therefore her representation of herself was a pearl. But, aware of what Guilhèm was waiting for, she returned to Rossa's lecture by the river bank.

'After telling us what the stone meant, Rossa told us how to care for it.' Esme closed her eyes. She could see Rossa insisting that they sit up straight and listen with all of their attention as she explained that there were a few rules they should never forget. They were never to bury their stone because that would deprive it of air. They were never to give it away or swap it, but to mind it always. And before they died, they were to entrust it to a consoled person or to someone they loved who would place the stone on the earth as a record of their life.

'Rossa called the earth God's garden,' said Esme. 'I asked her what would happen if I lost it. She made symbols, like you just did, and said that I was unlikely to lose it but if I did I would receive help. Then she repeated to me that I was never to give it away to anyone.' Esme thought for a few moments. 'Guilhèm, do you think she knew what I would do?'

Even as she asked the question, she knew the answer. Guilhèm remained in his meditative position with his eyes closed. Esme could hear Rossa's voice telling her that second time never to give her stone to anyone for any reason. She had been surprised that such a gentle person could even sound as stern as she had done at that moment.

Esme let the flushes of guilt subside before carrying on. 'We practiced on wooden models of our stones. One day, I was scratching a piece of wood and telling Raimond about our big hunt that day. I told him a story about how we brought the meat to Puivert Castle and how you didn't want to charge Serena much because you were in love with her, and how I interrupted and made a good bargain for you. I remember him laughing and saying that he loved listening to my stories. At that moment, I realised that I wanted to keep stories in my stone. I didn't know how that was supposed to reflect my soul but I liked the idea. I imagined that my stone was a pearl. I would scratch fissures into it and put stories into the stone through the fissures. A few years later, my father gave me my mother's pearl and the shading on the pearl was like the fissures on my stone. That's when I knew for definite that I had chosen the right image for my stone.'

Guilhèm prayed over Esme's cupped hands. She closed her eyes. He ended his prayers with a deep tonal hum that sounded unearthly. Esme felt heat in the palm of her hand where her stone rested. Then there was silence. After a lengthy pause, Guilhèm closed her hands over the stone and placed them against her heart. Esme felt the heat reach her heart.

'Look inside yourself and ask why you swapped the stones.'

'I was trying to force Raimond to leave the friar,' she whispered after a while.

'I ask you again, Esme, why did you swap stones?'

Esme imagined herself looking at the ray of heat between her stone and heart. 'Why did I do it?' she asked herself silently several times. She saw the ray of heat travelling up and out through the top of her head. She looked for the ray below her heart. She could see where it should go but there was a break and it stopped just below her heart. She got an image of people she knew and loved. She sought out Raimond. He was standing back, looking at the break and looking at her. Behind him, a woman who she knew was her mother, stepped forward. She rested her hands on Esme's stomach and heart. Esme felt a rush of love and the ray of heat flowed from her heart to the lower part of her body.

Tears fell from her closed eyes. 'I wanted Raimond to make me feel whole, Guilhèm, but I should never have asked him to do that. My mother is helping me.'

Esme remained in her meditation until she was ready to open her eyes. Looking over to Guilhèm, she smiled.

Guilhèm was not smiling. 'Esme, dear friend, you are eighteen years old. It is time for you to grow up and stop thinking only about yourself. You must accept the choices of others. You have been welcomed into a closed community but sitting around, unkempt and fretting about Raimond is unacceptable. You don't have to stay on Montségur but if you do, you must stay with all of your heart and you must participate in the community. If you choose to go, you must do the same. Anything else is a life half-lived.'

Esme let his words sink in. She did not rush to answer. Eventually she said, 'I'd like to stay on Montségur, at least until Raimond is better. I will make an effort, Guilhèm.'

'And I'll support you,' he said affectionately. 'Now let's go and find that fungus.'

It took them two days to find the yellow fungus. When they returned to Montségur, Rixanda looked at Esme closely. 'Her demeanour has shifted,' she said after Esme had left to wash and find clean clothes.

'She really is a wonderful young woman,' Guilhèm assured her.

Raimond responded well to the treatment and soon agreed to sit outside in the spring air where he could see the activity on the mountain.

Rixanda monitored Esme without saying a word to her. One day she invited Esme to accept three treatments to ease the stress in her body. Esme took it as an order and humbly agreed. During the third session, she felt something weighty lifting from her.

'Don't talk about it, just accept,' said Rixanda, when Esme queried what it might have been. 'Your mother is all around you. These treatments will help you to draw in her love fully.'

27

Montségur, April–May 1240

Esme blossomed, especially after Rixanda asked her to collect herbs from the forest for stocks in the healing room. Raimond, on the other hand, showed no interest in engaging with the people who greeted him and wished him well with his recovery. One warm spring evening, Raimond, Matina and Esclarmonde were watching the sun going down on the horizon. Esme was in the forest collecting herbs. Matina and José had married during the winter and she thought she might be pregnant. With some excitement and nervousness, she discussed the prospect with Esclarmonde, one hand resting on her belly. Raimond was slumped in a chair, off in his own world.

Spider ambled over, followed closely by Alayda and Julian. Spider laid his head on Raimond's lap and nuzzled him. Languidly, Raimond stroked the dog. 'Sorry, Spider, I don't have any food.'

Alayda reached into Julian's pocket. 'Here, give him this,' she said, handing him some bread.

Spider sat up, his tongue hanging out. Raimond broke the bread into pieces. Spider ate the bread messily, dropping most of it on the ground.

Raimond smiled: 'It's a waste, you eating food like this, Spider.'

'He's so old he can't eat much. Julian and I work extra hard to earn bread and other treats for him.' said Alayda. 'Raimond, when are you going to try walking properly? You barely move from the confines of the castle and I've got so much to show you.'

Raimond sat back. His eyes drifted off to the horizon. His foot still hurt when he stood on it but his muscles were in good condition. Rixanda allowed him to stay in the small bedroom attached to the healing room because there were no other patients. Sooner or later, however, he would have to leave that sanctuary. Maybe when he did, he would leave Montségur also; he did not belong here.

'Your foot isn't that bad,' Alayda sounded exasperated. 'You must try. Father was much worse than you and he walked all the way to Foix and back.'

The wind blew his hair over Raimond's face and he left it there. He had been thinking about his mother and father a lot lately. He knew what they must have gone through with Tiqué and he could not get the terrible images out of his mind. He wished he had had the chance to talk to Jaufré, to find out more about his childhood and his translation work; to ask him why he had not been more discreet with his work when he knew of the threat from Rome. Most of all he wanted to beg his forgiveness. It was his fault that his father had died. If he hadn't told Tiqué that he was still alive, the friar would never have found him. Why did he let Esme talk to him that day in Foix? He should have stopped her. She wasn't to know how dangerous it was to give information to anyone associated with the friars. Raimond pressed the fingers of his good hand into his eyes.

'Raimond?' Matina gently touched his knee.

Raimond pushed back his hair and looked up. Alayda had left with Julian.

'You drifted off again. Are you in pain?' Matina asked.

He shook his head.

'You can talk to me, you know. I am your sister. I looked after you when you were little. If you don't want to talk to me, you can talk to someone else, Esme or Guilhèm?'

Raimond turned away from her. 'Talk? No I can't, not to you dear Matina' he thought. 'You do not want my story to become part of the family you will have with José. And not Alayda, because she would probably want to kill me. Guilhèm would certainly listen but how would I start the conversation? Only a chatterer like Esme has long conversations with Guilhèm. And Esme, my Esme. How I wish I could talk to you. I know you could hear the truth and not condemn me. But I have brought you enough suffering and knowing the truth about me will only bring you more sadness.'

He groaned audibly and sank further into his chair. Matina and Esclarmonde tried to soothe him but he refused to respond to their concern.

♦ ♦ ♦ ♦ ♦

Alayda turned up with a crutch for Raimond two days later

and, after some cajoling, dragged him into a standing position. Raimond let Julian place the padded crutch under his armpit. The carved hand grip was at exactly the right height for him. He steadied himself on his right foot and slowly moved forward. Alayda talked him through each move while Julian stayed by his side, ready to catch him.

'Try the uneven ground. That's where the real test will be,' Alayda said.

Guilhabert de Castre appeared at the door of the castle above them. He was very frail but liked to step outside and look at the magnificent landscape around him. With one hand on his heart, he watched intently as Raimond struggled at first, then gained confidence.

Rixanda was pleased. 'You have the support of the entire community, Raimond,' she said as she outlined an exercise regime and fitted him with a padded boot. 'Don't reject it.'

After a slow start, Raimond found himself enjoying a sense of achievement as he made his way around the top of the pog. He visited each storeroom and workshop on the ground-floor level of the castle courtyard. He went up steps to the military quarters around the upper courtyard. From there he made his way out to the narrow passages and steps between the houses on the north side of the castle.

As he became more adept, he ventured down the narrow, rocky path towards the supply platforms, which were situated on a high cliff on the north-east of the pog. He found a spot where he could rest against a rock and observe the work of teams of people engaged in lifting wood and other heavy goods from below. There were two platforms with hoists fixed on the top of a sheer limestone cliff. At this time of year water jugs, the bottom encased in a rope basket and the top covered in weighted leather, were being hoisted in quantity. Alayda and Julian were among the runners who carried the heavy jugs to a depot close to the castle.

Raimond's overall condition improved. As summer approached, the prominence of the scar was greatly diminished by his healthy weight, deep tan and mass of black curly hair. He moved into the men's dormitory. Rixanda would have preferred it if he had moved in with his family but he refused. It was a long time since he had lived with them he said, and he no longer belonged there.

On Luisana's recommendation, he attended the community's daily prayers, rising before dawn for morning prayers and returning to the hall after the midday meal for the lengthy afternoon session. It was a demanding timetable but he did not object; he had become used to a monastic schedule with the friars and looked forward to the relief that this quiet time gave him. Unlike the friars, the elders and the consoled people on Montségur spent a lot of time in deep, personal meditation. He found that the dark thoughts and images that plagued him vanished when he was with them.

The only part of the day that made him uncomfortable was mealtime. Raimond wanted to dine with the consoled people because they ate in silence. However they followed a vegan diet and Rixanda insisted that he eat meat and other animal products. For this, he had to join the elderly widows in the dining room. He kept to himself, sitting at one end of a table and answering politely when addressed but otherwise not engaging with the diners, who respected his desire to be left alone. He ignored Esme, who helped Matina to deliver the meal.

Meanwhile, he was thinking about leaving Montségur. He would go to one of the big cities as soon as he was fit. His plan, which he kept to himself, was that he would change his name, swear whatever oaths anyone wanted him to swear, and earn his own living. Merchants were gaining power in the cities and he was sure that they would employ him for his literacy and language skills. Guilhèm had worked out how to establish himself in Carcassonne; he would ask him for help to set himself up in Toulouse or even further north.

♦ ♦ ♦ ♦ ♦

Esme was now preparing many of the midday meals for the widows in the communal dining room. Matina was often unwell with her pregnancy and everyone was happy for Esme to take over. She did not cook as well as Matina but she was organised and efficient. She told them colourful stories about her hunting trips with Guilhèm and asked them about their lives. The diners warmed to her. She, in turn, looked forward to seeing them. There were eighteen of them, two men and sixteen women. None had received the Consolamentum but, for various reasons, all had been given refuge on Montségur. One of her favourite people was Bertrana, a tiny woman of about sixty years old. Bertrana had a musical voice and a throaty laugh. She was unable to eat a great deal and, while the rest of the group were eating their dinner, she drank boiled water with mint leaves and ate crushed nuts and seeds that Matina or Esme prepared with guidance from Rixanda.

One day Bertrana asked Esme to sit down beside her after the meal had been served: 'You can't hear our stories if you are rushing around.'

'Why would you want to be bothering this young woman with our stories?' asked one of the men.

'Because we have stories to tell and Esme is interested.'

'You talk all day, Madam Bertrana,' said the man. 'Talk, talk, talk, while we're trying to eat.'

'You should wait until we've finished eating, then you can put us to sleep for the afternoon,' laughed the other man.

'You men are lucky that you have our charming company,' teased a woman.

The banter went up and down the table. Esme got herself a dish of rabbit casserole and sat beside Bertrana. Out of the corner of her eye, she could see that Raimond was watching her. She took her stone out of her pouch and held it in one hand while she ate.

'Now all of you be quiet for a moment. What story will we tell Esme today?' asked Bertrana. 'Maybe something about the French general, Simon de Montfort. You've heard of him of course?'

'We all have stories about that brutal man,' said another woman.

'Does she know that it was the women of Toulouse who finally killed him?' a large woman called Petrona asked.

'That is a good story,' said Bertrana.

Esme opened the hand in which she held her stone.

Bertrana acknowledged the movement with a smile then turned her attention to Petrona, who had started her story.

'It was 22 years ago but I remember it well.' Petrona spoke softly. 'He had attacked us before, twice, and come into the city once. He had done so much damage to our communities in Toulouse and in the towns and villages around us. We were tired.'

With the help of several others who had lived near Toulouse, Petrona described the long siege that began in winter and continued to the following summer. Everyone, including women and girls, was involved in defending the city. In spring, the people of Toulouse constructed a trebuchet to hurl large stones at the French army.

'In summer, during a battle, a group of women were in charge of the trebuchet. They spotted de Montfort and fired stones directly at him. They hit him and he died. I wasn't there but I heard about it. Very soon afterwards, the siege was ended.'

'But not the Crusade,' said Bertrana. 'That went on for some years but without de Montfort, it was not as vicious. When it ended, the Romans took a different tactic.'

'Their Inquisition,' muttered one of the women.

Further stories, recollections and comments followed. Esme absorbed them all; she felt the anger and sadness but appreciated the detail they offered. As she left the dining hall, she put her stone back into her pouch. Raimond was waiting for her outside.

'You have to stop that, Esme.'

'Raimond!' She smiled at him. It was the first time he had addressed her directly for so long.

Without returning the smile, he repeated what he had said.

'Stop what?'

'What do you think? Stop encouraging those people to talk like that.'

'But they know I am interested and they wouldn't talk if it upset them. You know that too.' She was startled by the anger in his voice.

'People shouldn't talk about those events. What if someone hears? Or if someone finds out that you know about those things?'

'When I hear a story, I put it into my stone. They are hidden there. I can't remember the stories in detail unless I call them out and I don't do that unless I'm safe.'

'You can't hide what you know in a few scratches on a stone. They'll force you to talk. You will end up betraying everyone.'

Raimond hobbled off to the prayer hall. Esme's good humour crumbled. She leant against a wall and closed her eyes. Tears slid down her cheeks. He would never forgive her.

'Oops!' She heard a scuffle beside her and opened her eyes. Brother Thomas, a consoled man, had stumbled. She rushed over and reached out her arm to help him.

'Thank you, my dear, my old bones are not as reliable as they used to be.'

She offered him her arm as far as the prayer hall.

'Perhaps you would like to sit beside me for afternoon prayers?'

Esme wiped her face with her sleeve. 'Thank you, Brother Thomas, but I think I will go for a walk.'

'What a very good idea. This afternoon when I am meditating

I will imagine myself there too.' He took her hands in both of his and bowed his head over them. 'You have great love in your heart, my dear, and we all have great love for you. Have faith.'

Esme's shoulders lifted slightly as she walked out to a rocky outcrop to think.

28

Montségur, June 1240

LATER THAT NIGHT, Raimond lay in bed. He was more restless than usual. He hated upsetting Esme. He thought of all of the stories she had heard and the number of people who knew she was gathering them. Tiqué was dead but there were many others continuing his work. As soon as one of them found out about her, he would extract every detail from her. Giving up hope of getting to sleep, Raimond got out of bed quietly, picked up a mat and put his blanket around his shoulders. The moon was bright. Slowly he made his way to the rock by the supply platform and placed the mat on the ground. With no clouds, it was a chilly night. He put the woollen blanket over his knees. In the distance he heard a baby cry. There was quiet again.

He felt for his stone with his left hand and studied it in the moon light. It was a slim stone with smooth surfaces. It was shaped like a diamond except for one longer side, which had a jagged edge. Soon after finding the stone, he had chosen the image of a diamond to represent his soul. He began engraving the lines of a diamond on one of the smooth surfaces but had only completed two lines when Friar Tiqué arrived in Labernoc and took his parents. He had not done any engraving since then.

Raimond placed his stone into the palm of his right hand and put both hands back under the blanket. Gingerly, he let the tips of his scarred fingers feel the stone. Even with the loss of sensitivity in his fingers, he could feel the engraving.

'God, I try but I am not worthy of you,' he said in a quiet voice, dropping the stone on his lap and looking up at the moon. 'I am not worthy of my parents or my sisters or Esme.' Agitated, he drew his nails over the scar on his face: 'Why did I not run away? What made me stay? Maybe I liked enough of their world to stay. Prayer and education. Isn't that what so many of the friars like? To pray and to learn.' He shook his head.

An image of Esme smiling at him appeared in his mind's eye. He dismissed it with an angry scowl. 'You don't know who I am now. Remember me for who I was. That me will love you forever and can never hurt you.'

A bird called out in the darkness. It reminded Raimond of a Roman cardinal who praised his script by exclaiming 'Bella!' repeatedly.

'"Bella!"' He mimicked the cardinal out loud. 'My handwriting describes torture of real people and the bishops say "Bella!"'

'The birds are talkative tonight,' said the voice of a man behind him.

Startled, Raimond turned around.

'Oh, Your Grace, I didn't hear you coming, I beg your

pardon,' stammered Raimond, attempting to jump up. He stood heavily on his bad foot and winced.

Bishop Guilhabert de Castres smiled at him. 'Dear Raimond, I am a man like you. Please call me Guilhabert. May I sit beside you?'

Putting the pressure on his good foot, Raimond moved the mat to make a seat for the elderly man. Guilhabert used his walking stick to help himself bend down slowly. He turned the mat sideways before sitting on one side of the mat and inviting Raimond to sit on the other. He took the blanket being offered by Raimond and arranged it so that it covered both their knees.

'Although I am an old man, Raimond, there is no need for you to be cold while I am warm.'

Raimond sat down. 'Are you comfortable, Bishop Guilhabert?'

Guilhabert de Castres settled himself against a natural hollow in the rocks. 'I don't often get a chance any more to sit under the stars. The beauty of this place will wipe away any discomfort.'

The bishop sat quietly. His breathing was laboured. Raimond worried that the night air might make him ill. But the bishop did not complain. Tiqué would never have tolerated such discomfort.

As the bishop's breathing slowed down, Raimond felt for his stone. It had fallen off his lap when he stood up.

'It is a beautiful night,' said the bishop after a while. 'Look at the way the moon lights up the rocks.'

Raimond felt around for his stone.

'What is it?'

'Nothing,' responded Raimond hastily, sitting back again.

'No, it is not nothing. You have lost something. There is plenty of light, let's find it.'

The bishop leant forward and tapped the ground with his hand. 'Is this it?' he asked, holding out the stone with its jagged edge and fingering the shallow etching.

Raimond took it from him gratefully.

'What have you put on it so far?'

'Not much, just a few lines that were meant to turn into a diamond but I never got to finish it.'

'You will, Raimond. It is a splendid image for you; you are a beautiful diamond.'

'No, not anymore! Oh Your Grace, I beg your pardon.'

'There is no need to beg my pardon for speaking from your heart.'

There was silence.

'Tell me about Rome. I believe there are some very fine buildings.'

'There are, plenty of them, but there is nothing fine about what goes on in them,' said Raimond. He had thought about Rome at length but had not spoken about it. How much could he tell the bishop? He glanced at Guilhabert, who was looking at the landscape in the moonlight.

'I would like to hear some of your thoughts about Rome. I expect there was a lot to take in.'

With a little further encouragement, Raimond described some of the magnificent buildings, the great wealth and beautiful objects, the rich food and wine, the delicate scents and the absence of poor people around the most important buildings. He talked about coming into contact with noblemen and senior prelates. 'As Tiqué's scribe, I was obliged to accompany him often. The men of the church are determined and clever and very polite to each other. But it's what they do with their power that is so terrible,' Raimond spoke rapidly. 'The real part of their work is controlling people. I've seen what they do to women as well as men. They claim they are teaching the words of Jesus but their methods revolve around torturing and terrorising. They talk as if … as if this violence is necessary and even good for people.'

'And you, Raimond? What was your role?'

Raimond took a deep breath before answering quietly. 'I took notes and wrote up reports. Friar Tiqué wanted to create a process for the Inquisition, for the interrogations really. He was very proud of the number of people he interrogated and he liked to assemble information about every aspect of those interrogations. I helped him to present those results and I think, sometimes I helped him to write the results in the ordered way. He said I was good at that – ordering information. But I think it was my script. It made his records more palatable, less ugly.'

'What do you now think of this man, Tiqué?'

'I try not to hate him for what he did to my family and the many people he hurt. What he did to me, I don't hate him for that. I had become one of them and I deserved that. Maybe he was like me once...' He trailed off.

'Let me see your stone again? Ah yes, the lines that will become a diamond. I would like to show you something. I will ask you to close your eyes and I will touch your forehead. Will you allow me to do that?'

Raimond nodded and closed his eyes. He felt Guilhabert's thumb on his forehead, then felt him flick it upwards before removing it.

'Now, when I say so, I want you to open your eyes and tell me what you see.'

Raimond sat with his eyes closed and a tingling in his forehead. He raised his head.

'Now open your eyes.'

As he opened them, the first thing he saw was a very bright star shining in the sky. 'It's a diamond,' he breathed.

'It's a diamond, just like you. That is in you, Raimond, and with time, you will uncover that in yourself and you will finish the image on your stone.'

Raimond imagined the light from the star penetrating the spot on his forehead and running through his body. He closed his eyes and felt peaceful for the first time in a long time.

The bishop broke the silence. 'Raimond, I think I need to get back to my bed. Would you help me up, please?'

Raimond assisted Guilhabert to the castle, up steep steps and through the narrow alleys. When he left him at his door, he looked back towards where they had been sitting and marvelled at how far the elderly man had come to talk to him.

Bishop Guilhabert de Castres died two days later. Raimond felt in some way responsible. He attended the mourning ceremony for the bishop the following day, then collapsed back into himself. That week he remained in the prayer hall for most of the day and the healer had to order him into the dining hall to eat.

Luisana asked him to come and talk to her. With a heavy heart Raimond went to the spacious, airy room in the main house where the most important meetings and ceremonies took place. Luisana was sitting upright in a wooden chair, which was covered with a thick white woollen blanket. She smiled as he entered, and indicated that he should sit beside her. Raimond was conscious that he had not washed for days. Luisana did not seem to notice.

'Raimond, just before he died, Guilhabert asked me to start your healing at once,' she said. 'And I agreed. We have been watching you make an excellent physical recovery but your mind is very troubled and we did not want to start the healing on this aspect of your being until you were healthy. I have prayed with the elders for guidance on this and they have agreed that the time is right. Are you ready to start?'

Raimond nodded politely.

'Raimond, this is not an order, it is a query. The choice is yours. But I know that Guilhabert had a conversation with you before he died. For some months he was anxious to help you but didn't want to rush you. When he knew he had only a few days left, he sought you out.'

Raimond looked up at Luisana, his eyes glistening. 'Bishop Guilhabert came down to the platform to talk to me. I thought it was the effort he made for me, and the cold that had killed him.'

'My goodness no, dear Raimond. Guilhabert made his own choices. He had a job he wanted to do and would have drawn in enough strength to complete that job.'

'To talk to me?' Raimond stared at the floor for some moments. 'Luisana. Many people have been helping me and I have not repaid their effort with my own. I will take your guidance and do what you suggest.'

29

Montferrier June 1240

THE DAY AFTER THE MOURNING ceremony for Guilhabert, Esme left Montségur. She had seen Raimond only briefly since he had snapped at her and had not spoken to him at all. Mindful of Guilhèm's words on their walk to find the yellow fungus, she tried to find balance within herself but she was struggling.

She told Guilhèm of her plans. 'I need to get away for a few days. I don't know where, I just need to think.'

'Good idea, Esme. But tell Luisana of your plans. This is a protected community and she needs to be aware of people coming and going from here.'

With blessings from Luisana, Esme left the mountain. After a two-hour walk down to the valley, she stopped by a river near the village of Montferrier. She listened to the flowing water and watched the bees flit around the blossoms in the trees. Two ravens who nested near Montségur flew overhead. She wondered how far they travelled in a day. She felt her body relaxing but all she could think about was Raimond and how he had spoken to her. After eight months together in a small isolated community, that was the only time he had addressed her directly. She did not blame him for being so angry but she desperately wanted to speak to him properly, to apologise to him. She had no idea what to do. She could not force him to talk but she could not walk away from him until she had apologised. She took out her stone and, using a metal nail she kept in her pack, she scraped at it to sharpen up the fissures.

In the afternoon, she opened the bulky parcel of food Matina had prepared. There were nuts, seeds, bread, fresh mutton, dried rabbit, two eggs, two blocks of cheese and two small pies. Esme smiled appreciatively; there was enough food here to keep her going for at least twelve days. She ate as she watched two ravens fly high overhead. As darkness fell, she gathered grasses and branches to make herself a comfortable shelter at the base of a large tree.

The following days were sunny and warm and Esme was content to remain by the river. Much of the time she sat looking at the birds and the river and the insects, her stone in her hand. She remembered the times when she was young and the visiting holy people had encouraged her to be still and let nature tell its story. As Esme became more absorbed in the river and the wildlife, her mind slowed down and she passed hours thinking only of what was happening in front of her.

On the fifth night, she slept deeply and dreamt vividly. She saw herself as an old woman in the company of a middle-aged woman and a girl. They were all sitting by a fire like a family. The old Esme took her stone out of the pouch and was showing it to the woman and child. Holding it up, it got bigger and bigger and images began to drift out of the fissures as if on wisps of smoke. In her dream Esme could see faces but couldn't identify them; some were laughing, some crying, some talking or singing or rocking children to sleep. There were many different locations, big stone buildings and small cottages, forests and towns. Esme watched the images floating around the room until old Esme commanded them to return to the stone. The girl pointed to the stone and seemed to ask a question. Old Esme brought one face out of a fissure. It was Raimond and he was smiling at her.

Esme felt blissful as she woke up. She reached for her stone and held it close to her heart. In her half-awake state she went back over the dream and drew it together in a coherent sequence. 'I was holding stories in my stone. I let them out and put them back on my command.'

Awake now, Esme sat up and looked closely at the stone. Could she really command stories to come out like in the dream? She held up the stone and summoned from it the story about the red-headed boys. Images of Tiqué on his horse herding three terrified boys in front of him, mothers trying to free the boys, Del Gurbe striking the mothers, Barca slashing the boys with his sword, all came to her memory in sequence. She ordered the story back into the stone and cleared her mind by watching a dragonfly with blue wings and a green body. Then she called out another story, one about her mother that Philippe had told her. Immediately she saw a small woman with long dark hair, almond shaped eyes and dressed in a shimmering deep green dress. She was singing in a castle accompanied by two men. A slight smile played on her lips as she sang; she looked adoringly at someone in the audience; it was Philippe. Esme looked at her mother again. She recognised her now. She watched her mother for a little longer and returned the story to the stone.

She sat back and remembered her foster mother saying that when her soul's purpose was revealed to her, there would be magic. Esme thought about what had just happened. Her dream had been vivid and had carried on into visions while she was awake. The stories she had just seen had been very distinctive and had contained details she had not remembered hearing about, like the way her mother looked at her father. Is that the magic that Ava had spoken about? And if it was, is this the way the spirit world was telling her that she could keep stories safely in her stone?

She spent the following days experimenting, summoning stories and putting them back. Although the images were not as strong as those on the first morning, her confidence grew. After twelve days by the river, she felt content and happy. It was time to return to the community on Montségur.

30

Montségur, July 1240

Esme rested under a tree before the final climb up the steep pog. She could see the houses of Montségur clustered against the castle wall. Today, she was particularly struck by the majesty of the limestone cliffs on the northern and western faces of the pog. She had never looked at them properly before. They were high and sheer with few ledges. The rock was the sort that might crumble in your hand. No one, not even the most skilled and brave climbers, could scale those cliffs unaided. She knew that the garrison had created several paths with climbing aids around some of these cliffs but secrecy surrounded them and, even with the hidden aids, they could only be climbed by a few highly-trained men.

An idea occurred to her. Helping Matina with the dinners was not very demanding but being part of the climbing team might be. Would the garrison accept her as one of their climbers? It would give her a solid role in the community as well as bring some excitement into her life. Esme's tiredness vanished and, with a burst of energy, she ran up the pog, greeted the soldiers at the defence lines and made her way to the castle.

When she reached the top, she was surprised to see many of the garrison members and their families going to afternoon prayers; seldom did the garrison attend prayers in such numbers. Brother Thomas was resting near the main door. 'I was waiting for you, my dear.' He took her hands. 'I have some sad news. Our sister, Bertrana, has passed on.'

'Bertrana?' Shocked, Esme's eyes filled with tears.

'She went very peacefully. I know you were close to her and she enjoyed your company. Will you come with me into the hall? We are gathering to celebrate her life.'

Esme took Brother Thomas's arm as he made his way to one of the chairs by the side of the crowded prayer hall. She sat on the floor beside him, feeling comforted by his concern for her. Bertrana had been a great friend to her and when she was at her lowest, the love and compassion of the older woman had kept her going. Esme dabbed at her tears with her sleeve. Light streamed in from the two large, south-facing windows. There were several hundred people already sitting here. The consoled, many in grey-blue woollen robes, sat cross-legged on the floor. Soldiers stood near the back while their families sat in clusters around the edges against the high stone walls. The widows and widowers who had eaten meals with Bertrana every day sat on chairs to one side of the windows where the gentle breeze cooled them. Older members of the de Pereille family, who owned the castle, sat with them.

The Montségur elders were praying in a semi-circle at one

end of the hall. There were eight of them including Luisana and they were deep in silence. Guilhèm had told her that if she repeated the elders' names like a prayer, it would take her into a special place in her heart. This seemed to be the moment to do this. Esme looked at each of the six men and two women in turn and, reaching into her memory, silently called their names: Luisana, Leyas, Luyon, Gerad, Dam, Yusu, Uswan, Dimaz. Relieved that she had remembered them all, she repeated the names until she was fluent. When she stopped, she noticed that her breathing had settled.

Esme spied Guilhèm; he was deep in meditation and looked like a ninth elder. It took her a little longer to find Raimond. He was sitting on the floor at the far side of the room. His face was at an angle to her but she could see that his eyes were closed. Her heart began to beat loudly again. She turned her attention back to the elders and repeated their names.

Bishop Bernard Marty, Guilhabert de Castres' successor, started the ceremony with prayers and a chant. As the holy people joined in, the rich sound of men and women chanting in unison filled the room and poured out through the open windows. Bishop Marty placed Bertrana's stone on a plinth with candles.

Absorbed by the sacred atmosphere, Esme did not hear Bishop Marty addressing her. Brother Thomas tapped her on her shoulder and directed her attention to the bishop, who was looking at her with expectation.

'Esme, widow Bertrana told you something about her life' Bishop Marty's gentle voice travelled over to Esme as if on a wave. 'Perhaps you would share a little of it?'

Brother Thomas gave her an arm to help her stand up. Without thinking about what she was doing, Esme reached into her pouch and took out her stone. She looked at it for a few moments and then spoke in a quiet voice: 'Widow Bertrana grew up in the town of Cabaret. She was from a long line of herbalists and healers. She had a happy childhood.' Esme could hear her voice in the silence of the crowded room. She was trying to think of nice things to say but as she looked at her stone, only the big and terrible stories would come out. She glanced at Brother Thomas. He smiled in encouragement.

'Bertrana was married with two children but then the crusaders attacked the nearby town of Bram and took the townspeople prisoner. One hundred men of Bram had their eyes gouged out, their noses and lips sliced off, and were pushed into a line. The man at the top of the line was left with one eye. He was ordered to lead the terrible procession to Bertrana's town of Cabaret.'

Esme heard a deep sigh run around the room. She wondered if she had said too much and upset people but another reassuring smile from Brother Thomas encouraged her to continue.

'Bertrana practiced as a herbalist and raised her children during the remaining eight years of Rome's Crusade. Bertrana's son was killed in battle. Her daughter married and had three children. When the friars appeared in the region, Bertrana was one of those who the villagers felt would be a target of the new Inquisition. She was a very good healer and often prayed in the traditional way when she was working with a sick person. Her daughter told her that she had to leave Bram before friars came looking for her.

'Widow Bertrana did not want to go but the daughter's husband said she had no choice; if she remained, her daughter's family would be in grave danger.'

Several heads shook sadly at the telling of this familiar situation. Esme thought of her father's baby on the way and her own responsibility as an older sister to protect the little one. Sadness gripped her and she struggled to recover her voice. With a rising panic, she looked around the room. Everyone remained attentive. She waited until she was ready to speak again.

'Bertrana found refuge here. She loved living here. She loved the conversation at mealtimes. She argued and laughed and told me some very funny stories as well as these sad ones. I pray today that I have honoured her with an accurate retelling of a little of what she told me.'

Esme sat down and put her stone away. She noticed Raimond looking directly at her. She wished she had had time to wash her face before coming to the ceremony. She met his look before dropping her eyes.

31

Montségur, Autumn 1240

THE ELITE CLIMBERS were reluctant to include Esme in their team. 'It's a waste of time,' one complained. 'We've never had a woman do this before. And anyway she's much too short to reach the hand holds.'

The leader of the group, a knight named Othon, let the men talk. Two men had fallen to their deaths over the past few years and he did not want to lose anyone else. Esme had charmed him when she asked rather breathlessly whether she could become a climber. He had spoken to Guilhèm, a man he had come to know and admire. 'She's been climbing high walls without any help since she was a child' was Guilhèm's response.

It was enough to persuade Othon and he instructed his climbers to start her on the lower reaches of the easy tracks. 'If she falls, she'll only bruise herself,' he reasoned.

After six successful weeks of training, Othon stood at the top of a sheer drop and watched Esme. She was concentrating hard, checking each grip before making another move. It was her first climb without the security of a rope on one of the more difficult paths to the top of Montségur. It had not taken long for Esme to impress the climbing men with her natural skill. At the beginning of her training, she was slowly guided up and down each section of a path on a rope, handholds and footholds pointed out to her. Her small fingers and light frame gave her an advantage as she could use crevices for leverage that the men could not use. There were artificial aids placed here and there, but only where the trained climbers needed them; this was to avoid unauthorised use of the paths. She had climbed this route on a rope numerous times. Now, without a rope, one slip and she would fall to her death.

Esme heaved herself over the top. Exhilarated, she jumped up and hugged Othon.

A bell rang and Esme ran off to help Matina serve the communal lunch. Flushed, she greeted each of the elderly diners with a kiss on the cheek. Raimond came in. Without thinking, she kissed him on the cheek too. She did not notice him blush as she returned to the kitchen. During the meal, Esme told the diners about the climb. Raimond ate silently but she could see he was listening. Whatever he was doing with Luisana and Bishop Marty had changed him. He did not speak much to her – or to anyone – but when he did, he was always pleasant. His fellow diners supported him with a smile, a kind word, a gentle touch and prayer. Sometimes it was clear from his eyes that he was distressed; Esme wished she could help him but found the strength to carry on with her own duties and did not ask him any questions.

After Raimond and most of the diners had left, Esme sat down for her usual after-dinner conversation with those who remained. Since she had spoken at the ceremony for Bertrana, the elderly folk were more than willing to share stories of their lives with her. Details of battles, atrocities, suppressions, the viciousness of the friars, the weaknesses of local bailiffs, and the rampant fear of ordinary people were shared and discussed openly. Esme would listen, interjecting occasionally to clarify a fact and to ask a question. Later she would discuss these stories with Brother Thomas before locking them into her stone pearl.

'This is a valuable service, Esme,' he said. 'There are very few safe places for all of these stories but it is important that they live on. Keep going; you have a wonderful gift for this work.'

32

Montségur, October 1240

One year after the Labernoc group had arrived at Montségur, Esclarmonde asked Esme to attend a meeting with Luisana, Bishop Marty and Raimond. It was early in the morning and raining heavily. Wearing a red scarf once owned by Ava and lent to her for the occasion by Matina, Esme walked with Esclarmonde into the large room with the south-facing window. She was surprised to see the eight elders and at least another ten people arranged in two concentric circles with a fire burning in a metal fireplace in the centre of the group.

Luisana, Bishop Marty, Brother Thomas and Raimond were already sitting in the inner circle. Esme saw Raimond look at the red scarf but he quickly returned his gaze to the flame. Esclarmonde directed her to a chair two away from Raimond in the inner circle. Moments later, Guilhèm entered and sat between them. Esme was relieved to see him. He still wore his red bearskin waistcoat but that was the only indication that he had ever been a hunter. His leggings and jacket were clean. She noticed his hands: in the past, they were working implements with all the signs of rough usage but now they were spotlessly clean and even looked soft. Yet his long, gentle face, attentive smile and big brown eyes had not changed.

When they were all seated, Luisana and Leyas, the senior male elder, led a lengthy chant. When Luisana's voice soared above the others, Esme thought it was the most beautiful sound she had ever heard. Now and then she glanced sideways at Raimond; he was deathly pale and his lips quivered.

As the chant faded to the background, Luisana spoke. Explaining that after many months of praying, talking and healing, she said that Raimond was now ready to talk about his most terrible deed in the service of Friar Tiqué. He had asked that his friends, Esme and Guilhèm, be present to hear it.

Esme felt dizzy. She told herself to listen to this story like she would any other story. She touched the pouch around her neck and looked at Luisana, who nodded. She took out her stone and held it in her open palm.

'During this healing, the chanting of our elders will create a sacred atmosphere so that Raimond's story is released into the heart of love. This will lighten his burden and speed his recovery,' continued Luisana.

After a while, Raimond started. He talked about accepting the necessity of remaining with Tiqué for the safety and protection of his father and his siblings. He had hoped that Tiqué would lose interest in him and he could slip away but soon learnt that Tiqué was the child of a heretical father and was determined to prove that children of heretics were not themselves heretics.

Raimond said that he learnt ways of coping. He had got on well with some of the friars and clerks although he was always careful around them. 'I dreamt of my mother often, and I imagined talking to my father and asking him for advice. I also composed conversations with Esme, at least until,' he hesitated, 'until this happened.'

Raimond stared at the fire before continuing.

'Esme, Guilhèm, do you remember when the friars went on their Inquisition outside Carcassonne? It was early in the summer. Tiqué had made it his mission to arrest everyone who might be considered a heretic in the villages around Carcassonne before the summer was over. He knew that the Pope was receiving complaints about the behaviour of some inquisitors. But he was very ambitious and was determined to impress the Roman officials. He wanted to be the man who led an Inquisition here, to Montségur.'

The elders made their tonal chant a little louder. Luisana threw some leaves on the fire; it blazed up to a purple flame and gave off a sweet scent.

Raimond clasped his hands together. 'Tiqué came up with ways of making the Inquisition efficient. He suggested that every inquisitor should have a standard list of possible offences and set punishments. He also wanted to standardise methods of questioning people. I know this because I wrote down everything for him. Then one day he said that it was time I learnt to take notes in the interrogations. It was the last place I wanted to go. I had heard the constables talk about what happened there.'

Raimond damaged foot twitched and he coughed. Luisana

walked over to him and, with a reassuring caress on his shoulder, gave him a cup of water. When he was finished, she placed the cup on a small table beside him and returned to her seat.

'I remember the first time I went into the dungeon. The only light was from the torches on the wall. There was a fire to one side like you would find in a blacksmith's. There were lots of metal implements on a bench. There were chairs and tables, and a rack. I was told to sit at a table in front of the rack where there were writing implements. The clerk was at another table; he was busy with ink and quills and was writing. I tried to be busy too, but I didn't know what to write. It turns out he was writing the date and the location and the people present; I learnt that later.

'Then the door opened. Constables Barca and Del Gurbe came in... came in dragging… those constables were brutes; I think Barca was the worst. I was very careful around them. They used to drink and pretend to hit me but in the end they never touched me; they were afraid of Tiqué.'

He glanced up at Esme realising that this could be the last time she might return his look. He held her eye for a moment and turned back towards the fire.

'Del Gurbe and Barca were dragging in a woman. She was crying. Del Gurbe threw her on the floor in front of Friar Tiqué, and she dropped there and sort of whimpered. She had golden hair, and when she moved, I saw a birthmark shaped like a butterfly on her neck.'

Esme stifled a gasp as she remembered the woman who had been in the procession of prisoners on the evening of the big fight in the courtyard. She had given the woman some water and, when the woman had lifted her head to drink, Esme had seen a butterfly mark on her neck.

'The woman's feet were cut and bruised. I wanted so much to go over and help her, but I did not move. Tiqué told her to sit in a chair. She managed to lift herself. Her face was dirty and streaked with tears, but her eyes were clear blue. Tiqué asked her questions like what was her name, the people in her family and their names, ordinary things. He sounded calm and I remember thinking that it wasn't too bad. But she was looking at the constable who was stoking the fire. All I could see at the time was her. She reminded me of my mother. She said she had children to look after and was expecting another.

'Tiqué bent down so his face was very close to hers and looked at her. She mumbled something but he just kept staring at her.

'"Ah there it is," he said standing up straight. He ordered two of the constables to take off her clothes, and put her on the rack. I hid my face. I had never seen a naked woman before, and felt ashamed. Tiqué came over to me and told me it was my job to watch and take notes. His voice was kindly; he sounded like a teacher. The woman looked at me pleading for help, like I was the only sympathetic person in the room. I was so frightened and shocked that I think my face looked like the stern mask that I saw on everyone else in the room. The woman started to weep and I ….'

Raimond gagged but recovered quickly after taking several deep breaths and a sip of water. 'Her name was Beatriz and at one point she cried out that she was with child, and her child would be called Loba.'

'So this is also the story of Beatriz and Loba,' said Luisana. She threw more leaves on the fire. The chant rose and the air was filled with sound.

'The woman, Beatriz, was tied to the rack, and Tiqué kept showing her implements to terrify her. Large lumps of metal, some of them were red-hot. There were pinchers and pokers, and tools... I later learnt that the intention was to get the person to confess once they saw these weapons. They called it the first degree of interrogation.

'Tiqué kept going to Beatriz and squeezing her chin with his fingers and thumb and staring into her eyes and muttering, "I want to know what you're hiding from me". She was terrified. I could see her whole body shaking. I looked away but I heard her lose control…'

Raimond looked at his hands.

'We understand, Raimond,' said Luisana, throwing more leaves on the fire. 'Perhaps continue from there.'

He nodded gratefully and went on: 'Beatriz was pleading with him, saying that she would recant, that she would do anything he wanted, that she could tell him who was in her village, that she didn't know any consoled people by name, but she would describe them, anything at all; she was pleading. Her stomach was extended with child. Tiqué kept pointing at it and saying that she was going to give birth to the devil. I could not understand why Tiqué kept going. She had nothing else to give him, but Tiqué didn't believe her. I could see she was struggling to think of things to tell him.

'Then Friar Tiqué turned around and asked me what he should do next, whether he should use water to get her to confess or if he should use fire. I remember my head racing. I didn't know what he was going to do. I didn't really understand him. He raised his voice, "Water or fire, you choose; which shall I use on this heretic, water or fire?" I said, "I don't know". He picked up a poker and pressed it to her skin. She screamed.'

Raimond could sense Esme close by. He continued: 'Friar Tiqué asked me again and I was so paralysed trying to work out what he would do with the water that he burnt her again. She fainted. He approached me with the poker and said, "Next time, make the decision when I ask."

'He threw cold water on Beatriz,' Raimond said her name deliberately. 'She became conscious again, and was moaning and struggling against the restraints. She was terrified and in pain and couldn't say anything.'

He stopped. His heart was pounding and he was feeling light-headed. 'I'm sorry that Esme has to listen to this but I have done these things, so I must tell the truth. Tiqué asked me again, fire or water, so now I said water. He poured the water down Beatriz's throat. She was still tied to the rack and struggling. She was drowning and I didn't help her.'

Raimond stopped again. He grasped his chest and gulped for breath. Before Esme could open her mouth to demand help, Luisana went to him and placed her hands on his lungs. She breathed slowly and loudly until Raimond's breathing slowed down. The elders continued to chant. She remained there, with her hands hovering over his shoulders, as Raimond resumed his story.

'Finally, Tiqué said that it was enough for the moment and we would start again later. He walked around the room, talking with Del Gurbe and Barca, who were grinning. He picked up some of the implements and appeared to study them. All the time Beatriz was lying on the rack, moaning and crying and choking. I wanted to go to her, cover her, help her down, but I couldn't move.

'Eventually another constable untied her, and she fell off the rack. The constables dragged her out of the room and put her in a dungeon. They dragged her by her arms because she couldn't walk. Her head was moving from side to side. Tiqué instructed the constables to chain her, and told me to follow her and give her back her clothes. I remember Barca laughed when Tiqué told me to do that. The constables chained her to the wall before she could put on her clothes and just left. I started to try and dress her but didn't know how. I draped her clothes around her so that she was covered and not sitting directly on the cold floor. I whispered to her, "I'm sorry"; she looked at me. I think she blamed me too. Barca came in and pulled me back. He pulled at her dress, and pointed out the burns on her body, and told me that they were my fault. I couldn't cry or make a sound. I said nothing. The next thing, blood and then something, which I now know was her child, burst out from between her legs.'

Raimond trembled. Luisana placed one hand on his chest and the other on his back.

'She cried "Loba, my child," and died'.

Esme felt unsure of where to look or what to do. Brother Thomas got her attention. He pressed his hand to his heart and mouthed 'Love'. Discreetly, she wiped her face with the sleeve of her dress and moved her hands to her heart as Raimond continued.

'I can't forget her. I let her down; I made it worse for her, she might not have been so burnt, and she might not have died, and her baby might have been born. I don't know if she heard me saying sorry; I don't know if she forgave me. I keep telling her I am so sorry, but she's dead now and can't hear me.'

He bent over and let out a series of heart-wrenching wails, rocking on his knees. Luisana kept her hand on his back. The fire was blazing purple. Esclarmonde threw handfuls of herbs on to it, causing green flame, then purple, then gold. The elders' chanting rose; Guilhèm chanted with them.

Esme closed her eyes. She felt like she was in a very powerful force and could not move. In the back of her mind, she tried to work out what it was, and the only word that came to mind was 'Love'. She let the sensation move through her. In her mind's eye, she saw two women: one was Raimond's mother, Ava, and the other was her own mother, Emersenda. They were both smiling at her. Ava then turned towards where Raimond was sitting. Esme went into her own mother's arms and felt peace. She rested there before opening one eye to look at Raimond. He was sobbing quietly, his head was resting on Luisana's breast. She had her arms wrapped around him and was stroking his head softly.

Bishop Marty spoke; his voice seemed to come from far away: 'And now, let us see if Beatriz is prepared to talk to us.'

The bishop looked towards the fire, then to the side of it. He smiled then spoke. 'She's here. I had thought she wouldn't be too far away.'

He smiled at the empty space. Esme saw a shimmer of something where the bishop was looking. Luisana looked at the space too, and bowed as if she was greeting an honoured guest.

'She is talking to you, Raimond,' said the bishop. 'She is saying that she could see your struggle. She is a mother. She knew you were being forced to do what you did. She says she is glad that you have released her story.'

'I am so, so sorry, Beatriz, I am so sorry,' Raimond pressed his hands together. 'I wish I could have… I am so sorry.'

Luisana passed him a handkerchief.

'Yes, she knows, she can see your apology and she forgives you,' said Bishop Marty, still watching the space by the fire. 'But she says you have to forgive yourself, she can't do that for you.' He paused. 'Beatriz wants to say something else,' he looked back to the space. 'She is saying that while she has forgiven the friar and his constables, she has not forgotten what they have done and one day they will be held to account, one day they will face justice. It is a Universal Law.'

'Then I too must be brought to justice.'

The bishop shook his head. 'She says that you, Raimond, were young and in a situation not of your choosing; you are not accountable in this case.' Bishop Marty smiled and nodded at the empty space. 'She says that you are not to confuse the need for speaking the truth and seeking justice with seeking revenge. You now need only to work to forgive yourself.'

The bishop stopped talking. 'Very good,' he said eventually, breaking the spell.

Luisana returned to her seat. 'Raimond, you invited Esme to listen to this story for a purpose and she has listened with an open heart and no judgment. The maturity shown by both of you is exemplary and you are clearly fit for the difficult lives that you have agreed to. Esme, I know you and Raimond have many things to talk about and, when the time is right, you will now find that you can talk freely and with love. Esme, as a dearly beloved friend of Raimond, we ask you to seal this healing, please, with a gift.'

Looking directly at Raimond, she said without hesitation, 'I want to give you the pearl my mother gave me.' She reached into the small pouch around her neck and took out her pearl. With a nod from Luisana, she stood in front of Raimond and looked at the pearl for a few moments. The chanting of the holy people was hushed. 'My *besson*, Raimond, I give you this gift from my heart. You are very brave and,' she thought for a few moments. 'It is my wish for you that the darkness lifts and you are free to be yourself.'

She held out the pearl and presented it to him. Raimond looked up and smiled at her; his dark green eyes, clear for the first time since their meeting in Carcassonne, sparkled. He took the gift and held it to his heart. 'Thank you, *bessa*,' he whispered.

33

Montségur, December 1240

Esme was nervous around Raimond at first. He greeted her with a smile, commented on the weather and thanked her for the food she placed in front of him. But nothing more. She wanted desperately to talk to him, to apologise for swapping their stones, to share stories, to restore their friendship. Guilhèm told her to leave the timing of their first big conversation to Raimond. 'It will come. He needs to adjust to his new freedom and rebuild his confidence.'

His advice gave her hope and she was relieved when Raimond addressed her directly on several occasions, asking about her climbing and talking about the forthcoming birth of Matina's baby. Early one evening, about two weeks after the big session with the elders, she was standing on a rock on the western point of the pog watching the setting winter sun. Raimond had encouraged her to talk about a big climb she had done that day and she was remembering every detail of the conversation, the smile that reached his eyes, his gasp when she mentioned that a handhold had crumbled, his spontaneous clap when she described her relief on completing the climb. She closed her eyes.

'Hello, Esme.'

Startled, Esme turned around to see Rixanda appraising her. She returned the greeting as the healer looked her up and down, assessing her. 'You have done very well, Esme. I can see you now. Yes, much, much better. Come to me tomorrow morning after prayers and I will straighten up your back. That will help you.'

Grateful for the stern woman's kindness, Esme thanked her and turned up promptly in the healing room the next day. During the treatment, Rixanda manipulated Esme, moved her arms and legs, her torso and shoulders and finally held her head in both hands. When Esme stood up she felt she was floating. She gave Rixanda a spontaneous hug and drifted off to the dining room, imagining herself to be a beautiful woman floating above the ground in a silk gown and rose-patterned slippers.

Raimond looked up as soon as she stepped into the dining room. She beamed at him. He smiled back, his smile lighting up his face. Blood rushed to Esme's cheeks and her heart glowed. Only a call for assistance from Matina broke the spell. She drifted through the meal, aware that Raimond was watching her.

♦ ♦ ♦ ♦ ♦

Matina and José's son was born early in January. The boy, named Johann, was small but robust and healthy, and was the cause of celebration in the mountain community. Several nights after the birth, José organised a party in the house. It started as a quiet affair with a steady stream of guests admiring the baby in hushed tones. As the spiced wine flowed and plates of small venison and vegetable pies were passed around, the presence of the sleeping baby was forgotten and the volume rose. One of the knights began to sing in a deep, resonant voice of distant battles and lost love. Another knight followed this with a song of more battles and nights of passionate love. More songs followed, with the men adding their own lines, boasting of their conquests or teasing friends on their failures.

'We're welcoming a boy,' protested one of the knights when his wife chided him for singing bawdy songs to a newborn. 'When José has a girl, you may lead the singing.'

Esme sat against the grass-matted wall enjoying the liveliness of a garrison party. It reminded her of the parties Jaufré and Ava had hosted in Labernoc when the troubadours visited. She was surprised when she saw Raimond coming through the door; he had never come to a party on Montségur before. He pushed his way through the crowd to squeeze in beside her. Alayda pushed a cup of hippocras into his hand and topped up Esme's cup. Smiling briefly at Esme, he tapped his good foot to the music and drank the wine. Sitting so close to him with their upper arms pressed together, Esme could barely breathe. Every nerve in her body tingled. She sipped her wine and sang, all the while wondering if Raimond could hear her heart pounding.

As the crowd began to go home and the squash eased, Raimond did not move away. The moon was moving to the west when the last of the knights were dragged away by their wives. Esme and Alayda tidied up quickly while José and Julian arranged the beds. Raimond stood up to leave.

'Don't go, Raimond,' insisted Alayda. 'This will be the first time we'll all be sleeping in the same place for a long time and, if it never happens again, it would be nice just once. That's your bed.' She threw a pile of straw beside Esme's bed and tossed a blanket and pillow on top of it.

Raimond had had two cups of spiced wine and, unused to alcohol, was feeling a little unsteady. He sat down on his allocated bed with relief and removed his padded boot. Esme, tucking into her own bed, tried not to look as he took off his outer clothes. When he lay down, he was so close to her that she could feel the heat from his body.

'Do you remember what our parents used to say before we went to sleep?' asked Alayda into the quiet of the dark room. 'You are your heart, Matina. You are your heart, Raimond. You are your heart, Esme. You are your heart, Julian. And I am my heart' she paused before saying, 'Good night, Mother, Father. We love you.'

Esme lay on her back and listened to the familiar snores of her foster family. She could hear Raimond breathing. She turned her head towards him. Sensing her movement, Raimond turned towards her and opened his eyes. He smiled and closed his eyes once more. Esme felt his hand seek out her hand under the blanket. When he found it, he shuffled in to lie beside her. She rested her head on his shoulder and sighed deeply. As he fell asleep, she could feel her heart beating in unison with his.

Early the following morning when Esme woke up, her back was to Raimond and his arm was around her. His eyes were closed. It was past dawn and morning prayers would have started. José, Alayda and Julian rose quietly and went off to fulfil their morning duties. Esme could hear Matina feeding her baby.

Raimond woke with a murmur, his arm still around Esme. He tightened his embrace and she squeezed his hands in response. They lay together without moving.

Soon winter sunlight brightened the room. Matina began singing to baby Johann.

'Oh *bessa,* I've missed you,' Raimond whispered in Esme's ear. 'Can you really forgive me? I have so much to tell you.'

Esme turned around to him and held his hands in hers. '*Besson,*' she whispered. 'Can you forgive me?'

Raimond looked puzzled for a moment. 'Later today, will you meet me to talk? Please?'

He kissed her hands slowly, his head bent, his eyes closed. Esme rested her forehead on his.

Eventually, aware that he was expected elsewhere, Raimond rose. He put on his boots and stood up. '*Bessa,*' he mouthed, before turning to Matina, quietly wishing her a happy day with Johann.

As soon as he had disappeared, Esme went to sit beside Matina, who could not contain her delight at what she had just witnessed.

34

Montségur, January 1241

RAIMOND AND ESME met that evening at the rock near the supply platform where Guilhabert had spoken to Raimond shortly before he died. They sat side by side, their backs to the rock, their arms touching and a blanket over their knees. Stars sparkled in the sky. Lopp was at their feet. After moments, their nervousness vanished as they remembered the times they used to sit under the moon in the forest above Labernoc. They remembered playing in the river, the evenings of singing and dancing in the family home, the feasts on special days when Guilhèm received permission from the bailiff to present the village with a couple of deer.

After a while, they stopped talking.

'Esme,' Raimond said into the silence. 'I am so sorry for everything. For not coming with you. For being so rude to you. For betraying you to Tiqué.'

'Betraying me to Tiqué?' Esme was surprised.

'I should never have even mentioned your name to him. I

am so very sorry.'

Esme sat up. 'Do you really believe you had betrayed me? Raimond, I saw what he did to you. If I had been there, I would have told you to tell him everything long before he hurt you. What? Why are you smiling?'

He told about how he had imagined hearing her in the dungeon saying just that.

Esme did not smile. 'It was my fault that he hurt you at all, Raimond. Guilhèm told me not to talk to you but I did. And if I hadn't taken your stone, he'd never have done those things to you.'

'And if you hadn't, I wouldn't be here. Truly, Esme, I wouldn't.' He took her hands in his. 'I was locked into their world. From the day I participated in the interrogation of Beatriz, from then, I belonged to them. And by the time I got to Foix, I was content. Not all of the friars were like Tiqué, some were very nice. I had accepted my life. Don't you see? If Tiqué had not turned on me, I would probably never have left.'

Esme took a little while to be convinced.

'Now will you accept that we have both done things we would never have done if the friar had not come into our lives?' Raimond took Esme's face in his hands. His green eyes were soft and loving. 'I love you, Esme. And now I am free to love you forever. Can we forgive ourselves completely so that we can love each other completely?'

The moon came out from behind a cloud and surrounded the young pair in its gentle light. 'Yes' she said, but the word did not come out. 'Yes,' she tried again. 'Yes.' The third time was strong and definite.

Raimond drew her to him and kissed her softly on her lips. Transported, Esme closed her eyes. Tenderly they held each other as the stars shone brightly overhead. Eventually, even the warmth of each other's touch was not enough to withstand the winter air and they returned to the house.

♦ ♦ ♦ ♦ ♦

Raimond spent each of the following nights in the family home, his arms wrapped around Esme. He even skipped early morning prayers so that he could continue to hold her. Each evening they sat together, their backs to the rock by the supply platform, and talked. Stories spilled out. The confusion and uncertainties and hurts of the past few years evaporated. Soon they could find funny tales to tell each other from their time apart and their laughter was a joy for their friends on the mountain to hear.

Matina asked Esme if he had mentioned marriage. Esme blushed and did not answer. 'Well why not?' Matina asked. 'You belong together and always have.'

Matina asked José to have a conversation with Raimond. Unsure of what he was supposed to say, José intercepted Raimond later that day on the castle steps. 'I can recommend marriage, Raimond,' he said without preamble. 'I love Matina and Johann and I'm very glad I married her and have a son. I hope that reassures you.' And he walked on.

Bemused, Raimond watched him disappear into the castle. Marriage? José and Matina? Reassurance? Raimond had been on his way to the family home, but instead walked down to their rock to think. José was trying to tell him something. The sun was setting in the sky and Esme's birds, as he now called them, were flying on the thermals. He watched them. They were always together, flying, swooping, hovering. Guilhèm said that they mated for life. They did not appear to have any young but maybe the young flew off and found their own mates as soon as they were able. Mates, like Esme and myself. He smiled and imagined what fun the two of them would have if they were birds soaring on the wind. He felt a twinge in his foot. But we could be married, Esme and I. Was that what José was trying to suggest? The birds picked up a thermal and swooped, one after the other. Suddenly, all Raimond wanted was to be married to Esme, to be as close as they were last night but to be together as a man is with a woman.

That night he slept in his own bed in the men's dormitory and met Esme by their rock the following day. He was feeling nervous; what if she did not want to marry him? He knew about Arnold. Maybe she would prefer to marry someone like him.

His proposal to her was hesitant.

Esme stared at him in response, her eyes filling with tears. 'Of course!' she breathed before embracing him with joy.

♦ ♦ ♦ ♦ ♦

Marriages were not common on Montségur. Some garrison members, including José, had married there. But, as most of the community devoted their lives to prayer, personal desires such as a union between two people were not part of their world. After nearly two and a half years on Montségur, Raimond and

Esme had become much loved and valued members of the community. It was for this reason that Luisana invited them to come and see her about the marriage ceremony.

Before the meeting, Luisana prayed for guidance. She had come to know Raimond especially very well. She had worked and prayed with him and, during that time, had seen aspects of him that perhaps Esme had not yet seen. She could see that he was very at ease in the world of prayer. She also believed that he understood the higher purpose of collective prayer. Whether he could reconcile that understanding with a marriage, even to his beloved Esme, was something she did not know. She would ask Guilhèm to attend the meeting; his presence and wisdom would help her with whatever choices or guidance she would need to make.

Luisana met Raimond and Esme in the ante-room where small spiritual ceremonies and meetings were often conducted. Guilhèm was already there. Luisana started their meeting with silent prayer.

Esme closed her eyes and floated happily in the peaceful atmosphere. That she was marrying Raimond felt easy and natural. The trials of the previous years had faded into distant memory and her life was perfect. She would have liked her father to attend the ceremony but with her baby sister, Lucia, only months old, she could not expect him to leave Andreva. She would visit him soon afterwards and tell him all about it.

'Esme and Raimond, your happiness is a joy to behold,' Luisana's voice brought Esme back from her reverie.

Esme reached for Raimond's hand and squeezed it. He took some moments to return from his meditative state.

'We are here to talk about a blessing from the community for your marriage,' said Luisana. 'As you know, when we bless a marriage in ceremony, we consider it very carefully. The blessing of this community, of the elders and our brethren, is powerful and we must be sure that the union can accept the responsibility that comes with the blessing.

'You know that we are all on earth to serve,' Luisana continued. 'Our love and duty to God is greater than love between one person and another. Sometimes we have to put our own desires to one side in order to fulfil our soul's purpose.'

They both nodded in agreement and smiled expectantly. Guilhèm could hear the reservation in Luisana's words and was glad that neither of them was really listening.

Luisana turned to Guilhèm, a query on her face.

'Raimond and Esme have been raised to be selfless in their love, Luisana,' he said. 'They have faced immense challenges as they matured and I believe they both now know truly what it is to love selflessly.'

Two small birds landed on the window sill. Luisana watched them silently. The birds pressed against each other. Chirping, one bird nuzzled the other with its head. They remained there for a few moments before flying away together.

A tear came to her eye as she smiled softly: 'Dear Esme, dear Raimond. Your connection of love is strong between you. Your awareness of your own souls and your souls' purposes is also strong. It would be a pleasure for our community to bless your marriage and to invite you to continue your work here with us. It is our tradition than when we are choosing a date for an important occasion, we consult one of our elders who has a deep understanding of astrology. With your permission, we will ask his help in choosing a date for you.'

35

Montségur, January 1241

RAIMOND AND ESME were married six days later. The elder had suggested the date because it would support fearlessness in their union and give strength to the love in their hearts. With such short notice, Matina, Esclarmonde and several other women helped Esme to prepare. They washed her in rose water, scrubbed her nails and cleaned her hair with lupins and vinegar until it was shining and smooth. Esclarmonde found a fine woollen dress and arranged to have it adjusted to fit Esme's small frame. Meanwhile Guilhèm made a quick visit to Philippe and Andreva to tell them of the news. Philippe sent Esme the veil that her mother had worn on their wedding day. Esme cried when she saw the precious object; it was a short veil of delicate ivory lace flecked with golden motifs. Andreva had sent a package with clothes, shoes and treatments for her hair and skin. On the night before the wedding, Matina and Esme sat by the small fire in their home with Johann sleeping in his cradle beside them. As they talked quietly, Matina treated Esme's hands and feet with oils and lotions from Andreva's parcel. The following morning, the women arrived to help Esme dress. Slowly, she stepped into the light blue dress. It fitted her perfectly. Esclarmonde draped a golden belt around her waist and gave her a pair of slippers decorated with blue flowers. Matina swept up her hair and fixed the veil with a comb.

'You look beautiful,' Matina kissed her on both cheeks. 'Your mother would be so happy for you today. No, no, don't cry, dear sister. Our mothers and my father would be very happy for you today. We must feel their happiness.'

Esme thought of all of the people who could not be here today: her mother, Ava and Jaufré, Agnes, Serena, Bonnie. She touched her mother's veil, which her father had kept all of this time, and smiled.

'I'm ready,' she said in a whisper.

Raimond was waiting by the northern entrance to the castle. He reached out his hands to her and kissed them.

'You are beautiful, *bessa.*'

Together they walked into the castle where Esclarmonde welcomed them. She led them through the entrance hall of the castle and to the airy meeting room where the elders were already assembled. Golden sunlight shone through the open shutters. Incense floated in the air and the chant of the elders filled the room. Raimond squeezed Esme's hand; Esme leant into him as they walked forward.

The eight elders sat in a circle with Leyas and Luisana at the centre. Guilhèm stood up and hugged them both. Esme rested her head against Guilhèm's rusty-red jacket for a moment.

'These prayers are for your happiness and joy' he whispered to her.

She smiled gratefully and turned to Raimond. Together they walked towards the circle.

Bishop Marty welcomed them, his broad smile accentuating his rosy red cheeks. Esme and Raimond sat on chairs in front of a table. There were two jars and a candle on the table. One jar was filled with a brilliant blue liquid; the other, a smaller one, was empty. The bishop invited Esme and Raimond to put their stones in the empty jar. He filled it with the blue liquid from the second jar.

'Tomorrow, at the ceremony with the whole community present, I will return your stones to you. Tonight they will remain with the elders to receive deep blessings.'

Esme and Raimond were reminded to spend the hours between the two ceremonies quietly. They could stay together but were not to be sexually intimate.

They left the room and went to their rock by the supply platform. The air was still. They sat side by side wrapped in blankets and said little. As the winter day closed in, Raimond put his arm around Esme to keep her warm. They went to their beds in the family home. Tomorrow night they would be in a new home, a tiny house that Luisana had made available to them.

The following day, Raimond went to the prayer hall while Matina once again prepared Esme for ceremony. Her hair shining and scented with rose powder, dressed in the woollen dress and ivory veil but this time with a delicate garland of snow drops around her neck, Esme met Raimond outside the prayer hall. Hand in hand, they walked in together. Most of the community had assembled and they were greeted with quiet words and hugs. Their friends from the communal dining room embraced them, the people from distant lands took their hands and blessed them in their own languages, and each of the climbing team hugged Esme. Guilhèm and Esclarmonde guided the couple to chairs that were facing each other. The blue jar, still containing their stones, was on a nearby table. The soft sound of elders chanting drifted over the hall.

Bishop Marty conducted this ceremony also. He talked briefly about Raimond and Esme, saying how they had been born at the same time in the same room over nineteen years earlier. He mentioned each of their parents, Ava, Jaufré, Emersenda and Philippe. Raimond glanced at Esme and saw sadness in her eyes. He missed them too but now he would look after her. He would be her husband, constant and loving for as long as God willed it. Bishop Marty concluded his speech by saying he was honoured to be celebrating a sacred ceremony of love for two dear members of the Montségur community.

The rich, harmonious sound of the consoled people chanting filled the hall as Esclarmonde carried a red ribbon to the couple on a golden pillow. Bishop Marty wrapped it around their joined hands. The beautiful voice of Luisana rose above the chant. Esme and Raimond held each other's gaze, their eyes shining with love, their hands held tightly. White and golden light filled their vision. It was a moment of magic.

Bishop Marty declared them married. He poured the blue liquid back into its original jar and dried the stones.

'For a short period, you will look after each other's stones so you will learn how to take care of one another's souls.' He placed Raimond's stone in Esme's hand, and Esme's in Raimond's hand.

The ceremony came to an end with more prayers. Raimond took Esme into his arms and kissed her. The crowd clapped and cheered. Matina and Alayda wrapped their arms around both of them. Pies, spiced wine and musical instruments were carried into the hall and a lively party with singing and dancing commenced.

Exhausted but happy, Esme and Raimond left as the party came to an end. Their new home was waiting for them. Alayda had lit a small fire and a magnificent bed made from gifts from their friends. There was a thick woollen rug, two soft feather pillows, and, when Raimond pulled back the woollen blanket, there was a fine wool blanket on top of the straw and wool mattress.

Taking Esme's hand, Raimond pulled her tenderly to the bed and slowly removed her veil and dress. He ran his left hand down the silk shift, which Andreva had sent her for her special night. In the smoky glow of the fire, Esme watched as Raimond took off his boots and clothes and slipped in beside her. She felt very shy, his naked body beside her, his hands caressing her.

'I love you, Esme,' he whispered into her ear.

She felt a tingle run through her body and turned to him, wrapping her arms around him. And with great tenderness, they gave themselves to each other. A tremendous peace descended on both of them that night.

Interlude
Foix January 1316

STÉPHANIE DID NOT WANT TO break the spell of William Bélibaste's telling of the story but she was concerned about Esme, who was lying on the pillow motionless.

She signalled to William to stop for a moment and stood up to check on her great aunt. There were tears seeping out from Esme's closed eyelids. Stéphanie dabbed them and Esme opened her eyes.

Esme whispered. 'Love.'

'Shall I continue, Esme?' William asked quietly.

Esme nodded and looked at Stéphanie. She looked down at her stone. Raimond, Matina and Alayda and Julian, Guilhèm, the elders, her friends, the garrison, she could see them all. William could also see them. She closed her eyes and nodded slightly.

William carried on.

Part 3

36

Montségur, Autumn 1241

THE SUMMER OF 1241 was a time of happiness for Esme and Raimond. Together they participated in activities on the mountain and enjoyed the quiet social life of Montségur. At night they lay in the warmth of each other's arms and watched the stars through the open door of their house. Esme felt complete.

Then word came through from contacts in Rome that the Inquisition had officially been restored. The news was received quietly on Montségur. The consoled people carried on with their daily routine of prayers and duties, and they helped distressed members of the community to find peace with the revelation.

Esme felt the old sorrow and uncertainty return. Since her marriage, she had truly believed that the persecution was over. She loved Montségur but she also imagined setting up a home with Raimond in Foix one day. Raimond could be a scribe and translator for the count and for the merchants. She would sew and hopefully get requests for fine embroidery from Andreva's friends. But as more reports arrived about the zealous activities of the Inquisition, Esme put her dreams away. She would not place Raimond in danger and he was safe in the middle of this protected community.

Early in autumn Montségur's network of informants brought some disturbing information. The Count of Toulouse, the most powerful lord in the region, was planning to besiege Montségur in a show of loyalty to the Pope and to the King of France. It was well known that the Count was desperate for a male heir and wanted to have his marriage annulled. He promised to destroy Montségur in the hope of receiving the annulment.

The commander of the Montségur garrison was Pierre-Roger de Mirepoix, a tall, broad-chested man with a booming voice. He was co-owner of Montségur with Raymond de Pereille and was married to Philippa, de Pereille's daughter. A military man, he was not given to small talk and was often abrupt in his manner. Now, with the safety of the community in his hands, his commanding presence was reassuring. He immediately ordered preparations to withstand a siege. Cisterns, wood stores and food larders were filled; arrows, stones and other weapons were stockpiled along the barbicans; and the approaches to the secret paths on the northern face of Montségur were given extra camouflage.

On an autumn day in 1241, word came through that the Count of Toulouse's army was on the move. Soon the peaceful air around Montségur was disturbed by a distant rumbling. Esme joined the garrison and others as they waited on the barbicans. All around the mountain peaks and forest covered slopes looked majestic and familiar but the air was filled with the sounds of an approaching army. Soon knights on horseback and hundreds of armed men marched into view. They were followed by mules pulling carts and livestock.

The Montségur community watched grimly as the camp took shape. Over the following day, Toulouse's army raised their tents, built their fires, set up their supply quarters and bought vegetables, water and wood from local villagers.

Climbers from Montségur went down the secret paths to gather information, especially about any of Toulouse's allies who might be joining the siege. Lookouts were placed on strategic peaks all around Montségur. Runners, including Esme, kept the line of communication open between them and Pierre-Roger de Mirepoix. Esme was relieved to be involved; at least this way she would know what was going on without having to wait for a community meeting.

Along the barbicans, the defenders were expecting an attack as soon as the French camp was complete. However the besiegers made no effort to mount an assault. Night fell with no movement from below. It was the same the following day, and the day after that. The garrison, alert, primed for battle, watched as the besiegers remained by their small fires. Days turned to weeks and still Toulouse's army did not make a move. Winter was approaching. Were they trying to starve the community into submission? How long would they stay? Would the soldiers return to their farms in spring when their military service was completed? Informants returning to the pog had nothing further to report other than the general opinion that the Count of Toulouse believed he was doing enough to impress the Pope by besieging Montségur.

The cold winter weather came early and the count's men could be seen moving closer to their fires. As the siege continued, the strain of food rationing and the constant need to be ready for an attack were taking their toll on the pog. The garrison was tired, children were hungry and their mothers were concerned. Some food could be carried up on the secret paths but there were soldiers stationed near the base of the supply platform so this could not be used. There was no spare food for the dogs and Spider, already elderly, passed away in his sleep. Julian buried him on the eastern side of the mountain as Alayda looked on, tears streaming down her face.

Esme was worried about Matina. Shortly after Toulouse's army arrived, she found her foster sister in the kitchen clutching her throat and gasping; her face was white and her eyes unseeing: 'I can't go through this again, I can't! Why have they come? What if I die? Who will look after my son?'

Esme tried to calm her down but, as Matina was in the early stages of her second pregnancy, she went to fetch the healer. After examining her, Rixanda was firm: 'Matina, I can give you a tonic to balance your nerves but you must build your courage or your son and your unborn child will pick up your weakness.'

Raimond, meanwhile, carried on as if the threat at the base of the pog had nothing to do with him. Prolonged walking caused him pain and this made him of no use to the garrison so he continued to work with Luisana on writing duties. Esme sensed that there was a new urgency about his work as he often continued late into the evening but he did not talk much about it and she did not probe.

One night, after a mission to spy on the army below, Esme lay restlessly in bed. Lopp was sitting by the door in his usual spot. The dog was only about seven years old but he was having difficulty foraging for food for himself. He had lost a lot of weight and Esme did not think he would survive if the siege continued for much longer. The conversations she had heard from the enemy camp that day had been dominated by complaints about the cold and the shortage of food while many also spoke of their desire to return to their wives and families.

It was very late when Raimond came home. 'Are you awake, Esme? I have something to tell you.'

Wearily Esme grunted. Raimond lowered himself on the bed using his good foot to sit down beside her. He seemed excited.

'I saw something wonderful today,' he said, taking her hands and pulling her into a sitting position. '*Bessa,* my dearest love, Luisana said I could tell you about it. I know you are tired but...' He kissed her lightly on her lips. His eyes shining.

'Tell me,' Esme sighed.

'You know it is said that the people of Montségur have sacred documents and precious relics in their care? Well, they do and today, I saw one of them. Esme, it was a document written by Jesus, a true document of Jesus written in his own hand.' He let out a deep breath. 'Guilhèm put the book on the table. I can still feel it.'

The tension vanished from Esme's body. Slowly, through

the silence, his words sank in. The written words of Jesus, here on Montségur, so close to where she lay.

'Are you sure? We've heard the rumours about sacred documents on Montségur. But we also heard that there are descendants of Jesus and Mary Magdalene living here and since being here, we've heard nothing at all about them.'

'It is real, Esme. It is an ancient document written by Him. Luisana and Elder Leyas and all of the elders were in the room. Guilhèm took it out of a box and laid it on a table, and Luisana allowed me to stand close to it. There was...' He searched for a word. 'I don't know how to describe it. There was something coming from it, a gold light that I could feel. It seemed to wrap itself around me and lift me off the ground. I have never known anything like that before. I felt I was standing beside Jesus himself.'

Despite her doubts, Esme was mesmerised. Raimond was glowing. She sensed a light reach out from his heart and, closing her eyes, she breathed it into her. She felt her heart fill with love. She did not want the moment to end.

When she opened her eyes, Raimond was looking far beyond her. 'I couldn't read the words. They are written in his language, in Aramaic, but I could sense them. It was strange. They felt like words of kindness and of love. Simple words. I know this sounds very odd, but now that I have felt the words, *bessa*, everything seems very clear to me. I can see the path to heaven. And it is so straightforward.'

He stopped speaking, his eyes becoming more distant.

Esme became uneasy. 'Raimond, can you be on the path to heaven and still be on earth?' she asked. When he did not answer, she squeezed his hands and repeated the question.

'What? Yes, my beloved, of course you can,' a frown flashed across his face. Slowly, almost reluctantly, he returned to her. '*Bessa,* we'll always be together. We are of one heart.'

He laid her down and covered her with the woollen blanket. She snuggled into him, holding him tightly. Gently he caressed her until she fell asleep in his arms. He stepped back into his vision again. The beauty and perfection of it enveloped his body. In the vision he looked for Esme; when he found her, their eyes met and they smiled at each other in true understanding.

As winter snow fell heavily and persistently, there was movement in the camp below. 'They're taking down their tents,' the news rippled through the besieged community. The army of Toulouse was indeed packing up. There was neither warning nor fanfare. As steadily as they had set up camp, they dismantled the camp and filled the carts. There had been no attack and Raymond VII, Count of Toulouse, had not received an annulment. But no one on the pog celebrated. The garrison watched until the last of them disappeared to the west. Everyone was exhausted. The food and water supplies had held out but rationing would continue until stocks were restored.

The departure of the army was too late for Lopp. Rixanda tried to help but she said that the lack of food had shut down his organs. Julian buried the dog beside Spider and, with Guilhèm, Raimond and her foster sisters beside her, Esme remembered Lopp's company and support over the four years since her summer in Carcassonne.

That evening, sadness overwhelmed her. She began to feel very unsafe and wanted to leave Montségur. Raimond held her tenderly but assured her that Toulouse's army had never intended to attack the pog and there was no reason to go.

'What if the Roman church sends another army? Raimond, you can't fall into the hands of the friars again.'

'Hush, my love, hush,' Raimond cradled her head. 'Let the peace surrounding this community fill your heart.'

Esme was not so easily comforted. 'Prayer won't defeat them. Please let's leave. We can go to my father or even to the south, to the village where José's family lives; he said it is safe there.'

'The writings of Jesus and his words of love are more powerful than any sword, *bessa*. We have been drawn here for a reason and I don't think it is time to leave yet.'

Unconvinced, Esme breathed deeply and dropped the subject. She wished she could see the world from Raimond's point of view, he was genuinely oblivious to the danger. Weary from the sadness of the day, she eventually fell asleep.

37

Montségur, Winter–Spring 1242

THE EXHAUSTION AFTER the departure of Toulouse's army soon gave way to a restful peace on Montségur. The chanting of the consoled people during periods of prayer filled the pog and went on longer than usual. The garrison and their families ate from the replenished stores and slept through the night. With plenty of snow and rain, water was abundant and washing was freely allowed. After strict rationing, the cleanliness of the entire community helped everyone to feel better. The laughter of children and the calls of their mothers echoed in the still air during the warm parts of the day. Social gatherings with music and dancing at night were soft and quiet. For Esme it was a time of happiness and tranquillity as she helped Matina with Johann, and nestled into Raimond's arms each night.

But as the snows melted, the unsettled world beyond Montségur intruded once more. Two knights and a representative of the nobility attended a lengthy meeting with Pierre-Roger and his lieutenants. This was not unusual in itself; Pierre-Roger often entertained important visitors on the pog. But over the following weeks, there were further noble visits and more meetings. During this time a steady stream of consoled men and women arrived. Two came one day, two came several days later, and two more several days after that. Esme gave up counting when the number reached 14. Then villagers appeared, seeking refuge with the community. Families, most carrying their belongings, wanted to come up the pog. Pierre-Roger placed a new security point further down the track to deter them. Some elderly widows and widowers were invited to take up residence with the community but most villagers were turned away. They were given directions to the lands of Aragon or Catalonia south of the mountains where they might find a safe place to live. They were also given provisions and other support if they needed it. Their intentions were included in the prayers on Montségur.

The peace of the winter became a distant memory for Esme as she once more struggled with unwanted thoughts and distressed emotions. She found herself lying beside Raimond at night, restless, her mind racing, while he slept soundly. Images of Ava on the pyre, of Jaufré as an angry, crippled man, of Nicholaus and Jacotina and the friends she had left in Carcassonne, of the red-headed boys and their parents in the village near Carcassonne, of Serena, Bonnie and Agnes with their bloody wounds filled her mind. She wanted to cry but could not. She tried to talk to Raimond but, while he was sympathetic and would caress her lovingly, he seemed removed from these memories.

One morning Guilhèm sought her out and, seeing the dark circles under her eyes, he suggested a walk. They went down the pog, past the security point, and up a steep slope to the south. There, Guilhèm chose a spot where they had a panoramic view of the countryside. Mountain peaks in the distance to the south were still covered with snow but nearby the forests on the rolling slopes displayed splashes of white blossom and new growth. The ravens flew overhead. Esme watched them as Guilhèm sat still, his breath deep and steady. After a little while, he asked her to talk to him about how she was feeling.

Esme did not need any encouragement. Speaking in rapid sentences punctuated by tears, she told him about the images and thoughts that had been haunting her.

'And here we are again, Guilhèm.'

Guilhèm chanted quietly and drew symbols in the air with his hands. 'Raimond told you about the sacred documents?'

Esme nodded. 'That's what the Romans want, isn't it? They have heard the rumours about sacred documents being here and have reason to believe they are true. These documents would challenge the Roman church and they're not going to be satisfied until they've got their hands on them and Montségur is destroyed.'

She waited for Guilhèm to contradict her but he did not.

'Guilhèm, I think we'd be safer away from here. If there's another siege, Raimond might not be able to escape easily.'

'I can't tell you what to do, Esme. But do you remember me saying that Montségur is more special than you could imagine? This is a very important time for our people and we are each here, in this place, for a reason, including you. You can choose whether to stay or go; and, if you love Raimond as much as I know you do, you must trust him to make his own choices.'

'We're married. Does that not mean that we should work together, make choices that are best for the two of us?'

Guilhèm did not answer.

'I know, you can't tell me what to do,' she said, a little frustrated.

'You are well able to find the answer by yourself. Just remember that this world that you can see is but a tiny part of the whole. It is sometimes difficult to imagine but when you make choices, try to be aware of that.'

Esme stared at the pog and beautiful landscape around it as she tried to work through the muddle in her head. Her thoughts drifted back to the marriage ceremony. She remembered that Luisana had said several things about their souls' purposes before she had agreed to bless their marriage. She had told them that sometimes they had to put their own desires aside to fulfil this purpose.

'Did you and Luisana know that Raimond would only ever see the love and the prayers and the holy world of Montségur, and not the dangers of living here? Is that why she talked about our souls' purposes before she agreed to marry us?'

'You have free will, Esme, we all do and for that reason we can't tell the future. You must make your own choices and allow your husband to make his choices. When you learn to do that, you can be married to each other without either of you being pulled away from your soul's path by the other's wishes.'

'But what if Rome sends its inquisitors to Montségur and he chooses to stay and pray. Is that the right choice for his own soul even if it puts him in danger?' She groaned. She was going around in circles and getting nowhere.

'The only choices you can be responsible for are your own,' said Guilhèm. 'Maybe focus on one question, make a choice and see how you feel. Take a few moments, don't rush, Esme, this is important.'

Esme sat up straight and looked at the blue sky. Whether she should stay or go was the question that was uppermost in her mind. She put Raimond's involvement in that choice to one side and focussed on herself, should she stay or go. She repeated the question over and over and gradually her mind cleared. Taking a deep breath, she asked the question out loud: 'Stay or go?' Instantly she answered herself. 'Stay. I want to stay on Montségur. I want to stay with Raimond and you and everyone here.' Her voice sounded strange to her but she carried on describing her choice. 'I want to be part of the work, part of the service, whatever may happen.' She lowered her gaze. 'I think I've made my choice, Guilhèm.'

'How does that feel?'

She scanned her body quickly. 'Clean, easy,' she smiled at him. 'At least that's what came to my mind. I don't feel any anxiety.' She scanned her body again. 'None at all. This means that my choice is the right one?' She looked at him for confirmation.

'It's your choice, Esme. It is what you feel.'

'I feel,' she sought for a word, 'I feel happy, happy that I am staying. It is what I want to do. It is the right choice.'

'And if Raimond feels the same way when he makes a choice?'

'Then of course he has made the right choice and I wouldn't try to persuade him otherwise. Oh thank you, Guilhèm, it's really very simple!'

The sun was setting when they returned to the pog. Guilhèm watched her as she strode up ahead of him, her back straight and her feet light. 'Courage and strength, little one,' he whispered. 'You have a true heart and are able for this.'

38

Montségur–Avignonet February–May 1242

During the early months of 1242, eight elderly widows were welcomed on Montségur. Willelma, a tall, lean woman from Saissac, north-west of Carcassonne, arrived in March. She had suffered much and her anger at the world was palpable. Now she had an audience, she was determined that her views would be heard.

'It is worse than ever,' she declared over dinner. 'I raised my children while de Montfort and his men slaughtered all around us but I think I'd prefer the openness of bloody battle to the friars' war.' She described how everyone in her village was interviewed by friars and asked for information about their neighbours: 'No one knows who has said what. All of the meetings with the friars are in secret. They write down everything. And then they can accuse anyone of anything. Even offering a holy person a cup of water on a hot day, or having once been in the same house as someone accused of heresy is enough to be called a heretic.'

With Willelma's encouragement, other new arrivals talked about experiences of accusation and punishment. Long-term residents used kindly words and made quiet references to the prayerful intention of Montségur to comfort the newcomers but Willelma held on to her anger. 'And how long have you been in this little paradise?' she rounded on a widow one day. 'You have no idea what is going on out there. Until the whole world is on their knees in front of these Romans, paying them money and giving them everything they ask for, they won't stop. And you are telling me we should stop talking about it!'

The anger was not confined to the dining room. Tension was also evident among the garrison. Men-at-arms, some of them recent arrivals, could be overheard relaying ugly tales about incidents involving the friars. A few even talked of war and revenge against the friars. Their voices might be low but their tone was sharp and their comments uncompromising. Pierre-Roger, his knights and visiting officials could be seen in animated, sometimes heated discussions.

Esme was no longer worried about living with Raimond on Montségur. She had made her choice to stay and she would do so with all of her heart. When she heard the long-term residents talk about this being a prayerful place, she understood what they meant. The anger of the new arrivals that was spreading into the garrison seemed out of place to her. She felt the peace generated by the prayers of the holy people and it calmed her whenever she heard angry sentiments.

Raimond was as sanguine as ever. 'It will pass, *bessa*. People will vent their rage and then find peace in themselves. We pray every day for this rage to finish its work.' She loved his tranquillity and rested in it after especially difficult days. Sometimes she even went to the prayer hall and sat with him.

Alayda did not share her brother's attitude. 'We all know only too well what will happen if we let the friars into our villages again. They have to be stopped,' she said one evening when the family were together.

'It will only bring more bloodshed, and it will never end,' said Matina.

'It will never end if the Romans are allowed to carry on. They are destroying the lives of every village they go near. All they need to do is pick on a few people like our parents and everyone else becomes scared and useless. Look at the bailiff; he was a friend of our family yet he helped the friar to kill our mother!'

'But remember he let us go,' countered Matina.

'He should never have let the friar stay in the first place. If he had shown a little bit of courage, our parents would be alive and we would never have had to leave Labernoc.'

Towards the end of May, a meeting was called. It began as usual with prayers, after which Pierre-Roger addressed the community. He confirmed what Willelma and others had been saying about the friars' interrogation and information-gathering activities in the region.

'The friars are going from village to village,' Pierre-Roger said in his booming voice. 'They are filling their ledgers with information, true or false, and moving on to the next village. This is a very sinister development. Although we on Montségur are not directly threatened, we have decided with reluctance to take action to protect our faith and our way of life. We will intercept an Inquisition party operating nearby and destroy their records, by force if necessary.'

There was a low gasp, mostly from family members sitting at the edges of the room. Esme heard her own intake of breath. She was shocked. The Montségur garrison was here to protect the community on the pog, not to go out and provoke a fight. She looked at the elders and the bishop. How could they condone such an approach? Most of the elders and the consoled people were sitting cross-legged, deep in prayer. Esme wondered if they had even been listening. Luisana, standing behind Pierre-Roger, had her eyes cast down. Esme thought Luisana looked sad. Could she not have dissuaded them from taking this action?

'The inquisitors will be staying with Hugh d'Alfaro in Avignonet,' Pierre-Roger was explaining. 'He is as angry as the rest of us about their actions and will help us to seize their records. It is our intention to destroy them immediately.'

The following morning Esme sat with Alayda and Julian on a lower barbican and watched 30 men, the knights including José on horseback, make their way down the mountain for the 70 kilometre trek, which would take them north towards Foix and on to Avignonet.

While they were gone, the life of the community continued but the atmosphere was tense. Esme helped Matina with the elderly widows and with Johann, and sat with her when there was nothing else to do. The remaining garrison members were on full alert, lining the barbicans and watching the surrounding countryside. The chant of the consoled people filled the air. From time to time, Esme sat near one of the windows of the prayer hall to let their prayer wash over her.

Towards the end of the second day, a horseman came charging towards the pog. Several more followed him. The garrison, families and lay people gathered on the south-western barbicans, eager for news. 'Success!' the cry word ran through the crowd. Three more horsemen followed the first. They were waving their arms.

Hot and exhausted, the four men left their horses mid-way up the pog and ran up the final stages. Esme pressed forward, Matina and Johann beside her. 'We are all safe,' she heard. 'And the records were destroyed.' A cry of relief went up from the women. Esme hugged Matina. There were laughter and tears and chatter as they waited for their men to return. In the background, Esme heard the chant of the consoled people rising up and thought they were especially loud but, with the excitement of the moment, she paid no further attention.

There was some time to wait before the main party returned. It was dark when the clatter of armed men could be heard. By then, the women had gone to their homes to prepare meals and put children to bed. The men were hungry and subdued. There were no shouts of triumph and questions from those still waiting on the barbicans were dismissed. Esme watched and listened. There was something wrong. She gave José and Matina a little time alone before she went to join them. Alayda and Julian were already there demanding to know what had happened.

'It all went horribly wrong,' José said quietly, finishing off the dish of rabbit stew prepared by Matina and pouring himself some more hippocras.

Despite Matina suggesting that they wait until morning, Alayda would not let him rest until she had heard what had happened. After a reluctant start, José answered Alayda's questions and a picture of the event emerged. Esme held her stone in her hand as he spoke.

'By the time we got to Avignonet, armed villagers along the way had joined us. We didn't want them but they were determined to come with us. They wanted a fight with Rome's men and it was too difficult, even dangerous, to send them on their way.' He explained that a messenger from Hugh d'Alfaro's castle guided a group of about forty men including José and some villagers into the tower where two inquisitors and their nine companions were sleeping. Pierre-Roger and the rest of the men had stayed in a nearby forest. Once in the castle, the intruders had burst into the bedrooms and dragged the Inquisition party out into a central hall. Their rooms were ransacked and records and documents were piled into the smouldering fireplace in one of the bedrooms. Some oil from a lamp was thrown on and the records blazed. One of the friars became very angry and pushed his way back into the room to rescue the documents. 'He was a strong man and he struck several of our men. A fight broke out.' He shook his head. 'Someone, I don't know who, pulled out a sword and struck the big friar. After that we could not control the situation. It was all over very quickly. All of the inquisitors' party were dying or dead.'

'Was it the villagers who killed them?' asked Alayda.

José shrugged sadly. 'We were all there so we were all responsible, Alayda.'

‘Hush, hush,’ said Matina, shooting a look at Alayda. ‘That’s enough for tonight. We need to sleep now.’

Esme went home. Raimond had just returned from the prayer hall and she relayed José’s account briefly. For the first time in a long time, Raimond became upset; ‘We have stooped to their level, Esme. What have we done to ourselves?’

39

Montségur, Spring–Summer 1243

A YEAR HAD PASSED since the massacre at Avignonet. Every day Esme thanked God for granting her happiness. She loved Raimond. She loved the community. Her stone pearl was filling with stories as consoled people, garrison members and their wives, and artisans sought her out to tell her stories about their lives. She would perch herself on the wall of a barbican on a warm day and talk to the soldier on duty. She would help a consoled person in the vegetable garden, then sit and talk to them. Consoled people from distant lands talked to her in broken Occitan. The visiting blacksmith would take a break from the heat of the forge and drink water while telling Esme of life in a nearby village. Everyone had a tale to tell about how they came to be living on or visiting Montségur. As she learnt more about the people who made up the community, it became clear to her that everyone was aware of the important role that Montségur played in protecting their deeply-held Christian traditions.

In her quiet moments, she hoped that the presence of these good people on this sacred pog would be enough to keep their traditions strong and pure for future generations. But after the siege by the army of the Count of Toulouse nearly two years earlier and the events at Avignonet the previous year, she was not convinced it would be.

Raimond too thanked God every day for his life. He was praying, working with Luisana, and living with his beloved Esme. He had nearly finished etching the diamond on his personal stone and each time he brushed away the scrapings, he felt his whole being become cleaner, brighter and stronger. During the long summer evenings, he often walked out to the supply platform with Esme and sat against their rock watching the night fall. He had not left the pog since he had arrived, partly because of his foot, but largely because he had no desire to do so. Esme visited her father, Andreva and baby Lucia every few months and Raimond loved to listen to the news from Foix and to enjoy the world through her eyes. He knew that Andreva was disappointed that Esme was not pregnant yet. As he watched Esme play with Matina's sons, two year old Johann and the new baby Pedro, he looked for signs of unspoken yearning on Esme's part, but could discern none. Meanwhile he prayed for his mother, his father, Guilhèm's family and for those whose torture or deaths he had witnessed. As time went on, he included without qualification Friar Tiqué in his prayers.

By February the spring flowers were appearing on Montségur. More consoled people arrived. Esme guessed that there must be nearly 200 people here who devoted their lives to prayer. She wondered where they would all sleep but the mountain seemed to expand with each arrival. Spring was a perfect combination of sunshine and rain. The cisterns filled, vegetable gardens were planted, houses were thrown open, and bedding and clothes that smelt of wood smoke were washed and aired.

Then on a peaceful afternoon in April 1243 a horseman came thundering up to the pog. He pushed his horse as far as the trees, dismounted and strode rapidly up the rest of the way.

Esme went to the south-western defences to see what was happening. She watched the man, panting from exhaustion, approach Pierre-Roger, who had come out to the castle door. They talked briefly and together went into the castle. In the early afternoon a community meeting was called. Esme went into the prayer hall, took off her shoes and walked over to sit beside Raimond. His eyes were closed and his hands were intertwined on his lap; he held his stone between his thumbs. He sensed her presence and turned to look at her. His green eyes sparkled in the light from the open window. Esme, married now for two and a half years, felt the familiar rush of love for her husband. She shifted slightly so that their knees touched.

When everyone was assembled, Pierre-Roger addressed the meeting. He told them that they had just received word that there was to be a determined effort by the Romans to destroy Montségur. An informant had learnt at a meeting of the Roman church in Béziers that the French army had agreed to attack this community. Hugues d'Arcis, the seneschal of the King of France in Carcassonne, was raising an army of mercenaries. Roman prelates were also supplying troops and resources.

'They say it is in retaliation for the actions at Avignonet a year ago,' he said, his voice loud and firm. 'We will hold our ground and defend our community. It is time to prepare ourselves.'

Esme felt her stomach contract. Matina stifled a sob as a ripple of anxiety ran through the women.

Pierre-Roger responded to the noise sharply, reminding everyone that they could leave if they chose to, but they must do so immediately and travel south with haste. Everyone who remained on the pog would be expected to do their duty, 'and that includes the children. This is a defended sanctuary and if you are not able to work with us, please leave and let us do our job.'

There was silence. Esme wished she could comfort Matina. At the same time, she noticed that Raimond had not even flinched; he was breathing steadily and his heart beat had not changed. She wondered if he had even heard the news.

Over the following weeks, the entire community worked energetically. Food, wood, water, missiles, arrows and other necessary items were stocked up. Esme worked with the climbers to secure the hidden paths. Together they ensured that access routes to the tracks at the base of the pog were well disguised and the camouflage at the base of the supply platform was improved. Some knights were trained to use the easier routes.

The consoled men and women prayed day and night. Raimond joined them when he was not working for Luisana. Despite the garrison's activities, the atmosphere on Montségur was hushed as the intensity of the prayer spread out over the pog. Now and then Esme caught a glimpse of a light over the pog, especially at night when there was no moon. When she mentioned it to Raimond, he said simply, 'Prayer can do that.'

The French army arrived in May. Esme joined the defenders on the barbicans as they watched the lengthy procession of knights on horseback, infantry, and heavily-laden carts being pulled by teams of mules come into view. A tall man sat motionless on his horse and looked at the defenders; even from this distance, Esme sensed the power emanating from him. He seemed to be staring at Pierre-Roger. Esme glanced over at the commander of Montségur, who was staring back. She watched them until the French man, whom she soon learnt was General Hugues d'Arcis broke the connection and rode off towards his own tent, which was being erected in the shade of some trees.

'Look!' exclaimed a knight. 'Friars! They're here too. And one of their bishops!'

A small procession pulled into view. Esme moved to the lowest barbican to study them. There was a senior prelate on a magnificent horse, four friars, two constables, and numerous servants, some sitting among the equipment in the many carts. Esme did not recognise any of them. The prelate was soon identified by his flag as the Archbishop of Narbonne. French soldiers directed them to a clear site to the south of the mountain by a copse of trees, where two servants provided chairs for the archbishop and friars, while others erected the tents and set up their camp.

Even more equipment arrived over the coming days, including stone-slinging machines, which puzzled the defenders.

'How can they expect to use those here?' A knight asked aloud.

A sprawling camp took shape at the base of the pog as troops set up tents, chopped down some of the trees and prepared their quarters. The dense band of trees and shrubs 30 metres from the base of the track was left intact. At the bottom of the slope, where the track up to the pog started, the quarter-master's stores were set up. A large tent was erected and, over the following days, local villagers began their deliveries. Once again bullocks and mules driven by local men pulled carts of wood and water to the supply tent; women with baskets in slings on their backs provided the vegetables.

Soldiers from Montségur donned the hooded-hessian coats of the locals and carried supplies to the quarter-master's tent. This access provided them with good information about the layout of the camp. They were interested in the area on the slope closest to the band of trees. Long sections of the stone-slinging machines had been placed along there with cloth hung over the horizontal beams. It was impossible to see in to the corral above the barrier but the garrison suspected that this was where the French stored their weapons, missiles and assault machinery. Pierre-Roger's informants estimated that the besieging army consisted of 10,000 troops and many were mercenaries. This latter piece of information was troubling: there was now little hope that the bulk of the army would depart after their period of obligatory service.

The first attack came seven days after the French arrived. As off-duty garrison members rushed to take up their position, the French troops emerged from the band of trees and ran up the narrow path. Hails of arrows and missiles rained down from the defences. The French reached the mule stop and returned fire, but the gradient of the slope was sharp, the accessible track narrow, and few of their missiles reached their targets. Nevertheless wave after wave of French arrows were fired but most casualties were suffered by the attackers. Eventually the retreat was ordered and the French withdrew to the safety of the trees, taking their dead and injured with them.

The mountain-top community was now alive with activity and all hope of a repeat of Toulouse's siege on Montségur evaporated. This was a real and determined attack. Pierre-Roger and the knights issued orders, rearranged their troops, restocked weapons, gathered French missiles that could be reused, and waited for the next assault. It came days later. The result of this and subsequent attacks was much the same. So long as the small Montségur army had enough armaments to fire at the vanguard, they could keep the sophisticated French army at bay. Stones and buckets of waste, including excrement and carcasses, which would attract flies and cause disease, were also flung at the attackers to force them back.

Other than exhaust the defenders with frequent assaults, there was little the French could do. The south-west was the only access point; it was simply not possible to launch an assault on the other faces of the pog because of the high, sheer cliffs. The sporadic attacks continued into the autumn. Several defenders died and more were injured, but the community was safe from being overrun for as long as its supplies could hold out. The camouflage around the base of the supply platform was still proving highly effective, and water, wood and food were still hoisted up on the darkest nights and in silence. The same local villagers who were supplying the French army were paid well to supply the Montségur community. Water and food were strictly rationed on the top of the pog. Climbers, including Esme, went up and down the secret paths carrying messages to potential allies, purchasing supplies and spying on the French.

One night Raimond and Esme rested in bed together. There had been a lot of fighting that day and the community was exhausted. Esme had just returned after a gruelling two-day trek into nearby forests to get medicinal herbs, and was dozing off; the French never attacked at night time.

Raimond was alert. 'One of Pierre-Roger's spies told him that the French won't leave until we hand over our sacred documents to the Roman church,' he whispered. 'Pierre-Roger was with the elders today suggesting that a compromise might be reached, that some items could be handed over, but Luisana and the bishop said that it couldn't be done at this time.'

'Maybe we should smuggle the most important items off the mountain before it's too late,' Esme suggested sleepily. 'I could help.'

He hugged her: 'The documents are not ordinary and they can only be carried by special people. I think they might be preparing Guilhèm to do that.'

'He's always been different. He even looks like one of the elders.'

'*Bessa,* we have to protect the documents. We can't let the Romans take them.'

Esme opened her eyes and looked at Raimond curiously.

There was an urgency, even a hint of panic in his voice. It was very unlike him. 'Did something happen?' she asked.

'Go to sleep, my love. You've had a long day.'

Grateful, Esme shut her eyes as she snuggled into her husband's warm body. Within minutes, she was fast asleep.

Raimond held her close under the blanket. He listened to the silence outside and remembered the second sacred document he had been allowed to see. It contained a lineage of the bloodline of Jesus and Mary Magdalene and their daughter Sarah right up to the current day. No wonder the Romans were desperate to get their hands on it; it would undermine their claim to be the true and only representative of Christianity on earth. As he had listened to the discussion between the garrison commander and the elders, he had felt an overwhelming sense of responsibility to protect Montségur's sacred treasure by whatever means. He hugged Esme tightly. Tomorrow he would tell her about this document.

40

Montségur, Winter 1243

THE DAYS GOT COLDER and snow fell. The French were suffering. While the tents used by the friars and the senior knights were protected from bitter winds by the retained sections of the forest, most were exposed and several soldiers died of illness or malnutrition every day. A shortage of dry wood added to the French soldiers' difficulties and the fires around which they huddled were small. Vegetable supplies, naturally low in winter, were limited and expensive causing numerous arguments between the local villagers and the army's quarter-masters. Soldiers were still being ordered up the mountain to attack but their sorties looked half-hearted. They had no hope of taking Montségur by force and there was little question now but that the French strategy was to starve and freeze Montségur into submission.

On the mountain, the situation was also deteriorating. As the French became more familiar with the terrain around Montségur, they extended their camp and placed tents close to the track leading to the supply platform. It now became impossible for suppliers to approach it safely and the community's supply of fresh food was cut off. Rations were reduced. Children were fed first, then the defenders, followed by the women and other lay people. The consoled people were the last to accept food.

Pierre-Roger ordered that the easier paths down the north-eastern side of the pog were not to be used and obstacles were placed at the approaches to their bases to make them unidentifiable. The consequences of accidentally showing the besiegers one of the mountain's vulnerable access points were too grave to risk. Only three secret routes were left intact and these were so difficult that Esme was one of the few people who could use them.

Messages of support from enemies of the King of France, which hinted at possible reinforcements for the besieged, boosted morale on the pog as the days turned colder. Rumours circulated that the Count of Toulouse, once more out of favour with Rome, or the armies of Emperor Frederick II, also currently an enemy of Rome, were on the way. But by mid-winter, no reinforcements had appeared. Attempts to purchase the services of mercenaries were also a failure. The French, on the other hand, received a small body of reinforcements under the command of the Bishop of Albi, a prelate of Rome and a known expert on assault weapons. General d'Arcis and his knights could be seen meeting at length with the bishop. The Archbishop of Narbonne had departed some months earlier, leaving four friars to represent Rome's interests.

There were no attacks by the French for days after the

bishop's arrival. Esme watched Pierre-Roger looking down on the French camp from the lowest barbican. At one point, General d'Arcis stood back and seemed to be staring at Montségur's commander. Esme wondered if they were somehow communicating with each other.

The following night she spied two of Pierre-Roger's closest confidants going down the mountain on one of the easy tracks. She could not think what they might be doing; Pierre-Roger had specifically forbidden the use of these tracks. Given the seniority of the two men, she thought it unlikely that this was a betrayal. Nevertheless this track was unguarded and she felt obliged to wait and watch until daylight. They returned a few hours later; Pierre-Roger was waiting for them at the north entrance to the castle. He listened intently to what they had to say. Had they done a deal with the French? Might the end of the siege be in sight? The three men went their separate ways, Pierre-Roger into the castle, the two knights to their homes. Esme would have to wait. The commander was generally open with the community about strategy and developments; no doubt he would call a meeting.

But no meeting was called. Confused, Esme carried on through the day, helping Matina with the communal meal. Eleven of the elderly folk had died over the previous months. The surviving diners made a point of encouraging good humour among the mothers and young children, who now ate at their table. Often Esme saw the older people slip a little of their modest ration onto the dishes of the children. How much more of this siege could the community handle? How would it end? Would everyone have to die? She had heard enough tales from the time of the crusade commanded by Simon de Montfort to dread the possible outcomes of defeat.

That night she waited impatiently for Raimond to return and asked him if he knew what was going on.

'Pierre-Roger is very frustrated. I think he wants to negotiate a surrender but Luisana says that it is not time yet.'

Unable to sleep Esme clung to Raimond. He whispered a prayer into her ear and stroked her head. Eventually she fell asleep.

'Attack! Attack!' the urgent cries woke them up. It was still dark. The pog came alive with the familiar sounds of off-duty soldiers scrambling for their weapons and running to their position. Raimond hurried off with the aid of his stick to join the holy people in prayer. Esme ran to help Matina, who was shaking with fear. They roused three-year-old Johann and eleven-month-old Pedro who were both cranky at being woken up.

'The French are very early this morning,' whispered Esme, as she wrapped Pedro in a blanket.

Through the crack in the door, they could see dawn breaking. Carrying a child each, they went to the castle kitchen where the other mothers were gathering. After the children were settled, Esme returned to the house to get their day clothes. On the way, she saw Pierre-Roger and two of his knights striding rapidly towards the eastern barbican. Esme followed them and in the distance she saw about twenty men on top of the sheer 80-metre cliff called Roc de la Tour on the eastern side of Montségur. As they watched, four more men appeared on top of the cliff. The French! How did they get there? She moved closer to Pierre-Roger.

'There were only three of our men on duty at Roc de la Tour overnight,' she heard one of the garrison report to Pierre-Roger. 'I'm afraid they are dead now.'

As the sun rose, Esme could see the invaders more clearly. Armed men appeared to be coming up on fixed ropes. How had they got up there without ropes in the first place? She had often looked at that exposed rock face to imagine how she would climb it but could never work out a route.

Pierre-Roger sent fighters towards the cliff, which was several hundred metres from the barbican. They launched their arrows but the response from the French drove them back. They were too late; by now there were enough French at the top of the Roc to defend their position. Pierre-Roger issued rapid instructions to maintain forces on the south-west face and keep only the minimum number required on the eastern barbican. The approach to the eastern barbican was narrow and the men of Montségur would still have the advantage.

It took the invaders several days to consolidate their position on the top of Roc de la Tour. The ferocious attacks on the south-west face continued but the French made no attempt to launch a full-scale attack on the eastern barbican. Esme witnessed several animated arguments among the defenders. At one point Alayda shouted at Pierre-Roger.

'Sire, we have to push them off there, somehow. We know this mountain; they don't. We have to attempt to stop them.'

A knight answered for Pierre-Roger, explaining heatedly that there were simply not enough defenders to go around and ordered her to back to her post.

The French strategy became clear as the first pieces of a trebuchet were hoisted up. It would take them a few days to assemble the large wooden catapult and collect stone missiles. The trebuchet was known to have a firing range of between 150 and 200 metres. Once in action, they could move closer to the eastern end of the castle walls and perhaps even bombard the roof of the castle; if that happened, it would be impossible to defend the castle and village.

Watching the French stacking rocks at the base of the partially constructed trebuchet, Esme trembled with fear. She tried to control herself but could not. For the first time in her life she felt truly trapped. With her teeth chattering and her body shaking, she stumbled back towards the castle where she bumped into Guilhèm.

'Gently, gently,' he hugged her. 'Come into the prayer hall with me.'

'They're coming! I must do something!' she hissed.

'The most practical thing you can do is come to the prayer hall with me.'

With his arm around her shoulders, he brought her into the hall. There were at least two hundred men and women there. Luisana sat on a chair to one side. Bishop Marty was on a mat on the floor. Everyone was deep in prayer.

Guilhèm and Esme took off their shoes and sat on the floor. Esme could still hear the cries and crashes of the battle going on the south-west face. She sought out Raimond. He was sitting at the far side of the room beside Esclarmonde. She wished he would come and put his arms around her but he was in another world. Guilhèm put his hand on Esme's back and looked at her tenderly. She met his eyes. A part of her wanted to keep hold of the fear because she felt it would keep her on alert but she closed her eyes and concentrated on slowing her breathing.

It took some time before the stillness of the prayer hall reached her heart. She rested for a little while longer then opened her eyes and stood up, retrieved her shoes and left the hall.

Guilhèm followed her out: 'It's going to become more frightening, Esme. Whenever you feel fearful, go into the hall. The consoled are fighting the battle their way and there will always be a large number of people praying in there.'

◆ ◆ ◆ ◆ ◆

Sustained attacks on both fronts commenced several days later. From dawn to dusk, the French archers maintained a barrage of arrows towards the defence lines. The Montségur garrison was exhausted but held its position. There were casualties on both sides. Wounded and dying defenders were attended to by Rixanda.

In the mid-afternoon on the second day, Rixanda called Esme in to help her sew up a wound on an unconscious soldier. When she had sealed the wound, there was a crash. She gasped. Rixanda looked over at her briefly. Esme remembered her peace in the prayer room and refocused on her task. There was another crash, and another and another. Shouting could be heard from outside the room. She stayed steady and carried on with her work.

A woman walked in and quickly shut the door. 'The stone slinger is in operation,' she whispered. 'The stones are hitting the wall of the castle and some of the houses.'

'Any casualties?' asked Rixanda.

'None so far as I know. Missiles are damaging houses but not having any impact on the castle walls.'

By now the French were using Montségur's own supply hoist to haul up stone missiles and were maintaining a steady bombardment on the eastern end of the castle. They only stopped at dusk and during heavy rain. The assault on the defences by French archers was also constant but it too ceased during rain and after dark. The consoled people included prayers for a storm so that their defenders could rest.

Day after day, week after week, throughout January and February, the assaults continued. The Montségur soldiers were holding their defences but the strain was overwhelming. The village houses had been abandoned and everyone slept in the castle. Food rations had to be further reduced as the only tracks still safe to use were the dangerous ones to the north of the pog; carrying supplies in any quantity up those tracks was impossible.

By the end of February, the community was reaching its limit. It would be a matter of weeks at the most before starvation and disease would take their final hold. Montségur was on the brink of defeat.

41

Montségur, February–March 1244

At the end of February, a prolonged thunderstorm with giant hailstones drove the French into shelter. A meeting of the Montségur community was convened. Only the knights and sergeants on sentry duty remained at the barbicans.

With nearly 400 people present, the hall filled up. The men-at-arms clustered near the doors, their weapons beside them. Bishop Marty was standing at the top of the room with Luisana and Elder Leyas beside him. The other elders sat behind them in a row. Raimond, Esclarmonde and Guilhèm were sitting together but when Raimond saw Esme, he came over to sit on the floor beside her.

After brief prayers, Bishop Marty handed the meeting over to Pierre-Roger.

The commander did not waste time explaining how serious the situation was: 'There are no rescue parties coming to help us. No reinforcements from friends in distant lands. Our local lords, who might have helped us, have capitulated to the King of France. We have no expectation of any real help to relieve us. We are nearly finished.'

Esme glanced at Raimond; he had his eyes closed.

Pierre-Roger continued: 'The French can do much worse to us if they want to. They fire stone missiles at our walls. They could fire many more. But they are sending enough to let us know that they can maintain this barrage indefinitely. They are wearing us down and very soon we shall die, if not of the arrow or stone, then of starvation and illness. We face defeat.' He hesitated. 'It is time. We must surrender Montségur.'

Looking around, Esme saw relief mixed with fear on the faces of garrison families. Matina was struggling to maintain her composure and fussed over Pedro. The expression on Luisana's face was unreadable, while Guilhèm, Esclarmonde and the consoled were absorbed in prayer.

Bishop Marty stood up to support Pierre-Roger. 'We have prayed for guidance and now, to save as many of you as possible from death, we are ready to negotiate terms with the French commander. We will endeavour to give them the victory they and their masters wish for. Every effort and every prayer will be directed towards as peaceful a settlement as possible.'

'They'll kill us all and, if they don't, they'll put us in dungeons until we die,' said Alayda from the back of the hall. 'We've all heard stories about what the French do in victory and I've seen what the friars are capable of when there isn't even a war.'

Bishop Marty was on the point of replying when Pierre-Roger intervened: 'We are still in a position to negotiate,

Alayda. And times are different, quite different. The King of France is in charge of this and he is unlikely to want one of those gruesome displays that de Montfort was so fond of. Hugues d'Arcis is a man we can do business with.'

'How do you know that? We all know that the Romans and the friars are really in charge. We have to go on fighting them.'

'And we will definitely lose, Alayda. Do it this way, and people may live on.'

Luisana stood up slowly. Her hip had been giving her trouble for some months and she used the back of the chair to balance herself. 'Alayda, I am grateful to you for bringing your wisdom to this meeting. What you say had to be said but I am in agreement with Pierre-Roger.' Her gentle eyes scanned the crowd. 'My dear friends, we are facing horrifying choices but we must remember who we are and why we all chose to live in this holy place. We have deep faith that goes far beyond the limits of this life and ultimately it is this faith we must honour and serve.' She drew a breath. 'We have given our requests and recommendations to Pierre-Roger for the surrender negotiations and we pray that the French commander will truly negotiate with Pierre-Roger and his trusted men and that the most important of our requests will be honoured.'

Luisana sat down, exhausted. Julian took Alayda's hand as she bowed her head.

The following morning, Pierre-Roger stood on the battlements as several of his knights stepped out on each flank waving white flags on their lances. The French commanders acknowledged the signal and responded. It was the second day of March, 1244.

A knight and a sergeant went down to the French camp to commence negotiations for surrender. From her place on the uppermost barbican, Esme could see the four friars stride to the general's quarters. The Bishop of Albi had not remained long and she presumed that these men had the responsibility of representing the Pope's interests. The same four had been there since the beginning of the siege and Esme knew them all by sight. There was the one with the large belly who was in charge; there were two tall friars, a thick-set one and a neat one; and then there was a fourth one, a small man one who prowled around the camp and frequently stared up at the pog.

The community's messengers returned with terms. As Pierre-Roger discussed them on the barbican, Elder Leyas placed small branches with red berries in the shape of a cross on the ground nearby. The negotiations continued all day, with messengers going up and down the mountain several times. Eventually the commanders reached agreement. Pierre-Roger looked down at General d'Arcis. The general stood away from the friars and looked back. After a few moments, Pierre-Roger turned and followed Leyas into the hall. Esme and others who had been watching the negotiations went in after them.

The mood in the hall was sombre. The garrison left their weapons outside and sat protectively beside their families. With little preamble, Pierre-Roger announced that the agreed date of surrender was the sixteenth of March, a date chosen by the elders in consultation with those among them who had a profound understanding of astrology. By the terms of the agreement everyone would be obliged to take an oath of faith to the Roman church and renounce any faith that was not in accordance with the dogma of Rome. They would be questioned by the Inquisition and allowed to go free without punishment. An amnesty was offered for all of those involved in the raid at Avignonet.

'My friends, anyone who does not wish to renounce their own faith will face death on a pyre. Those are best terms we could arrange. I am sorry.'

There was barely a sound in the hall. Pierre-Roger waited for some moments before continuing. Several of his men would go to the French camp as hostages and, as the day drew closer, garrison families would be allowed to leave in advance of the final departure if they wish. After a little muted discussion to clarify points, the meeting dispersed. Raimond remained in the hall to pray. Esme wanted to stay with him but felt that Matina might need support. She followed her to her house.

'What can we do, Esme? We have no choice. You heard Pierre-Roger; we either swear an oath to the Roman church or die on a fire like our mother. We have to live for our little boys. We can't leave them. We'll have to take the oath. Oh, Esme, they'll torture us!'

Esme put her arms around her sister-in-law and stroked her hair: 'No, my love, Pierre-Roger trusts the French general to uphold the terms of the surrender agreement. And we have to believe that.'

'But after Labernoc, they won't let us go,' she cried. 'They won't let Raimond go.'

Esme assured her that they would not recognise her and urged her to concentrate on her family, answer the friars' questions and go south to José's family as quickly as possible.

'What are you going to do, Esme?'

Esme did not answer. She knew she could escape but Raimond could not, not with his foot. But nor could he face the Inquisition; they would be sure to find out who he was. She hoped that Guilhèm and the elders had a plan.

42

Montségur, 2–7 March 1244

After nearly ten months of noise, tension and anxiety, Montségur became silent. The hostages went down to the French camp and were greeted by General d'Arcis. They were led to a large tent and, shortly afterwards, a meal was carried in by servants. The French sent dried meats and fruit, cheese and hard bread to the community in a gesture of goodwill. The women prepared soups and distributed food with Rixanda's guidance.

Up on the pog a quiet rhythm was established over the following days as garrison families prepared for a long journey to wherever they would next call home. Using the abundance of water now in the cisterns, they washed their possessions and Esme made herself useful by mending clothes. She was struggling with her sorrow as her gaze lingered on the men and women she had grown to know and love, and who would unquestionably choose the fire. She still did not know how Raimond was going to escape and, when she asked him, he had said that the elders were meditating on it. Esme, meanwhile, was working out ways in which he could be carried down the pog during the night.

On the fifth of March, Esme and Raimond sat on their bed with the door open, pillows propped up against the straw-lined wall. It was a cloudless night and the stars twinkled in the sky. They could hear a man and several women singing softly in a nearby house.

'Please let me talk to Othon about lowering you down one of the cliffs,' Esme begged. 'I know he can do it. And I know how to get to Foix through the forests. You'll be safe there.'

Raimond did not answer.

'*Besson,* we are running out of time', Esme tried to hide her anxiety.

'Please don't worry. The right solution will present itself. There are more important matters to concern ourselves with than my safety.'

'Not to me!'

Raimond caressed her legs, which were resting on top of his. 'You know I've been making copies of holy documents to give to the French? The day before we all have to leave, we will hand over a few real documents and the rest will be incomplete copies.'

'Won't they spot that they are not real?'

'They will spot the difference when the documents get to Rome but none of their experts have shown up here. I met two of them in Rome; they are not the sort of people who would tolerate even one night in a tent.'

Trying to follow his train of thought, Esme asked. 'So do you think the friars might go away once they have the documents?'

He shook his head and took out his stone. 'No, no, I don't think so. They have made their conditions and I think they particularly want some of the people who are here.'

'Like who?'

Raimond rested his stone in his open hand. Even in the dim light, she could see that the image of the diamond on it was perfectly formed. 'Esme, do you remember when we got married, Luisana said sometimes we have to make sacrifices to follow our soul's purpose.'

Esme's heart began to thump. 'What are you saying?'

He studied his stone. 'I don't know, *bessa*, I really don't know. In my meditations in the past few days, and last night my dreams, I sensed something I can't quite reach and when I try, all I see is my stone.'

Esme felt an old panic rising. 'Raimond, we don't need to see the Inquisition. Luisana and Pierre-Roger will let us escape, I know they will. You're different to everyone else here because the friars won't let you go.'

Raimond touched the diamond etching with his scarred fingers. '*Bessa,* what if escape doesn't serve my soul's purpose? Because,' he took a deep breath. 'I don't know what I am to do but I don't think it is to escape.'

Esme stared at him in horror.

'Oh Esme, I wish I knew. Please will you help me?'

Esme wanted to burst out crying for Raimond, for herself, for the community. Instead, hearing the anxiety in her husband's voice, she reached into her pouch and took out her stone. Raimond placed his alongside it, the jagged edges interlocking.

Esme began to shake uncontrollably. Raimond cradled her hands in his, their stones together in the centre, and prayed silently. Slowly Esme steadied herself and her mind slowed down. She looked at their hands. The familiar sense of peace and love that she felt when she was close to Raimond helped her to relax.

They sat silently for some time, each in their own thoughts.

'Raimond, I know how it feels when I have made the right choice. Two years ago, I wanted to leave Montségur for this very reason, I was afraid of what would happen if Rome sent an army here to get the sacred documents. But with Guilhèm's help, I chose to stay and when I made that choice, I felt clean and the choice felt obvious and simple.'

'And all I want right now is to be with you forever,' whispered Raimond.

'Is that the choice?'

Raimond stared at their stones and shook his head slowly. 'I think we will be together forever, but I don't think that is the choice that is coming to me.'

Uncertain of what he meant, Esme hurried to reassure him. '*Besson,* I trust you to make the right choice for your own soul's journey, and I will accept it,' *even if I don't like it*, she added to herself. But the love she felt in the moment stopped her from thinking further.

♦ ♦ ♦ ♦ ♦

Two days later, on the seventh of March, Raimond asked Esme if she would come with him to see Luisana and Bishop Marty after the midday meal. Hearing something she could not identify in his tone, she was nervous when she went with him into the large meeting room. Since their conversation, Raimond had spent considerable time in meditation with the elders. He had been loving to her at night but she guessed that he had been exploring his choices. She prayed that he meant to escape with her and now she was about to find out. She was a bit surprised to see at least twenty people sitting in two concentric circles waiting for them.

Luisana welcomed the young couple warmly. Esme's heart went out to her; she looked so frail, yet her strength had been crucial for holding the community together. Brother Thomas, Guilhèm and Esclarmonde were seated in the inner circle. Bishop Marty and Elder Leyas were sitting on either side of Luisana, and the six other elders, Luyon, Gerad, Dam, Yusu, Uswan and Dimaz, were in the outer circle. Esclarmonde's older sister, Arpais, was there. She was a quiet woman who prayed a lot and seldom spoke.

Bishop Marty led them into a meditation. When it finished, Esme opened her eyes and turned to Raimond. Sensing her move, he turned and smiled at her. She tried to read the look in his eyes.

Luisana spoke. She talked of the many sacred items that were on Montségur, some of which would be handed over to the Roman church, as agreed, and some which would be taken off the mountain for secret locations; among these latter items were the stones of all those who would go to the pyre.

'We know that the stories are safe in your stone, Esme,' continued Luisana. 'This is very important. As you know, under the terms of the surrender, everyone is obliged to present themselves to the Inquisition to take the Roman oath or suffer the fires. However we ask you now, if you are willing, to make your own way down the mountain on a secret path and carry on into the world, taking our stories with you and gathering more as you go.'

Esme closed her eyes for a moment. The elders were giving her permission to escape. With quiet humility, she opened her eyes and agreed to the request.

'Esme, there is more. Guilhèm?'

Guilhèm stood up and went to a chest. The elders' chanting rose and filled the room. He lifted the lid and took out another chest. From that he took out a silver box. He brought it to the table, bowed, drew symbols with his hands, and opened it. Taking two ancient documents out of the box, he laid them on the table.

Esme held her breath as a powerful presence seemed to step out of the leather encased papyrus and come towards her. Sunlight filled the room. Every muscle in her body relaxed. She felt she was floating. The stillness was perfect.

'Here are our most sacred and precious documents,' Luisana's voice drifted into Esme's consciousness. 'These are the writings of Jesus Christ and Mary Magdalene, our beloved teachers. The documents have been passed on through their descendants for 1200 years. We have translated and copied many others but these documents cannot be copied. They radiate a truth and love that go out far beyond our little community. These documents are precious to all of humanity and while they are in our hands, we share that truth and love with the whole world through our prayers.'

There was silence. Esme knew that Luisana was speaking the truth, that she was in the presence of sacred documents of Jesus and Mary Magdalene. No wonder Raimond had been so calm during the siege; he had known this feeling of peace ever since seeing these documents during the first siege. She breathed slowly, enjoying the stillness.

'Esme,' Guilhèm was calling for her attention. He waited until she was ready. 'Esme, these documents carry great power and few people can hold them safely. I am one of those people; Esclarmonde is another. Esclarmonde will be coming with me and together we will take these documents off Montségur and away from here.'

He explained that his true father was not the man who had raised him but a man from a distant land of noble heritage who had met his mother when she was working at Queribus. When Leyas approached him in the forest after the death of Serena, Bonnie and Agnes, the elder had asked to see his feet.

'After many months on Montségur,' Guilhèm continued. 'Leyas brought me to a monastery. The monastery held an ancient ledger that had record of the marks on my foot. The marks identified me as being of the bloodline of Jesus and Mary Magdalene. The marks also said that I would have a special task to undertake during my lifetime. All of my training since coming here to Montségur has been to prepare me for this task, which is to save Montségur's sacred documents from being taken by the Romans.'

Guilhèm, of the bloodline of Mary Magdalene and Jesus? Esme listened in startled silence.

'There is a problem, Esme, which is one of the points

of our meeting here. We have learnt that when I was at the monastery, one of the monks was a spy for Rome. He saw me look at the ledger through a crack in the library wall. Rome fears people like myself because, by our very existence, we undermine their teachings.'

With a slight hesitation Guilhèm continued: 'Esme, we have learnt through our network that the Roman church believes that I am here on Montségur, and they want to arrest me or see me walk into the pyre. We have learnt that the spy at that monastery said that I have soft hands, that I wear a ring with a red cross on my finger and that I have a red waistcoat. He also found out that I ate meat so had not received the Consolamentum. We think that this is all they know. However friars will be monitoring everyone who comes down from the mountain and are likely to be looking for me using that description.'

'So I will take his place,' said Raimond, speaking for the first time. He turned and looked directly at Esme. 'I will take the Consolamentum and go down the mountain as Guilhèm so Guilhèm can carry the sacred documents to a safe place.'

Esme kept her eyes on Guilhèm as she turned her head slowly towards Raimond. Her heart stopped beating as her body went into shock. In the distance she heard Raimond's voice: '*Bessa,* I am the only one who can do it. My hands are soft, and I eat meat so I don't look like a consoled person.' Raimond paused. 'I have prayed and meditated and when I finally made the choice, I knew that for me, my love, it was the right one. Guilhèm is travelling with Esclarmonde so they can't take a secret path down the north face. I will take the

Consolamentum and will go into the fire so that they believe Guilhèm is dead.'

Esme looked at him now, her eyes wide open in horror. She tried to speak but no words came out.

'*Bessa,* for the sacred words of Jesus and Mary Magdalene to stay out of the hands of the Romans, it needs to be Guilhèm who carries them to safety. It is a sacrifice we need to make. Both of us, my dearest love.'

Esme felt herself beginning to shake. Raimond reached out his hand to her. Blindly, Esme took it. Her Raimond was going into the pyre.

43

Montségur, 8–14 March 1244

IN THE DAYS THAT FOLLOWED. Esme was in a daze. Raimond spent some time with the elders in prayer to prepare for his final day but the rest of the time he spent with Esme. Sometimes they sat in the prayer hall, at other times they sat, their backs against a rock, in the sunshine looking at the spring buds appearing on the trees. They held hands and said very little. Esme often felt dizzy with knots in her stomach and her throat. She wanted to scream and cry out but could not find her voice.

Life on Montségur was now taken over by spiritual ceremonies, deep prayer, quiet conversation and music. Already a few families had left by agreement with the French. The communal dinners were quick and functional. Two elderly widows were among the twenty or so lay people who chose to take the Consolamentum and die rather than renounce their faith. Raimond would be one of the last to take the Consolamentum so he could spend his remaining nights with

Esme in their little house looking at the stars through the open door.

On the twelfth of March, Guilhèm sought out Esme while Raimond was with the elders. He led her to a point where they could sit in the sun and look out over the rolling plains to the north-west of Montségur. In the distance they heard the knocking sounds of the stockade-style pyre being made in a large, open field at the edge of the French camp. Facing the other direction, they watched the ravens whose wide wings and soaring movements were now so familiar to Esme.

Sitting upright, Guilhèm closed his eyes.

A small bird landed at Esme's feet and hopped around, displaying its red tail. She felt for her stone and took it out. The scratched fissures were distinctive and gave the grey stone a shimmering texture. To Esme it truly looked like a pearl. It was full of stories, so many of them sad. Even Guilhèm would be gone in a few days. She remembered the many times when they had sat together like this. Tears welled up in her eyes. She wiped them away. If she started crying now, she might not stop.

'Dear Esme,' Guilhèm said her name softly, his eyes open. 'I have a message for you. It may not make sense at the moment.' He turned towards her: 'Our hearts and souls are all born free. It is our mind that creates walls and boundaries and limits. If we always follow the wind and the clear mountain stream, we will find that our life is content but we won't be complete; but if we get out of the wind and streams and stop and look carefully, we may just see the little forest tracks that lead off to beautiful, happy, magical places that we would have missed.

And if we missed them, we would have missed the keys to make us complete, for it is only in the silence and peace that we can hear ourselves and find our happiness.'

Transfixed, Esme could not speak.

'We all have the light of God in us,' Guilhèm said. 'But many of us can't see it. Can you see the light in my eyes?' She nodded. 'Well, I can see the light in your eyes. You have a beautiful heart and the light shines out through your eyes. This is who you are and how you look. Always remember that.'

He relaxed and sat back against the rock.

'I don't think I'll forget this moment, Guilhèm. You are so different but you are still the same.'

They looked out at the clouds drifting across the sky.

'Guilhèm, I've always had you to talk to, to help me. Without Raimond, and you not being around, I don't know how I am going to... to...'

'Esme, you are surrounded with love and support. You have a family in Foix. Matina and José and their little boys are your family too and Aragon is not far. And Alayda and Julian will be somewhere too. Gather stories and secure them in your stone. Do it for your baby sister, and for Matina's boys, and their descendants. It is a tough road, Esme, but you will have support.'

'I'll miss you, Guilhèm.'

Guilhèm smiled, but tears of sadness glistened in his eyes.

44

Montségur, 15 March 1244

ON THE FIFTEENTH OF MARCH, Raimond said farewell to his family. Matina, José and the children were going to walk down the mountain with Guilhèm the following day. Esclarmonde was going with them. In order to hide her from any future interest from Rome, Esclarmonde's half-sister, Arpais, was going to go down the mountain and say that she was Esclarmonde. Arpais had already taken the Consolamentum and was prepared. Guilhèm was confident that, by some means, his small group would avoid having to meet the friars but he did not have a precise plan. Once they escaped, he would travel north-west with Esclarmonde and the documents. Matina and her family would walk south through the mountains to José's family in Aragon. Alayda and Julian would join them and Esme would catch up with them along the route.

'Let's walk out to our rock; there will be no one there,' Raimond suggested when they left them. They made their way through the empty, narrow passages and ruined houses and sat down with their backs to the flat rock near the supply platform.

Sitting beside Raimond, Esme's mind was still and her heart beat gently. Occasionally one or the other would squeeze a hand or an arm. Esme wanted to stay there forever.

Raimond took two small bundles of red cloth from a pouch in his belt and opened one of the bundles. It contained his stone and her mother's pearl, which Esme had given him at the end of the healing session with Luisana three and a half years earlier. He let both rest in the palm of his hand. 'Esme, I love the pearl like I love you.'

She touched it with her finger. It looked like the moon. 'I am so pleased that you have it.'

'I wanted to give you something special so I asked one of the men from the east to make this for you.'

He placed the other bundle in her hand.

She opened it carefully. It was a small pendant on a delicate gold chain. The pendant was a gold disk with a diamond and a pearl sitting side by side in the centre of it. She gasped. 'Raimond, it's beautiful.'

'The moon is you, the diamond is me and we are united in the sun.' He picked it up and put it around her neck.

She rested her hand on it. 'Thank you.'

She took out her own stone and put it beside his.

'*Bessa,* my Esme,' Raimond gulped. 'I am so very sorry that I am doing this to you, leaving you here to...'

'No *besson,* no, don't, I know, I know.' Esme desperately wanted to avoid crying.

'Please, *bessa,* let me tell you how sorry I am.' Still holding his stone and the pearl, he wrapped his hands around hers. 'To hurt you so much, to condemn you to carry on, I wish with all of my heart that there was another way.'

'This is how it has to be because of... of everything. How can we not, you and I? We have to do this and you have made me very strong. I will be able to go on. Really, truly...'

'Keep my stone with you. The elders have given me permission to give my stone to you to help you. This way you know I will always be with you, my *bessa*.'

He took her stone and laid it on his hand beside his, the jagged edges together. After a while, he put the pearl back in his pouch and placed the two stones in her hand, folding her fingers over them.

'It is time, my beloved Esme. Remember, I will always be with you, helping you, loving you, you will never be alone.'

Squeezing the stones in her hand Esme rested her forehead on Raimond's and closed her eyes. She wanted to memorise every touch, every breath, every feeling of this moment but her mind was blank.

'We must go to the hall, *bessa*.'

Whispering words of love, they embraced.

Everyone still on the mountain had assembled in the prayer hall for the final Consolamentum ceremony. Four people, including Raimond, were to be consoled. They sat inside a circle in the centre of the room. A chair with a heart-shaped seat, which Esme had seen on a few occasions, was in the middle of the circle. The piece at the tip of the seat was missing. After lengthy prayers, Leyas and Luisana stood up and walked into the circle. Luisana held up a small triangle made of the same stone as the seat. With reverence, she slotted the piece into the tip. It fitted perfectly. Esme could see writing on it. She had heard it said that the first names of the apostles of Jesus were written on the small piece. Her eyes were on Raimond. She felt tears rising.

She felt a soft tap on her shoulder. It was Guilhèm. He held out his hand and indicated that she was to follow him into the circle. Leyas cradled her left hand in both of his and Luisana took her right hand. Closing her eyes, Esme felt herself being transported to another world, a place of perfect peace. Then Leyas spoke. His voice was very quiet.

'Esme, beloved child, you are very special. We honour you for accepting your path selflessly in this world of illusion.' He blessed her, drew a symbol on her forehead and put an imaginary ring on her finger and a bracelet on her arm. Both Luisana and Leyas drew a symbol on each hand. 'Esme, your mind might try to persuade you that you have been abandoned but your heart knows all. If you feel lost, look for signs, a cloud, a bird, a small animal, a kindly stranger, and these will remind you that you are never alone.'

After another blessing from the elders, Guilhèm guided Esme back to her seat.

Shortly afterwards the Consolamentum ceremony commenced with prayers, during which Bishop Marty intoned the names of the eight elders: Leyas, Luisana, Luyon, Gerad, Dam, Yusu, Uswan and Dimaz. The first person to be consoled was brought to the circle.

When it was Raimond's turn, Esme clasped her hands to her

heart. Bishop Marty intoned the names of saints and ascended masters, and led prayers. He called on everyone in the room, including children, to close their eyes. There was silence and Esme opened one eye to look. She saw Leyas and Luisana place their hands on Raimond's head, then on his shoulders and on his feet. They drew symbols at each point and, returning to his heart, they drew a symbol resembling a flower. She closed her eyes as Bishop Marty read from a parchment a series of questions in a quiet voice, to which Raimond answered 'yes'. He returned to his seat, now a consoled man.

Esme was only barely aware of the final ceremony of the afternoon during which each of those going to the pyre, except for Raimond, came forward and placed their stone on a table. Their journey on earth was finished and, as was the tradition of their people, their stones would be taken to a special place as a mark of respect to the earth and as a way of placing their lives on record. Four men had agreed to leave Montségur that night using one of the secret paths, and to travel north, south, east and west respectively with the stones.

After the ceremony, the garrison families dispersed and the consoled continued their meditation. Esme walked slowly over to Raimond. They bowed to each other, kissed each other's hands, embraced lightly and Esme left the room. It was dark outside. Without pausing, she fetched her bundle from their little house and made her way to a secret path. At the top, she took one last look at the castle and the houses nestled in the shade of its north wall and made her way down the path with the aid of hidden ropes and handles. She walked for a couple of hours to skirt the troops stationed at the base of the pog.

They were clustered around fires and talking quietly among themselves.

Esme ignored the profound sadness in her own heart as she doubled back and found a safe place to hide in the dense trees that had been left standing to shelter the tents of the commander, knights and friars. Before dawn, she would make her way through low shrubs and position herself up in a tree. She had plotted this route carefully; there were few leaves in her selected tree but the branches were thickly tangled and would hide her. From here she would be able to see Raimond coming down the mountain and walking to the pyre in the field. As she settled herself in the base of a tree, she finally gave in to her pain and wept.

45

Montségur, 16 March 1244

THE MORNING OF THE SIXTEENTH of March was misty and damp. Esme climbed the tree and settled on a wide branch. Aware that her body had frozen on the day eight and a half years ago when Ava had died, she had brought food and water for the long vigil. She could see the friars' tent, which, this morning, was busier than usual. She had heard that two more friars had turned up but had not bothered to look. Tiqué was dead so it did not matter who they were. She watched the small hooded friar walk in and out of the tent in an agitated way. Two friars stepped out of the tent but, at that moment, several soldiers stopped under the tree for a conversation. She buried her face and kept absolutely still.

The soldiers eventually moved on and, cautiously, Esme raised her head. The two friars had disappeared but the small friar, the one who skulked around the camp and spent time looking up at the castle, was making his way purposefully to the pog. Dozens of soldiers were standing around a long, narrow corral that had been set up beside the dense band of trees. The density of these trees packed with prickly shrubs and undergrowth had deliberately been maintained by the French to keep their weapon store safe from spies and saboteurs. Now these trees were being used to form one side of the corral; the beams of unused stone-slingers were used for the other sides. Esme guessed the soldiers planned to hold those who chose to live in this corral. It was not especially secure but with so many soldiers around, escape would be extremely difficult. Further up the pog, she could see scores of soldiers climbing the path. Some had nearly reached the top.

Esme watched the small friar making a nuisance of himself with the soldiers at the separation point. A sergeant was clearly telling him to leave. It was equally clear the friar had no intention of going. With a start, Esme guessed that he was probably the one who was charged with finding the members of the bloodline. How many holy people on Montségur had been of the bloodline of Mary Magdalene and Jesus? She had heard that Rome believed there were three. She knew about Guilhèm. Maybe Luisana or Leyas or Esclarmonde?

The cry went up that the prisoners were leaving the castle. The remaining three friars stepped out of their tent, smoothed down their clothes, adjusted their gold-coloured belts, and grasped small bags that contained their rosary beads and a bible. Looking proud and authoritative, they made their way to the foot of the pog near the quarter-master's tent to await the first procession.

♦ ♦ ♦ ♦ ♦

Luisana and Arpais de Pereille were in the first group of people to be taken down the mountain. They walked two by two. A rope ran down the middle of the group, from one end to the other, and each had a hand tied to the rope. Soldiers walked in front and behind the sad procession. Tall and elegant in a burgundy dress trimmed with golden thread, Luisana walked awkwardly. Her hip was giving her trouble and a soldier was helping her. As they came to the mule stop, she spotted two bulky friars sitting on the ground pulling meat from chicken legs. Luisana shuddered, then stumbled. The party came to a halt as the soldier helped her to stand again. Without looking at the friars, she made some swift symbols with her hands and discreetly sent them in the friars' direction. The group carried on. Many of those on the rope walked in their bare feet. They were thin, gaunt, and dressed in their poorest clothes, having given anything of further use to survivors. Behind them came more soldiers followed by the family members of some of those on the rope.

As they made their way along the narrow track through the trees, Luisana looked at the trees around her and smiled at the beauty of the natural world. A tit sang merrily. 'Good-bye, little one,' she whispered, looking at the bird. 'And thank you for all the joy you brought to our lives.'

They emerged from the band of trees and were confronted by thousands of soldiers spread out on the hill below. Two tight lines of armed men formed the final walk to an expanse of flat ground on which the stockade had been erected. The families were immediately forced into the makeshift corral. Loud protests turned to scuffles as they tried to embrace their loved ones.

'Sergeant,' Luisana's voice took on a commanding tone that cut through the noise. 'Please release us from these bonds. We shall walk to your pyre without protest but allow our families to say farewell. I will remain here. These are my friends and they will listen to me.'

After a hesitation, the sergeant ordered a man to untie them. 'But Madam please keep everyone moving. Don't make me have to use force.'

Giving their names to a record keeper, Arpais said she was Esclarmonde de Pereille. Esme could see the small friar peering closely at her and Luisana but when the elder made a jerking movement with her hands, he stepped back as if he had been pushed. Luisana and Arpais embraced and Arpais moved down the slope. As each person was untied, Luisana took their hands lightly. Gently she urged family members to keep their farewells brief.

As family members were driven into the separation area by the soldiers, Esme watched the friar look at every man quickly. He spent a little more time on those dressed as soldiers and those who did not have the gaunt appearance of a consoled man. Even after the ten-month siege and poor rations, it was still possible to distinguish the consoled from the meat eaters. He looked at their hands, occasionally stopping a man whose hands were not visible and demanding that he display them.

Another party of condemned friends arrived, accompanied

by family and garrison members. Once more the friar insisted on looking at every man closely, especially those who were being directed into the corral.

As the procession continued and the condemned were untied, the corral was filling up and the cries of sorrow were rising. Oblivious to the frustration of the soldiers, the small friar continued his work, studying men, grabbing at hands and peering into eyes.

From her perch Esme forced herself to keep watching. She had seen Arpais and the first group go through the narrow door of the wooden stockade. The walls of the stockade were three metres high in places and her friends were invisible to her now. She sensed sadness in the soldiers who lined the path. Many looked to the ground as the condemned people passed slowly by. She saw a few blessing themselves with the sign of the cross and a few surreptitiously touching their heart.

Esme scanned further up the mountain and saw a group of twelve people being led down on a rope followed by families and friends. There was still no sign of Raimond. Looking up the mountain, she noticed two friars struggling up the track. They stopped, turned and looked down the mountain. They must have been the two who had left the tent that morning. Looking at them now, she sensed something familiar about them, even from this distance. With a flash of horror, Esme realised they were in fact constables Del Gurbe and Barca.

Sweat broke out on her forehead. 'Oh Raimond! Oh no! They can't find you. God please, they will do terrible things to you. I know they will,' a wave of panic gripped her and she started to shake. She tried to think clearly. She would never make it back up the pog before they reached the top. She had to warn him. And she had to warn Guilhèm as well! The sacred documents – they mustn't get them!

One of the two ravens swooped down in front of her tree. The other was hovering above it. She was startled out of her panic; neither of them had ever come so close to her before. She gripped the tree branch. The bird swooped down low again.

Guilhèm can talk to the birds. 'Go to Guilhèm, please,' she whispered. 'Warn him that Constables Del Gurbe and Barca are going up the mountain.'

The bird swooped once more and flew away, followed by the other one. Esme watched them fly towards the top of the pog.

On the mountain Raimond was outside the castle entrance waiting to take his place on a rope. Beside him Guilhèm was adjusting his hood when the birds, one after the other, swooped over his head. A shiver went down his back. He sent Raimond back into the shelter of the castle; the healer, Rixanda, and Brother Thomas, who were staying with him, followed.

Moments later, Guilhèm came in with Matina: 'Barca and Del Gurbe are here,' he said. 'And they most certainly are looking for us.'

Raimond went white.

Matina was trembling. Rixanda gripped her and held her eye firmly: 'Courage, woman, courage. This is bigger than you.'

Moments later, Pierre-Roger and José appeared at the doorway: 'Alayda has run up to the parapet and is shouting at two friars who've just arrived,' said José.

'Oh Alayda! Thank you, brave woman,' muttered Guilhèm grimly. Explaining who the friars really were, he sent José to monitor their movements. There were still about fifty people left to be taken on the narrow path to the bottom of the pog on ropes and a crowd of about sixty to follow them. Several infirm people were waiting to be carried down on chairs by men of the garrison.

'Cowards, cowards,' Alayda shouts rained down from the parapet. On the way she had grabbed a discarded metal visor, which covered her forehead and nose. 'Friars, you are false. You say you are men of God but you are not. You have free will. You choose this life. You choose to commit terrible sins. You will be accountable. You will be condemned for your choices. Cowards!'

The soldiers ignored her. Alayda had shouted out accusations at the soldiers many times over the past ten months.

Del Gurbe and Barca, breathless from the climb up the pog, became very angry. How dare a woman shout profanities at them in front of others and especially when they were dressed as friars? They had killed people for less than this.

'Silence her,' snapped Barca to a soldier.

'Sorry, Most Reverend. Orders are to get these people down the mountain. A few more groups to go, including some invalids. We have to be finished by sundown.'

On the parapet, Alayda moved around the corner and continued to shout abuse at the friars. Julian appeared beside her, also wearing a metal mask. In their fury, Del Gurbe and Barca forgot about their mission and followed them around the castle walls, waving their fists and ordering her to be silent. Once they were out of sight, José signalled to Guilhèm to usher Raimond out. Raimond and Brother Thomas were tied to the rope together; Rixanda was tied behind Thomas and Elder Leyas insisted on being tied behind Raimond. Four more people including a knight and his wife were also tied on and the small group moved off down the mountain. Some chanted the Lord's Prayer. Raimond tried to join in. He had spent the night in prayer and had been feeling at one with the consoled people until the bird arrived. Now he was thinking of Esme and his family and what he was leaving behind. He felt panic rise in his throat. His foot hurt. He did not want to die; he wanted to live and love Esme and write Esme's stories, and watch Matina's children grow up, and maybe have a child with Esme. Thomas reached for his hand over the rope.

A woman sang, her pure voice carried across the air and wrapped itself around Raimond. He sensed his mother walking beside him minding him.

Matina, José, Guilhèm and Esclarmonde followed Raimond's group. Guilhèm, the sacred documents hidden in his sleeves, carried Pedro while José carried Johann. Esclarmonde walked with Matina. Their sadness was immense. They could hear Alayda still shouting loudly in the background.

Pierre-Roger gathered the remaining garrison and ordered them all outside the castle. A large group of twenty people was already filling the track as the soldiers tied them to a rope. These included Esclarmonde's mother and grandmother, both of whom needed to be carried down on chairs. Pierre-Roger ordered his men to make a fuss over them.

When Barca returned to the front of the castle, he was confronted by a large, milling crowd. 'I command you to bring that woman down here immediately,' he roared at the French sergeant.

'We are nearly finished, Most Reverend, I will send my men to get them shortly. We know that woman and her friend. They are warriors and will put up a fight. Please put up with it a bit longer.'

'I'll go and get her myself,' growled Barca, pushing his way towards the entrance of the castle through the crowd.

'Remember why we are here and let them sort her out, Barca,' said Del Gurbe, as he returned to the task of examining the faces of those being tied. 'We don't want to miss any of them.'

Finally the last of the condemned left the castle and started slowly down the track on the rope. Pierre-Roger and his most senior knights, who were prepared to face the Inquisition, followed them. The castle was empty except for Alayda and Julian. Pierre-Roger turned and saluted the pair before he left.

'We can get them now,' said the sergeant.

'Bring them to us,' snapped Barca, angry at the wasted effort. 'We're in charge here, and that woman is a heretic. If you don't get them to us, I will have you up for association with a heretic. Understand?'

At that Barca and Del Gurbe turned to go down the mountain, leaving the sergeant and his men to fetch Alayda and Julian.

At the separation point near the bottom of the pog, Esme could see the small friar twitch anxiously, even grabbing the hands of some of the emaciated consoled people to see if they had recently been wearing a ring. And then Raimond appeared. Esme's heart turned over. Brother Thomas, beside him, was stumbling to cover Raimond's limp. The friar moved towards them and hovered as Raimond was untied. Then he stepped up to him, prodding at Raimond to force him to look at him. Esme felt sick. She saw Raimond turn his head and look into the eyes of the friar. The friar stumbled backwards and would have fallen to the ground if a soldier had not caught him. Raimond looked at him for a moment longer, then turned back to Brother Thomas.

The friar regained his footing, his fists clenched.

Esme's heart ached. She could see Raimond trying to walk without a limp. The pain in his foot must be excruciating. She watched as Matina pushed in to hug him. She wished she could embrace him and take him away from there.

By now there were about 170 people, soldiers and their families and other lay people who had lived on the mountain, crowded into the corral waiting to be led away for questioning by the friars. As each new group of people arrived on a rope, the waiting crowd swelled, as did their cries and shouts to their loved ones who were going to the pyre.

Esme watched as the cloaked figures of Esclarmonde and Guilhèm, who was carrying Pedro on his hip, appeared at the very end of the group and merged quickly into the crowd. The friar's attention, now filled with fury, was fixed on Raimond. Esme could see José, carrying Johann, put his hand on Matina and guide her backwards, away from Raimond. Cries went up from the family of a consoled knight and again the crowd surged forward, threatening to swamp Luisana before the soldiers managed to push them back.

By the time order was restored, Matina, José, Esclarmonde, Guilhèm and the children had melted into the crowd. From her tree, Esme watched them disappear unnoticed into the dense band of trees. Esme wanted to cry with relief. Guilhèm had found a way out. He would lead the party through the forest and emerge some distance away. José would take Matina and the boys across the mountains to the coast and south to safety. Guilhèm and Esclarmonde were going north-west to islands, parts of which neither the King of France nor his allies had control over.

'Farewell, my dear and wonderful friend,' she whispered. 'Please, please God, I will see you again one day.'

Raimond and Brother Thomas stumbled down the path towards the pyre. The friar kept pace with them on the other side of the soldiers. Esme's heart lurched as Raimond approached the narrow doorway of the high stockade. Brother Thomas went in first; then Raimond went up the few steps to the thick platform of wooden logs, followed by Leyas. Esme wished that the tree would swallow her up. The sides of the pyre were too high to see Raimond now.

She looked for the ravens. They were hovering over the top of the pog. A movement caught her eye. It was Alayda and Julian and they were being marched down the track by soldiers, their hands tied behind their backs.

Even in captivity, Alayda was still abusing the French soldiers: 'Why do you serve those friars? You are the puppets of Rome' she was saying as they came around the corner and confronted Barca and Del Gurbe, who were leaning against a rock just above the mule station.

'There she is; put her up against that rock so I can see her,' demanded Barca.

Pressed against the rock, with soldiers on either side of her, Alayda stared straight into Barca's eyes.

Del Gurbe stood behind Barca, and looked over his shoulder.

'It's one of them!' exclaimed Del Gurbe.

'You're the she-wolf from the village,' spluttered Barca. 'I knew it. Where's your brother?'

Alayda spat at Barca. He let out a roar, grabbed a sword from a soldier and rammed it into her stomach.

Alayda's face froze. She swung towards Julian and whispered 'Love'. Barca withdrew the sword and she slumped to the ground.

'No!' howled Julian, and drawing on all of his massive strength, he snapped free of his ropes and hurled his full bodyweight against the two constables. Together the three of them went over the side of the cliff and tumbled down. They landed on a ledge below the track, Julian on top of the two fat men. With an extra heave, he rolled to one side and pushed them off the ledge. He rolled back onto his stomach and watched them as they crashed through trees, their heads banging against boulders. They ended in a bloodied heap. The soldiers looked down. Julian was motionless on a ledge about 20 metres below them. Barca and Del Gurbe had landed on a ledge 20 metres below that again.

'Well, go after them,' snapped the sergeant. 'The friars, that is.'

‘What about her friend, he may be alive.’

‘Leave him to me. We’re obliged to look after the friars. Go, now!’

The sergeant looked over the cliff at Julian. The big man’s body was not moving. His soldiers reached the friars; ‘both dead,’ one of them shouted.

‘Carry them down,’ the sergeant shouted back. ‘We’ll let the crows eat the other two.’

A dove landed on the ledge beside Julian’s body. Julian twitched, rolled onto his side and slowly sat up. Esme could see him check his limbs. He appeared to be uninjured. He lay down again and shuffled behind a shrub to wait.

46

Montségur, 16 March 1244

LUISANA WAS THE LAST to go through the narrow entrance to the pyre. Logs were stacked to close off the stockade. Esme gripped the tree trunk. Her beloved *besson* was behind those logs, alive. The men outside it were going to set fire to it and he was going to die. She could cry to the heavens but nothing was going to stop this now. She knew that. She closed her eyes and called on her mother and Ava to help Raimond, to bring him peace and protect him from pain. She heard chanting rising from inside the stockade.

Hugues d'Arcis stood nearby watching his soldiers finish their preparations. His heavy cloak sat back on his broad shoulders. The small friar sidled up to him.

'General, stop them chanting, it's blasphemy,' he demanded.

D'Arcis did not respond.

'General, I insist you get your soldiers to stop them, in the name of God and the Holy Church!'

'Don't be ridiculous, man; you've got what you came

for. Now let my men get on with their job,' d'Arcis growled without looking at the friar.

Inside the stockade, over 200 people were crushed together. Brother Thomas and Luisana had their arms around Raimond. The chanting rose like a wave. There were no cries. Surrounded by loving people, Raimond's heartbeat slowed. He thought of his mother and his father. He looked up to the sky. A cloud drifted overhead. It shifted into the shape of an angel and stopped. Two more clouds, also shaped like angels, drifted and stopped. Raimond smiled.

'Esme, *bessa,* my most beloved,' he breathed. He closed his eyes and rested into the arms of Luisana and Brother Thomas. He heard the crackling of the fire on the outside of the tree trunks. There was a rustle through the mass of bodies.

The smoke drifted slowly towards Esme in her tree about 50 metres away. She held her sleeve over her mouth to prevent herself from coughing. The wood at the base of the pyre was now smoking. The chanting had ceased. Guilhèm had said that the lack of air would kill them before the flames reached them. Esme hoped that it was so. The flames soared into the sky suddenly. As the smell of burning flesh reached her, she resisted the temptation to run away.

47

Montségur, 16 March 1244

Esme remained in the tree, twitching her limbs every now and then to make sure they would not freeze up. Time had no meaning. The lay people, including Pierre-Roger and his knights, walked off in an untidy procession to the east. Esme had no idea where they were going. They had not been restrained but were guarded by a large armed detail.

French knights and infantry, their horses and more carts loaded with tents and military equipment joined the procession. The camp was clearing fast. Six empty carts remained in place to carry away the charred remains. The friars mounted their horses and departed, leaving others to gather their belongings and take down their tents. The bodies of Barca and Del Gurbe were loaded onto a cart and left in the charge of servants.

Esme watched the section of the forest where Guilhèm and Matina and their party had disappeared. The army had walked away from there. Matina and José and their family would get to Aragon safely; and Guilhèm and Esclarmonde would escape with the precious documents.

By dusk several hundred soldiers remained, sitting close to their campfires. The pyre had collapsed inwards and was still smouldering.

Esme decided it was finally safe to go to Julian on the mountain. They would have to move Alayda's body in the dark and Julian did not know the paths on the mountain as well as she did. She slid out of the tree and shook her body to bring life back into it. Carefully she skirted the soldiers' camp and climbed up one of the easier secret tracks. She found Julian carrying Alayda tenderly towards the abandoned defence wall. Before he buried her, he took her stone, cut off a lock of her hair and put them into a pouch, which he wore around his neck.

'She loved it here, Esme,' he said when they buried her in soft soil beside the people who had died during the siege. 'She was so passionate about justice; she kept saying that everyone had free will and they chose to do what they did. She would never listen to excuses.' He paused. 'I loved her.'

'And she loved you, Julian,' said Esme.

'I sometimes thought we could have a little cottage and be close forever. Was that silly to think?'

'No, not at all silly. I dreamt too of a happy life with Raimond. Alayda needed you by her side; you made her whole. We were lucky to have beloved friends. Even for a short time.' Esme looked towards the pyre, which was now glowing in the dark. 'We have to keep going, Julian. We have to be strong and do all that is needed of us.'

Julian buried his head in his hands. Esme put her arms around the big man.

They remained together on the pog until morning.

'I'm going to wait until they have all moved off; then I'm following Matina and José south before working out where I go from there,' said Esme.

'I will come with you, Esme,' said Julian. 'I don't want to go back to Labernoc.'

Over the next few days the soldiers closed up their camp. The carts were loaded with the smashed bones of the consoled people of Montségur, and driven away to be dumped in a distant and unmarked place. Hugues d'Arcis was one of the last to leave. Having walked around the remnants of the camp, he looked up at the castle at the top of the mountain. The light was bright and dazzled him.

With his long cloak flowing behind him, he strode over to his servant who was holding the reins of his horse. His job was done.

Esme watched him from her perch in a tree on the lower reaches of Montségur. Birds tweeted in the dense foliage. When everyone had gone and the landscape was peaceful once more, Esme walked out into the empty fields feeling the muddy ground beneath her feet. Standing on the ridge between the pog and the pyre, she turned around slowly, taking in the familiar mountains. The ravens flew together above her. A donkey brayed soulfully in the distance. A flock of small birds swooped around her before returning to the trees. Their song filled the air. As Esme's eyes blurred with tears, the pog shimmered before her, throwing waves of gentle light in her direction. She bowed deeply in acknowledgement and wiped her eyes.

After one more lingering look at Montségur, she turned and joined Julian for the long walk to the south.

Epilogue: Foix January 1316

WILLIAM BÉLIBASTE finished Esme's story before dawn. Barely breathing, Esme opened her eyes slightly as William took Raimond's stone out of her pouch. He laid it beside Esme's stone, which was sitting in the palm of her hand, and joined them together along the jagged edge. He closed her fingers over the stones for a few moments, then opened her hand again and took both stones.

Unable to give Esme the Consolamentum because of his impure lifestyle, he gave her a blessing and departed. Later that day, with her great niece, Stéphanie, beside her, Esme passed from this life.

William placed Esme's stone in a sacred place near Montségur and returned to the safety of his community in Catalonia.

Five years later, in 1321, William Bélibaste was betrayed by one of his community and arrested as he crossed the Pyrenees into Languedoc. He was tried by the episcopal authority in his native Corbières and burnt to death on a pyre.

Author's note
June 2017

Interest in the Cathars grew in the twentieth century, gaining momentum with the publication in 1982 of *The Holy Blood and the Holy Grail* by Henry Lincoln, Michael Baigent and Richard Leigh. 21 years later the novel *The Da Vinci Code* by Dan Brown brought the Cathars to a vast international audience. Today, Montségur and other sites associated with the Cathars attract visitors from all over the world. The Department of Aude, which encompasses Carcassonne and Puivert, uses the term Pays Cathare [Cathar Country] to promote the region.

In 1998, the Mayor of Toulouse and other influential people in the region wrote an open letter to Pope John Paul II entitled 'Manifeste pour la Réconciliation' [Manifesto for Reconciliation]. Although Pope John Paul II made many apologies, he never referred to the Albigensian Crusade against Christians or to the Cathars. In 2016, following an initiative by local religious authorities, Monsignor Jean-Marc Eychenne, Roman Catholic Bishop of Pamiers, held a ceremony of apology at Montségur on 16 October. He said, 'Nous demandons pardon, d'abord à notre Seigneur, mais aussi à tous ceux que des membres de notre Église ont alors persécutés.' ['We ask for forgiveness, first of all to Our Lord, but also to all of those who have been persecuted by members of our church.'] The emotional ceremony was attended by 600 – 700 people and finished with music at the site of the pyre.

In May 2015, I added my petition for an apology from the Pope. In the letter, as follows, I asked Pope Francis to issue an apology specifically for the Albigensian Crusade and the persecution to the death of the people now known as the Cathars:

8 May 2015

Most Holy Father, Pope Francis

I am an Irish writer living in the south of France and for the past number of years I have been studying the history of the Christians who lived here in medieval times; today these Christians are known as the Cathars. My research has focussed on Montsegur, a mountain in the foothills of the Pyrenees. It was here in the thirteenth century that the most holy elders of the Cathar people gathered to pray in the face of persecution coming from those following the orders of Roman Catholic prelates.

During my research I have learnt about the Albigensian Crusade, which was called for by Pope Innocent III and commenced in 1209. This brutal campaign began with the slaughter of every man, woman and child in Beziers on 22 July 1209. After many tragic events, the Crusade formally ended in 1229.

Four years later, Pope Gregory IX appointed inquisitors to prosecute and punish Christian heretics. The friars of the Order of Preachers came to the Languedoc region of France and, in the execution of their duties, brought terrible sadness and heartache to many local communities. The community on Montsegur, protected by a small garrison, stood out as a beacon of light and prayer in this misery. As yet, they had not been attacked by either the crusaders or the inquisitors.

This changed in Spring 1243 when, after a Conclave in Beziers, a huge army laid siege to Montsegur under the leadership of General D'Arcis, Seneschal of Carcassonne. Peter Amiel, Archbishop of Narbonne, was present during the early days of the siege. The Montsegur garrison held the besiegers back for ten months but in February, 1244, they had to surrender. Under the terms of the surrender, a fifteen day truce was called. Those who agreed to submit themselves for questioning by the Inquisition were let go. Those who would not compromise their own faith were to come down the mountain on 16th March and die on a pyre. Of the 450 or so people surviving on Montsegur in March 1244, about 221 men and women chose to die on the pyre rather than forsake their beliefs.

Today many people climb Montsegur and the sense

of residual sadness is palpable. My own disquiet, which I experienced on my first visit to Montsegur in 2008, has deepened with study. I have discussed it with family and friends, most of whom like me were raised as Roman Catholics and many of whom are devout. Despite the 800 year gap between those events and today, responses range from shock and sorrow, to disgust. There is a huge and continued interest in the Cathars and Montsegur, as is evident from the number of people of all ages and fitness levels who trek up the steep slopes of the mountain each year. I have witnessed ceremonies and deep distress on the mountain on many occasions.

My reason for writing to you, Holy Father, is because I believe that there remains to this day a great deal of pain and sorrow associated with the persecution of the Cathars in the thirteenth century. I also believe that healing, forgiveness and love can seep through time and can bring peace to everyone, dead and alive, who is connected in some way with the sad events of that time.

And now I ask for a great blessing, Holy Father, in your capacity as Representative of all Roman Catholics throughout the world today and across time. I ask you with gratitude and love in my heart to issue an apology specifically for the Albigensian Crusade and for the persecution to the death of the Christian people known as the Cathars.

I cannot speak for others about the power of such an apology coming from you, but for me, it would bring a profound healing to a deep and mysterious wound. It would allow me to accept the events of that time and move on confident that love is the most potent force at the heart of all Christian churches.

With love and humility,
I am yours very respectfully,
Catherine de Courcy.

The actions of the Roman Catholic Church against these good Christians in the thirteenth century reverberate to today. Many raised in the Roman Catholic faith, including myself, have difficulty reconciling its teachings of love and forgiveness with these actions that remain without repentance in the Church's history. I believe an apology from the Pope will make a difference. At the time of writing, we still await such an apology.

Acknowledgements

My study of the Christians of Montségur began in October 2008 when Paddy McCoey invited me to join a group to explore the story of the final days on the pog. I continued the research with Paddy and Neil McCann for a couple of years. I wish to express my deep gratitude to both of them for drawing me into the extraordinary story of Montségur, and for the knowledge and insights they gave me during the time we worked together.

In March 2011, I began to write this book. I immersed myself in the story, reading whatever had been published in English, and gathering information and insights from many other sources. As the story is embedded in the landscape, I spent a lot of time on Montségur. I walked many of the tracks mentioned in the book and rested in forests, by rivers and in caves associated with the story.

I received enormous encouragement, support and advice along the way and am very grateful to all of those who helped me over the past six years. I wish to thank especially Maria Rawlins, John Rawlins, Sheila de Courcy, Jenny Brown, Noeleen Behan, Paddy Molloy, Irene Hayden, Nathalie Andre, MaeveAnn Austin, Sean Keighran, Yvette Monahan, Mary de Courcy, Mary McWilliams, Siobhan McDonald, Daragh Curtis, Declan Curtis and Aileen Fennessy. As a non-fiction writer,

I needed a lot of help to redirect my skills. I am immensely grateful to Kevin McGee, who gave me a masterclass in novel writing, and Brigie de Courcy, who read many drafts and gave me invaluable advice and direction. A huge thank you also to Clodagh Lynam, Rosanna Cooney and Beryl Hill for editing at various stages of the manuscript, to Anna de Courcy for the final edit, to Eoin Cooney and Telma Cooney for much-needed help with web technology, and to Karen Carty, Stephen Marcus, Jamie Jauncey and Brendan Foley for the timely help they gave me in bringing this story to publication. Very many thanks to Jessie Hayden who drew the map. Thank you also to Luc Tibor Erdos for directing me to many interesting places associated with the Cathars, to Andrew Smith for detailed astrological readings, to Kathleen Evans for information about medieval food and to Max Marty for information about the landscape in the thirteenth century. My thanks also to those who gave me much-needed encouragement after reading versions of the manuscript: my mother Mrs Sheila de Courcy, Terri Gover, Breda McEnaney, Monica McWilliams, Gilly Adkins, Gertrud Keavor, Julie Anaiya Sophia and Pete Wilson.

I received help, support and information from many other people, some of whom I don't know by name. The publication of this book is, I hope, a way of acknowledging and thanking them all for the information and insights they gave me.